OCT 1 0 2018

Also by Nicole Helm

BIG SKY COWBOYS

Rebel Cowboy

Outlaw Cowboy

True-Blue Cowboy Christmas

NAVY SEAL COWBOYS

Cowboy SEAL Homecoming

Cowboy SEAL Redemption

Cowboy SEAL Christmas

D1051941

Cowboy SEAL Christmas

NICOLE HELM

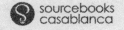

sourcebooks
casablanca

Copyright © 2018 by Nicole Helm

Cover and internal design © 2018 by Sourcebooks, Inc.

Cover design by Dawn Adams/Sourcebooks, Inc.

Cover art by Rob Lang Photography

Sourcebooks and the colophon are registered trademarks of Sourcebooks, Inc.

All rights reserved. No part of this book may be reproduced in any form
or by any electronic or mechanical means including information storage
and retrieval systems—except in the case of brief quotations embodied
in critical articles or reviews—without permission in writing from its
publisher, Sourcebooks, Inc.

The characters and events portrayed in this book are fictitious or are
used fictitiously. Any similarity to real persons, living or dead, is
purely coincidental and not intended by the author.

All brand names and product names used in this book are trademarks,
registered trademarks, or trade names of their respective holders.
Sourcebooks, Inc., is not associated with any product or vendor in this
book.

Published by Sourcebooks Casablanca, an imprint of Sourcebooks, Inc.
P.O. Box 4410, Naperville, Illinois 60567-4410
(630) 961-3900
Fax: (630) 961-2168
sourcebooks.com

Printed and bound in the United States of America.
OPM 10 9 8 7 6 5 4 3 2 1

Chapter 1

GABE CORTEZ LIKED TO THINK OF CHRISTMAS AS A ritualized torture simulation that would ultimately prepare him for any horrible war zone he found himself in.

If I can survive Christmas, I can survive anything.

And he'd survived his fair share, but this Christmas was seriously testing his limits, even with all war zones firmly in his past. Because the only thing as tortuous as Christmas was a *wedding*, and he was smack-dab in the middle of preparations for both.

"I don't see why Jack and I have to sit through this," Gabe announced, crossing his arms behind his head and kicking his legs up on the coffee table in front of him. Like the little army general she was, Becca was standing in front of the group discussing timelines and the chore schedule for a wedding that was something like weeks away and after Thanksgiving at that.

Becca's green eyes moved to him, and if Gabe hadn't spent almost fifteen years in the military, many of those being a Navy SEAL, he might have wilted at that look.

"You and Jack are part of this wedding," Becca replied calmly, though her gaze was fierce and not at all *calm*. "*And* a part of this ranch."

Gabe didn't allow himself any time to dwell on the soft, weak swell of pleasure that gave him. *Part of this ranch*. Well, of course they were. He, Alex, and Jack had shown up on Becca's doorstep over six months ago to start this little venture — Revival Ranch, a place for wounded veterans to heal and find purpose — and all five foot nothing of this shy little woman had whipped three injured former Navy SEALs into shape.

Mostly though, she'd helped Alex out of the depression and PTSD that had plagued him after their accident and injury discharge. Gabe could only ever be grateful to Becca for that. He'd spent nearly all of his fifteen years in military service at Alex's side and he'd never had a better friend, a better SEAL brother.

And now he's Becca's.

Well, so be it. Gabe had learned a long time ago that people didn't stick, especially when loving someone else was involved. At least Alex had chosen wisely. So had Jack, much as Gabe was loath to admit it. Rose might be all mouthy, sharp edges, but she made Jack happy, and Jack deserved that happiness.

If it left Gabe on his own, well, he'd been used to that before he'd joined the navy. He could get used to it again.

"Think of this like a mission, Bec. You give us orders. We'll follow them," Jack offered, sitting on an armchair, his increasingly pregnant woman sitting on his lap. "But we don't need discussions or meetings."

Becca frowned. "I will not think of my wedding as a mission."

Alex grinned at her from his seat on the far side of the couch Gabe was on. "You know you want to."

Becca grunted in frustration.

"That's actually smart," Monica offered from her seat on the other chair. "Weddings are a bit like war, at least in my experience."

Gabe tended to forget that Monica Finley, Revival

Ranch's on-site therapist, had been married before. No matter that her ten-year-old was currently wrestling with Star and Ranger, the two ranch dogs, over by the fire. She seemed like such a solitary, no-nonsense figure to Gabe. It was hard to think of her getting caught up in all this wedding planning.

Mostly, he tried not to think of her at all. She didn't belong here. Oh, she might be helping Alex and Jack with their PTSD, but she wasn't part of the *group*, their unit. She was an outsider. A *shrink*. Even before his military discharge, Gabe had learned to distrust mental health professionals and the lies they were willing to spew when the right pressure was applied.

He hadn't realized he was glaring at Monica until her gaze turned to him and she smiled that empty therapist smile. Blue eyes blank and vast as the Montana sky. He returned it in kind, because he knew how to deal with nosy people who thought they could tell you what you thought and felt.

"Besides," Monica continued, turning her attention back to Becca, her blond ponytail swinging with the movement, "this isn't wedding by committee. It's your wedding, and whatever you and Alex want is what matters. We'll do whatever you two need."

"Could you tell that to my mother?"

Monica laughed. "I'll try. But don't lose sight of the fact it's *your* day. And it's a symbolic day, but it's not a do-or-die day."

Becca blew out a breath. "Okay. You're right, and the best maid of honor ever." Becca smiled. "Maybe I'll just have Alex make up one of his binders with instructions."

Gabe groaned, and so did Jack. Alex's binders were

legendary. Even though Alex had relaxed a lot in the six months since his iron grip on controlling everything had nearly killed him, figuratively and maybe even a little literally, he was still his uptight self.

"I'm going to need a beer if we're going to start talking about binders. Anyone need anything?" Gabe got to his feet, committed everyone's drink request to memory, then headed for the kitchen.

Once inside the small room, he gave himself a minute of quiet and silence to just breathe. He felt…tense, and he wasn't sure why. An edginess had been creeping into him for months now, and he was having a harder and harder time being his pretend-nothing-matters self.

If he told anyone, they'd assume it was PTSD and insist he have a session with Monica, but Gabe knew better. While Alex and Jack grappled with the after-effects of the accident they'd survived, Gabe only suffered physically. He didn't have nightmares of the grenade being thrown into their vehicle and Geiger shielding them from the blast with his own body. It had caused Alex to crash the vehicle, and so all three of them suffered either from the blast or the crash. None of that, not even Geiger's death, affected Gabe mentally the way it had Alex and Jack.

But his shoulder and hip still bothered him off and on, more so since winter had set in. He'd left military life behind, and while he missed it like a lost limb, it didn't haunt him.

But other things did, and it seemed living civilian life brought them all back to the forefront.

He pushed those thoughts away and jerked open the fridge, grabbing himself a beer. He'd down one first in the quiet of the kitchen, away from that odd flutter of panic he got whenever Becca and Alex discussed the wedding, or Jack and Rose discussed the baby who'd arrive in the spring.

Gabe popped the top of the beer and then drank deeply. He tried channeling that inner center of calm that had gotten him through war zones and physical rehabilitation.

"Can I have one?"

Gabe eyed the kid, who'd entered the kitchen soundlessly. Impressive, really, the way he'd learned to sneak around. Gabe had hit it off with Colin the moment he'd met him, and he enjoyed having someone around who was young and eager to experience things. Whenever the kid's mother unclenched a bit, Gabe got to spend time with Colin at the ranch, and in the six months Colin had been here, Gabe knew the boy had grown to look up to him.

It felt good. Gabe might not trust the mother, but he had a soft spot for Colin. The boy was desperate for a place to belong and a little desperate to stir up trouble, and reminded Gabe so much of himself at that age it physically hurt sometimes.

He'd been a fatherless kid too, but Gabe's mother hadn't been like Monica. Which meant Gabe had to be careful where and how he stepped with the boy.

"And what do you suppose your mom would do to me if I gave you a beer?" Gabe asked casually.

Colin shrugged. "It could be a secret?"

Gabe merely raised an eyebrow, and the boy's shoulders slumped. He might not care much for Monica's profession, but she was a hell of a mom.

"Yeah, yeah, yeah. She'd find out," Colin groused.

Gabe reached into the cabinet where he knew Becca hid treats she didn't want to be demolished by the rest of them. He found a Twinkie and tossed it at Colin. "Here's a compromise."

The boy grinned, immediately tearing open the wrapper. "Mom never buys these," he said through a giant mouthful of junk food.

"And there's a good reason I don't," Monica said primly right before she stepped into the kitchen.

"Busted," Gabe muttered as Colin shoved the rest of the Twinkie into his mouth and looked up innocently at his mother. But Monica only stared at Gabe.

He refused to squirm, though he was sure that look was supposed to make him do just that. Instead, he grinned at her with as much careless charm as he could muster. "Did you want one?"

Monica smiled sweetly. "Sure," she said, because she never did quite what Gabe expected her to do, and that irritated him as much as anything—as much as her being a good mom and pretty besides, which sometimes made him forget she was not to be trusted. Not a part of the group. *Shrink*.

Yeah, he never forgot for long. Monica Finley might not be your average snake in the grass, but she was still a snake.

———

Monica took the proffered Twinkie and delicately unwrapped the plastic from the moist, tasteless cake. She hated these things, but surprising the people around her was something of a favorite pastime these days, and she knew taking the crappy excuse for cake would shock both her son and the large man who stood imposingly in the kitchen with him.

Even if she didn't know the basics of Gabe's military background, his body, his posture, his assessing, quiet way *screamed* military. She'd grown up with these men, married a man just like them, knew them.

Mostly.

Gabe was proving to be quite the enigma. It shouldn't have haunted her like it did. Shouldn't have mattered that there was one person on Revival Ranch she couldn't figure out.

But she found, when he grinned at her with all that fake charm, no matter that she *knew* it was fake, her stomach jittered in that old, silly schoolgirl way that could only ever spell trouble.

Monica Finley had *never* done trouble, and she didn't intend to start.

"I thought I'd help with drinks," she said, trying to surreptitiously slide the rest of the Twinkie in the trash while Colin chewed the lump he'd shoved into his mouth. "I'll grab the pops." She skirted around Gabe, trying to ignore the fact she felt compelled to give him a wide berth, for her own peace of mind. She pulled the two cans from the fridge.

She turned to her son, focusing on him instead of Gabe, and held the cans out to Colin, who'd finally finished swallowing. "Take these into the living room and give them to Jack and Alex."

"Why do *I* have to?" Colin demanded in that way that was increasingly getting on her nerves. As though every time she asked him to do something it was an epic insult of the highest order. Heaven forbid he do anything she asked without a metric ton of attitude. Weren't the teenage attitude years supposed to be a ways off yet?

"Why wouldn't you want to help your mother and your friends?" Monica returned calmly, smiling sweetly at her precious baby who would someday grow out of this obnoxious prepubescent stage. *Please, God*.

Colin rolled his eyes, but he took the cans of pop and exited the kitchen. Which Monica realized belatedly was quite the mistake, because now she was left with Gabe. Alone. In a very small room where his body seemed to take up far too much air.

"You guys have been in Blue Valley for almost half a year. Are you ever going to trust him *alone* around us?"

Monica startled. "I... What?"

"If you don't think we notice you popping up every time he's with us alone, well..."

"Colin wouldn't be anywhere near any of you if I didn't trust you," she said, ashamed there was a bit of defensive snap in her tone. Irritated with herself that he was right and she hadn't quite realized it. She didn't love Colin being alone with someone who wasn't *her*.

It wasn't Gabe or Alex or Jack she didn't trust. It was life. It was Montana. Cows and horses and whatever lurked in the mountains. It was all this *space* that could eat up a little boy and spit him out, and men who might not fully understand how vulnerable a little boy—*her* little boy—could be when they felt so physically invulnerable themselves.

No matter that she knew giving Colin the space to explore and grow was necessary for both his happiness and his well-being, Monica hadn't quite gotten a handle on her own insecurities and fears. Or rote reactions.

But she was working on it. Life was a work in progress. Et cetera. Et cetera. If she said it enough, she'd believe it. The power of positive thinking.

She blew out a breath. "That being said, it isn't easy letting my only child out of my sight in a new place. It isn't easy trusting when…" She'd heard such terrible things in her job. The abuses and accidents and neglect that had shaped some of her patients over the years. The cruelties of war that seemed so close when she watched someone relive them. Then there was the fact she'd learned how precious life could be when she'd lost Dex.

"It's not so new, this place," Gabe replied, not unkindly and yet not kindly at all. He had somehow mastered a neutral way of talking that grated on her nerves because that was how *she* talked.

She frowned at him in spite of her inner admonitions to remain stoic. "Is that for you to say?"

"No. Not at all," he returned, but there was something like a *challenge* in the way he backed down. Somehow that challenge always seemed to exist in their interactions.

There was a contentiousness with Gabe she didn't have with the other two men, and definitely not Becca. Oh, Jack had vocally objected to her presence, and it had taken him some time to agree to therapy. Alex had been as opposed to it as anyone, but they never acted as though they existed to challenge *her*. It was a distrust of the process, a worry that needing help equaled weakness.

With Gabe, she couldn't figure it out, and she was certain her body's reaction to him was rooted somewhere in that. He didn't feel like a patient.

She wished she could make him feel like one. After all, he was the lone holdout in the injured SEAL trio here.

So, maybe instead of focusing on the way her body sometimes reacted to Gabe Cortez or that she couldn't figure him out or the way her heart got a little mushy whenever she saw how he and Colin interacted, she should focus on earning his trust.

He'd been through an awful incident and seemed to fall somewhere between Alex's minor injuries and Jack's more substantial injuries on the physical side of things. But she could not get a read on his mental state, and that was what she was here for.

Revival Ranch was supposed to help wounded veterans heal. Men like her father, who'd come home from war someone else. Someone had helped him eventually, and she wanted to have that kind of effect on people and their families. She wanted to be that agent that helped them heal. It was why she'd uprooted her son and herself and embarked on this unknown journey—to help.

"Do you find being in the presence of children more comfortable than being in the presence of adults?"

Gabe laughed, that hard edge of bitterness at odds with the cheerful, charming exterior he so often put forth. She'd sensed that bitterness in him from the beginning, and it came out more and more these days.

It was something like a sign. He needed someone to talk to. He didn't trust her, and therapy wouldn't work without that trust. She'd have to work harder on being his friend, instead of letting her own reactions keep him at a distance.

"Don't shrink me, shrink," he said, grabbing another beer out of the fridge before closing the door a little too hard.

"I think that's my job, SEAL." *Not friendly, Monica*.

"Former SEAL," he said, holding up the beer in mock salute. "I'm a cowboy these days."

"And I'm more than just a shrink."

"Noted." He took a long pull from the bottle, looking out the doorway of the kitchen. "For the record, I think you're a damn fine mother." He never looked at her as he spoke the words, and then he strode out of the kitchen.

Monica stood in the kitchen, alone and far too shaken. It shouldn't matter what Gabe thought. He was a coworker at best, a rather surly person she had to put up with at worst.

It wasn't often that she got any sort of pats on the back these days, though. Her parents were still miffed at her for moving. Dex's family had never been particularly involved in her or Colin's life. She'd never had a lot of friends because she'd been so dedicated to her education and then her career.

Becca was an amazing friend to have here, but Monica felt so *old* sometimes in comparison. She'd been married and widowed, raised a ten-year-old almost alone, and while Becca certainly hadn't lived an easy life, she was still youthful. Sweet and strong and driven, but youthful nonetheless.

Gabe's opinion might not matter in the grand scheme of things, but damn if she could deny it felt good to be praised, to be called a *good* mother. Even if she didn't believe it coming from him…

Someone saw she was trying, and he'd gotten over his animosity toward her profession to verbalize it. It was hard not to be a little shaken about that.

But she never let herself be shaken for long. She'd turn it into action. Gabe Cortez needed a friend, and then he needed a therapist. She'd set out to offer him both. One first, then the other.

And then maybe she could stop getting those silly flutters in her stomach whenever he grinned at her.

A girl could dream anyway.

Chapter 2

GABE HADN'T THOUGHT A MONTANA WINTER WOULD be that much different than a New Jersey one. After all, they were both northern-ish. And he'd survived desert nights and hellish landscapes all over the world. Not to mention BUD/S training.

November in Montana was proving to be tougher. Or, worse, he was getting old and weak. He snorted as he hefted a bale of hay onto the UTV that would get him through the hard-packed snow of the pastures.

He pulled his hat a little lower on his head, then slid into the driver's seat. He was about to turn the ignition, but a female voice called out.

"Oh, there you are."

Gabe frowned over at Monica's approaching form. It was fairly early, though it was the last day of school before Thanksgiving break. Gabe imagined she'd been up getting Colin off to school.

She didn't stop until she stood right next to the vehicle, looking something like a ball of fabric with arms and legs.

"Is there a human being under there?"

She wrinkled her nose at him. Maybe she made some other facial expression, but since he could only see her nose and a little bit of her eyes, it was hard to tell.

"It's in the single digits. I put on every coat, scarf, and pair of gloves I own. Plus, I'm wearing three pairs of yoga pants under my jeans."

"You do yoga?"

"No, I do yoga *pants*." She pulled the pile of scarves off her mouth and smiled at him.

Oh, he did not trust this woman or this approach at all, especially when that smile lodged somewhere in his chest as if it had anything to do with him, when he knew better.

"I was hoping you could help me."

Gabe looked her up and down. He might not know Monica on a personal level, but he'd been around her enough in the past few months to know that asking for help was not something she did often or at all. Which meant she had an ulterior motive.

"I've got cows to feed and frozen water to break up. Can it wait?"

"Let me just tell you what it is, then you can think on it."

"It's the kind of favor I'm going to have to think on?"

She blew out a frustrated breath. "I need some help getting a Christmas tree. I was hoping to do it on Thanksgiving, just so I could get it up and ready the day after. Colin and I always do, but there's no place around here to go buy a tree. Becca says they just cut them down off the property."

When it was clear she wasn't going to say more, Gabe shrugged. "So?"

"So Jack and Rose will be at the Shaws' on Thanksgiving. Becca and her mom will be busy cooking, and I'm sure Alex will be on hand to help with preparations. I thought you could give us a hand. You don't have any Thanksgiving plans before Becca's dinner, do you?"

"No."

"Then it's settled."

"Is it?"

"Becca won't want us all underfoot while she's so generously making dinner. This way, we can go do something, and you'd be helping me *and* Colin. I know he'll appreciate it."

Underfoot. Yeah, he wasn't too keen on being underfoot or feeling like he was thirteen and unwanted again. "I wasn't planning on being underfoot. I may not even go to Becca's dinner."

Monica frowned, wisps of blond hair being tugged out of her hats by the hard, cold wind. "Where are you going?"

"Nowhere."

"But…" Monica smiled indulgently. "Becca is hardly going to allow you not to go. You'll be there if she has to drag you to the house herself."

Which was true, but that didn't make him any keener to pretend like he belonged at their Thanksgiving table. Monica might not either, but she at least had a kid to not belong with.

"Would it change your mind if I offered to pay you? Think of it as a little side job."

Insulted, Gabe slid out of the driver's seat and stood, glaring down at her. "I don't need your money."

"But I need your help," she returned, so damn calmly. "What can I do to get it?"

"Why am I surrounded by stubborn, inherently practical women?" he grumbled. Because he didn't know what to do with it. Becca, Monica, even Rose didn't back down until they got what they wanted. Like their very own band of sisters, dedicated to the prospect of driving him insane.

"Surely there's something I could offer you that would be a fair barter for your help."

He glanced down at her, holding that spring-blue-sky gaze of hers until she blinked. He couldn't tell if it was the cold or if there was an actual blush staining her cheeks, but he had a feeling his long, unrelenting stare made her feel *something*.

But she didn't back down.

"Maybe it's Montana that breeds this incessant stubbornness in people," Gabe muttered, tired of people wanting things from him. Alex and Jack wanted him to get therapy. Becca wanted him to be excited about the wedding. Monica wanted a favor. Everyone wanted something from him and he wanted…

Well, he supposed that was the problem. He didn't know what he wanted.

"I don't think it's Montana, since I was born in Texas and I've lived just about everywhere. I'm as much a Montanan as you are, though I don't own a cowboy hat yet."

"Better get on it. I hear they kick you out if you don't."

She chuckled. "You won't distract me."

"Of course not. Fine, I'll help you." How long could it take, after all, to chop down a tree? Which gave him an idea. "On one condition."

"All right."

"Colin gets to cut down the tree."

Her jaw dropped in outrage for a moment before she smoothed her expression into something calm. "Colin is ten. He's too young."

"That's my condition. Take it or leave it."

"He cannot chop down a tree!"

"Of course he can. With the right instruction. I bet Alex was chopping down trees out here before he could walk."

"I don't care what Alex was doing," she returned through clenched teeth.

Gabe was enjoying this. Monica was usually such an iron fortress of calm, but anytime he got on her about being too overprotective of Colin, she snapped. He liked being the one who made her snap.

She blew out a breath, drawing on that inner sense of calm she always seemed to be able to find. He wondered if it was a never-ending well.

Everything about her looked wrapped up and cozy. He'd certainly like to see what she looked like out of control and decidedly *not* cozy and—

What the hell was wrong with him? She was pretty enough, but he didn't get mixed up with women with kids or dead husbands they'd loved. Most importantly, he didn't get mixed up with *shrinks*. She'd have a field day if she ever found out about his childhood, and he wasn't the least bit interested in reliving that.

"Those are my terms," he said, wincing a little at how harsh his own voice sounded. She wasn't to blame for his thoughts taking an idiotic detour. So he tried to soften it with a smile. "The kid'll be fine."

"The *kid*," she scoffed. "*My* kid. My little boy."

"Who's going to spend the next few years at least hacking it through a few Montana winters. Give him the skills to do it. You'll both be happier in the long run."

"You sure have a lot of opinions on children and parenting," Monica returned, cool but certainly not placid as she crossed her arms over her bundled chest.

His grin didn't fade. If the kid was a way of poking at her, well, he wouldn't mind poking now and again. *Not* because of that little tickle of awareness or the unwelcome pang of attraction, but because he wasn't about to let her think she had the upper hand when it came to him.

"Why is that?" she continued, cocking her head with that kind of clinical study he thought they must teach in shrink schools.

"I didn't have a dad either," Gabe returned, because he knew giving her something would throw her off, surprise her—and it wasn't the big something he'd never, ever tell her or anyone.

Some of that clinical detachment faded. "A boy doesn't need a father. Plenty of kids don't have fathers."

He almost felt sorry for her, because he knew it was what she told herself. Much as Gabe recognized it as true, that a man could grow good and strong without a father, he could tell she didn't believe it. Not yet. Someday she would, when Colin was off being the good man he'd inevitably be. But she wasn't there yet.

Damn her for softening him toward her. "No, a kid doesn't need a dad," he said, looking her straight in the eye, hoping she'd see the truth in that. "But he does need the opportunity to spread his wings, usually far before the people around him are ready for it." Hell, he knew it wasn't his place, but he had a soft spot for the kid. And maybe even a little soft spot for how hard Monica tried to be a good mother. He'd been that little boy—not coddled or overprotected, but not given the freedom to make his own choices, learn his own skills. "Let him chop down a tree, Monica. I promise you, it'll be good for both of you."

She stared at him and, for one moment, all those masks she wore simply slid away. There was something like naked emotion and vulnerability on her face—so clear, Gabe *had* to look away.

"Be at our cabin at nine, then," she said, her voice suspiciously scratchy. He didn't look up until he heard her footsteps retreating.

Then he mentally kicked himself for opening his big, dumb mouth.

Monica didn't like having a session when she was emotionally worked up. But she refused to let those emotions bleed into her patient's time, especially when it was silly.

Why on earth would she let *Gabe Cortez*, some childless former Navy SEAL she barely knew, give her parenting advice?

If she needed advice, she asked her mother. She mostly didn't need it though, because she knew a ton about child development. She'd read all the books and lived the parenting life for *ten years*.

But Gabe's words shook her. She muttered a few curses just to get it out of her system. Then she stomped her foot on the snowy ground for good measure. She had ten minutes before she was supposed to meet with Alex for his weekly therapy session.

She needed a clear head. She was ready to suggest Alex move to once-a-month sessions instead of these weekly ones. He'd improved vastly, and much of it was due to the woman he was marrying and his willingness to communicate with her.

After all, as was the case with so many men she'd worked with, they had never learned how to verbalize fears and worries, especially after spending their early adulthood conditioned into *not* doing that. They had to learn or relearn the importance of laying down their burdens, even if it made them vulnerable.

She blew out a breath and closed her eyes. And didn't she need to take some of her own advice?

"Fighting with Gabe again?"

Monica jumped at the sound of Becca's voice. She hadn't realized Becca had approached. "We don't fight," she said automatically.

Becca cocked her head. "Then what do you call it?"

"We don't always see eye to eye."

Becca laughed. "You rub each other the *wrong* way. Maybe because you want to rub each other the right way."

Monica fisted her hands on her hips. "You did not just say that to me."

"I did. And I one hundred percent stole it from Alex." Becca grinned. "I'm too sweet and innocent to ever think of such a thing."

Monica snorted. "Ha!" She eyed her friend, who wore maybe half as many layers as Monica did even though she was a tiny little thing. "Are you heading in?"

Becca nodded.

"Could you tell Alex I'll be about fifteen minutes late?"

"Sure. Everything okay?"

"Yeah, I just need to make a phone call I'll probably talk myself out of if I don't make it now."

"No problem. I'll let him know." Becca took the stairs of the porch and Monica frowned after her.

"I don't want to rub Gabe any which way," she said, trying to sound sure and maybe even a little superior. As though Becca was a silly girl reading into things. And maybe Alex was a bit of a silly girl too.

But Becca only smiled. "Sure you don't." Then she disappeared inside.

Monica scowled. Having the *occasional* physical fantasy because of Gabe.'s *outward* appearance did not mean she wanted to actually act on it. Technically, Gabe was a potential client. That put him in an off-limits box.

And that was most certainly that.

But she couldn't deny that his words this morning had affected her, and now she was going to act based on what he said.

Monica pulled her cell out of her coat pocket and walked over to her truck. She turned the ignition, willing the heater to warm quickly. While she shivered in the driver's seat, she dialed her mother's phone number.

"Hello?" Mom's voice answered.

"Hi, Mom."

"What's wrong?" Mom demanded.

Monica chuckled. "Nothing bad. Just…I've been thinking, about what you and Daddy suggested."

"Which thing?" Mom asked, with enough humor that Monica smiled.

"Colin coming to visit on his own." Just saying the words aloud nearly ripped her chest open. But Gabe's words kept repeating in her head, an endless loop, because she'd thought them herself. She'd talked herself out of them based on her own insecurity and fears.

"*Oh*, that suggestion. Well."

"You sound surprised."

"I am. You shut us down so hard and so fast I didn't think there was any chance of you thinking about it further."

"I…" Monica took a deep breath. She'd called Mom

to do this thing but also to talk. To verbalize her fears. "Do you think I shelter him too much?"

"You moved him to the middle of Montana to start fifth grade in a school he's never even heard of, all so you could follow your dream job. I don't think he's coddled, sweetheart. And I don't blame you for doing it. You did the right thing for you, and that'll be the right thing for him."

"Daddy doesn't think so."

"You know your father. He can be a hard man when he's made up his mind, but he can also change it. Eventually."

Monica laughed in spite of her melancholy. Her father had not approved of Dex. *Why can't you marry an army man? What does the air force know?* Sometimes, when she was mad at Dex for getting himself killed, those words haunted her.

"You're a wonderful mother. A wonderful human being," Mom said in that gentle, sure way that had gotten Monica through so many rough patches. "But you have both been in each other's pockets pretty much since Colin was born, even when you lived here. Let the boy have some time to be the center of someone else's attention. Let *yourself* have some time to think only of yourself."

That sounded *horrible*. Why would she want to do that? But if Colin spent a week of winter break with Mom and Dad, Monica would be able to get some Christmas shopping done, some end-of-the-year cleaning, and she'd still work, of course. It would be sensible, and it'd be good for Colin.

So why did it hurt?

"Let us spoil him. Without you."

"Ouch."

"Oh, hush. You know I want to see you too, but don't you remember how much you loved visiting your grandmother by yourself when you were little? What confidence it gave you?"

Those summers had been the highlight of her childhood. They'd moved so much when she'd been growing up that Grandma's house had been home. It had given her a sense of freedom, a sense of self.

Grandma had been gone for twelve years now, and still the thought of her brought tears of grief to Monica's eyes. Normally she'd swallow the next words down, but verbalizing them was healthier. Was healing. "I wish she'd met him. I miss her."

"I know. Me too. Give me and your dad a chance to give Colin what Grandma gave you, huh?"

Monica wiped the tears from her cheeks with her bulky gloves. She looked out the windshield at Revival Ranch spreading out before her, the awe-inspiring mountains in the distance.

It had been a hard choice to move here, to uproot Colin from what he'd known in Denver. She'd done it fully for herself, and that selfishness had been necessary. She knew it had been necessary, but it didn't negate all the guilt.

"I'll ask him tonight."

"Ask him or tell him?"

Monica scowled, since her mother couldn't see her to scold her over it. "It'll be a discussion. He should have a say." She'd never had a say in things as a kid. Mom had run her house as strictly as Daddy had run his troops, and she'd demanded the same amount of respect. Monica had vowed to give her child more say, more autonomy.

Sometimes she failed, but this was going to be a discussion. "I have to get to work, but I'll call you tomorrow and we can figure out details."

"Why'd you call today then?"

Leave it to her mom to ask the hard questions. "Honestly? I was afraid I'd change my mind about it if I waited. But I do have to go. I love you, Mom."

"I love you too. Talk soon."

Monica hit End on her phone and allowed herself some silence to breathe in, to breathe out, to take strength from the mountains. Gave herself time to compartmentalize her emotions away so she could be someone else's sounding board.

When she turned off the ignition and stepped out of the truck, breathing in the icy cold, she was ready to don her therapist hat. *Therapist* and *Mom*. Those were the two labels that encompassed her whole life. And okay, maybe *Daughter* too.

Let yourself have some time to think only of yourself. Monica shuddered at Mom's words rattling around in her head. But she shoved them away and stepped toward her job.

Chapter 3

THANKSGIVING MORNING DAWNED GRAY AND COLD, with the threat of precipitation in the air. Gabe half-heartedly hoped that might keep him from having to help with Christmas-tree selecting.

God, he hated Christmas. The twinkly little lights, all the damn tchotchkes. The same song playing over and over and *over* again. Weird warm or sweet drinks when he'd much prefer a shot of whiskey.

Maybe he'd make his way down to Pioneer Spirit tonight. Hanging out at the bar wasn't quite as entertaining as it had been when Jack had been his companion, but he could find himself companionship.

For now, he knew he needed to get through the day ahead. "Suck it up, Cortez," he muttered to himself. He did not abide moping, and this felt perilously close.

So he put on his winter gear, downing the rest of his coffee, and focusing on the mission that lay before him: help a woman and her son get a Christmas tree. A clear goal, easily achieved, and all he had to do was put up with a slightly irritating woman.

Monica wouldn't know what tools she'd need, and while he was certainly no expert on Christmas-tree cutting, he figured he knew more about it than she did.

Gabe tramped across the snowy ground between the bunkhouse and the barn. The trees on the property were mostly on the outskirts, so it'd probably be easiest to take the truck out to the north pasture, then hike around for the right tree.

But as he stepped into the barn, he already heard voices. Female voices.

"This is everything you'll need. Gabe will know where to take you," Becca was saying as she stood next to some ridiculous contraption that looked suspiciously like a damned sleigh hooked up to her horse, Pal.

"What the hell is that?" Gabe demanded, not even trying for polite.

Becca didn't so much as flinch. She turned and smiled brightly at him. "Isn't it adorable? Absolutely perfect for a Christmas-tree-getting excursion. We're going to use it for the wedding, so Hick has been working with Pal to pull it."

"We can take the truck," Gabe returned gruffly.

"Take the sleigh. Colin'll get a kick out of it and you won't get stuck."

"I'm not driving a *sleigh*."

"That's okay. Monica can handle the horse portion. You're just along because you know where you're going. There's rope in the back to tie the tree down, and the saws you'll need. It'll be fun. Don't be such a grinch."

"Being a grinch is fulfilling a lifelong dream, Bec. It'd be cruel to take that dream away from me."

She rolled her eyes. "Take them out. Enjoy yourself. Be a good little Christmas-tree scout and have everyone back by two-ish. Thanksgiving meal is at three. Sharp. Don't be late. You know how my mother gets when people are late."

"I'm not scared of your mother."

Becca only laughed and waved as she walked away.

Which was fair enough. Sandra Denton was a scary lady, and Gabe would never admit *fear* per se, but he doubted they'd be late.

He turned to Monica where she stood at Pal's side, gently rubbing the beast. The kid was nowhere to be seen. "Thought I was supposed to meet you at your cabin."

"Yes, well, I got to thinking it made more sense to leave from here, and with all the right tools." She stroked the horse fondly. "Becca made us a big thermos of hot chocolate. Colin's inside getting that and I'm sure sneaking a few other treats."

"Like the Twinkies you don't like."

Her mouth curved, and she looked at him from behind the horse's head. "Just because I don't buy them doesn't mean I don't like them."

"You're not half as sneaky as you think you are. I watched you throw it away."

She sighed. "Sometimes, as a mom, you make sacrifices. And sometimes, as a mom, you lie so your kid doesn't know the real reason you won't buy Twinkies is you think they're disgusting and don't want to have to watch him eat them, not that you're worried about what chemicals might be inside."

"Being a mom sounds hard." And if he was honest with himself, it was kind of fascinating to watch her do it. Maybe because, though she'd dealt with somewhat similar circumstances, there weren't a lot of similarities between Monica and his own mother.

"You have *no* idea." She nodded toward Pal. "Becca mentioned you're not a fan of the horses."

"Not that I'm not a fan," Gabe replied, hiding his irritation at Becca's big mouth with the best smile he could muster. "Just never been around them much. Weird little bastards."

"My late husband's family had a horse farm," she said, her gaze on the horse as she continued to stroke it. "We met in high school on the base, and he used to get to go visit his aunt and uncle on the farm on the weekends. Then I started going with him. There was nothing quite like it."

Gabe didn't have a clue what to say to any of that. Monica never seemed uncomfortable bringing the dead guy up, even around Colin. It was so different than Gabe's upbringing, where he'd had to beg his mother to even find out what his late father's name had been.

"No farm animals in your childhood?" she asked casually.

"Grew up in the city, then the burbs. Being deployed taught me something about wide-open spaces and how to enjoy them, but not a damn thing about animals."

"It was one of the pluses of moving here for me, that Colin would get to be around horses and other animals. I didn't exactly have roof-climbing goats or roosters who won't die in mind, but he certainly gets a kick out of Becca's menagerie."

"Yeah, it's a menagerie all right." Gabe studied the sleigh. "Gonna be a tight fit." There was one broad bench down the center where they'd all have to huddle together to fit.

"Colin's small," Monica returned, clearly as married to this dumb sleigh idea as Becca had been.

As if on cue, Colin appeared at the barn entrance, two big thermoses in his hands. "Woah! Are we really going to ride that, like, around?" Colin asked, some mixture of skepticism and delight in his tone.

"Till we get frostbite, I guess," Gabe muttered, eyeing the horse when it made one of those patently weird horse-breathing noises.

"Don't be a coward, Gabe," Monica said too cheerfully as she gave the horse one last loving pat. She grinned up at him. "It doesn't suit you."

"Trust me, sweetheart, I've been brave in the face of a hell of a lot worse than a farm animal."

Something in her face went soft, and he felt himself soften with it. Till she spoke.

"I'd like to hear about that sometime."

He flashed one of those grins that was far more *bite me* than *aren't you funny*. "I don't think I can afford your hourly rate, Doc."

She closed her eyes and winced a little. "Sorry. Bad habit."

Gabe didn't say anything to that. He moved into the sleigh, scooting next to Colin, who was all but bouncing from excitement. Gabe made a joke about having a great view of the horse's butt, which made Colin giggle hysterically. At least that lifted his mood.

"What happens if it poops?" Colin asked, still laughing brightly.

"I think it means you get a shit sandwich for lunch."

Colin absolutely howled at that, and Gabe ignored the stern look Monica gave them both as she slid into the other side of the sleigh. She took the reins in her gloved hands and gave them a little flick.

The sleigh lurched forward and Gabe grimaced. He felt like a damn fool riding around in a *sleigh*, but Colin was looking this way and that as Pal led them down the hill and out toward the north pasture, the sleigh easily cutting through the hard-packed snow.

It certainly wasn't fast moving, but it was prettier than any ride in the truck might have been. Some of his irritation at Monica's switch back to nosy therapist eased. It was hard to hold on to it as Colin's small, freckled face slowly morphed into big-eyed wonder.

Gabe was only doing this for Colin, and he'd put up with the shrink for a few hours for the sake of that.

But this was the last favor he did for them, and that was that.

About halfway out to the area of Revival Ranch that boasted trees that could be cut down and used for decoration, Monica felt whatever guilt had been niggling in her stomach lift. It was hard to stay ashamed of her own actions when a beautiful white-and-gray canvas stretched out before her.

The ride was surprisingly smooth as Pal trotted along the fence line. Every once in a while, she glanced at Colin, who looked possibly as happy as she'd seen him since they'd moved here last summer.

She tried not to look at Gabe, even when he instructed her to turn here or go there. But when her gaze did drift his way, he was sitting next to Colin looking hard and stoic. Unreadable. Untouchable.

She should heed those looks. She'd only ever had patients who'd come to her because they wanted to or been forced to, so she hadn't quite learned the delicate task of just…waiting.

Then again, she was friends with Becca just fine

without any attempts to psychoanalyze, so maybe it wasn't so much history as her own perceptions. She'd decided Gabe needed therapy because of what she knew had happened to him. Maybe that wasn't fair.

"Stop here," Gabe instructed as they came upon a small clump of evergreens. Some cattle were huddled together around the trees. When Monica had expressed some dismay at the poor cows in all this frigid weather, Becca had laughed at her and explained the cows were fine. They were fed and watered and had trees to block the wind.

Monica was sure Becca knew what she was talking about, but it still made Monica feel a bit sorry for them. No matter that they looked content huddling there.

"Well, pick a tree," Gabe instructed, clearly not looking for a leisurely outing.

Monica looked at the trees and wrinkled her nose. "They're all so tiny."

Gabe's eyebrows lifted until they were hidden underneath the stocking cap he wore. "Did you move into a mansion with twelve-foot ceilings without my knowledge?"

She scowled at him. "No, but surely we can fit something taller than this."

"They look smaller out here. In your cabin, you'll wish you'd gone smaller."

"Impossible."

"Tell me you've got a little more sense than your mom, runt."

Colin straightened in his seat, then looked at her very seriously. "We should at least check them out up close, Mom."

Monica tried to hide a smile and replied just as seriously. "You know, I think you might be right."

They piled out of the sleigh and walked through the little cluster. Close up and right next to them, Monica begrudgingly realized Gabe was right. Most of these wouldn't even fit in the cabin, let alone something bigger. There were maybe two possibilities, and they looked so regretfully tiny.

But then again, their cabin was tiny. Teeny tiny.

"I think this one would fit," Colin said, hands on his hips, looking very serious and adult as he studied it.

"I think you're right," Monica said, trying to be just as serious. "Let's get the tools then, and Gabe can cut it down for us."

"Aren't you going to let Colin chop it?" Gabe asked, smiling lazily as he stood next to the sleigh.

Monica tried not to scowl. It was the deal they'd made. Damn it.

"Seriously? I get to use a saw?" Colin asked, so awed it almost made Monica forget a saw was, you know, a sharp blade of potential death and dismemberment. Almost.

Gabe happily pulled a saw and an ax out of the sleigh, and suddenly it looked less like a picturesque novelty and more like a little wagon of destruction.

"First an ax, then a saw."

Colin's jaw actually dropped and his head seemed to move in slow motion toward her. "Are you really going to let me?" he asked.

It was that shock that had her relenting no matter how her gut revolted at the idea. He was *so shocked* she was going to let him use two very simple tools, and she clearly needed to unclench a little bit.

Does unclenching really have to involve sharp, unwieldy potential weapons?

"She's really going to let you," Gabe chirped, striding over to the tree. "Now, with sharp tools and cutting things down, safety is key. You have to listen to my instructions and do what I say, okay?"

Again, Colin's head swiveled back to her, then to the tree and Gabe. "O-okay. Yeah, I'll do whatever you say."

Maybe it made her a coward, but Monica turned away. She could not watch her baby wield an ax or a saw. She could barely *breathe* listening to Gabe instructing Colin on how to hold the ax, how to angle the blade away from him.

She stared hard at the mountains, calling on a few techniques she taught her patients. Breathing. Visualizing. Centering.

So, yes, she'd developed a certain level of anxiety about safety since Dex had died. After all, Dex's helicopter hadn't crashed because someone had shot it down. It had been some safety failure during a routine drill.

It was quite normal to fixate on safety from then on out because safety *mattered*. Her worries weren't uncalled for.

But she couldn't let them overshadow the life her son would need to live.

They were sawing now, and Monica cringed at the sound. Sharp metal teeth against heavy, living tree trunk.

Why had she agreed to this?

She focused on the mountains and the fact they'd endured for centuries. Those peaks had seen a million Christmases and stood through them, never crumbling, never bending. Mountains didn't get anxious over what they couldn't control. They stood there looking majestic, *being* majestic.

She pulled her phone out of her pocket and took a picture of the beautiful mountains surrounded by bright winter blue, the sleigh sitting there in the forefront. A Christmas postcard come to life.

"Seriously?" Gabe muttered.

She turned her head and stared straight at him. He would not make her feel foolish for taking a pretty picture. "Seriously." Then she lifted the phone and snapped a photo of him and Colin next to the cluster of trees.

He scowled. "Delete that."

"Never," she replied sweetly, not at all threatened by that stern military order. She'd grown up with stern military orders. Let him *try* to intimidate her.

Gabe grumbled something, then turned back to Colin. The tree they'd chosen lay in the bed of snow next to the stump.

"You'll want to search it for bird nests or other wildlife before you put it up at your place."

Colin peered at the branches as Monica stepped closer to do the same.

"Shouldn't we have checked before we cut?"

Gabe shrugged. "They'll find some other place to live."

"That isn't very—"

In a quick move she didn't see coming at all, Gabe snatched the phone out of her grasp and immediately began scrolling.

"Hey! Give that back!" But when she reached for it, he only held it up higher, out of her reach, looking up as he continued scrolling.

"Gabe, give that back," she demanded, using the sternest mother voice she had. She held out her hand, considered counting to three as though he was a toddler.

Gabe only grinned at her, and she *refused* to let that all-too-charming curve of his mouth with the faintest dimple under his dark-whiskered cheek do *anything* to *any* part of her. Especially the particularly female parts of her.

Gabe jerked his chin toward the tree in the snow. "Go stand in front of the tree with your kid."

It took her a moment to put together what he meant by that, and then she could only blink at him. "Oh." Somewhat taken aback by the thoughtfulness, she tramped over to Colin and stood next to the fallen tree. She slipped her arm around his shoulder.

"Now smile. Both of you."

"Oh, he never smiles for pictures anymore. Too big and tough," Monica said, giving Colin a grin and squeeze.

"Funny. I got one," Gabe replied, holding the phone out to her. She snatched the phone and looked at the picture Gabe had taken. Colin was grinning. Monica herself had her mouth open, was looking down at Colin, which made her chin all but disappear. She looked ridiculous. "I'm talking."

Gabe shrugged. "Them's the breaks."

She almost demanded Gabe take another one, but she stared at the picture of her smiling son, then the man in front of her she did not understand at all. There were too many emotions fighting for prominence, and most of them made no sense to her at all.

He clapped his hands together. "Let's load up. Colin, I'm going to teach you how to tie a knot."

"I know how to tie a knot."

"Not a lame baby knot. A real knot."

Monica could only watch in shocked silence as Gabe

went through the basic steps of some military knot, and then he and Colin tied the tree to the sleigh.

She swallowed at her constricted throat, because for the first time in six months, she knew for an absolute fact she'd made the right decision to move here—not just for herself, but for her son.

And it was hard not to cry over that.

Chapter 4

"SEE?" COLIN HELD UP A WELL-TIED SQUARE KNOT TO THE room of adults who oohed and aahed over his skill.

Gabe was getting a kick out of how excited the kid was over tying a *knot*. Gabe had enjoyed teaching him this afternoon while they'd waited for Thanksgiving dinner to be ready. Everyone else had been in the tiny kitchen stepping on each other's toes as they prepared the food.

Colin had nimble fingers and an eager mind. It hadn't been easy for him in the beginning, and he'd been ready to give up, but Gabe had given him a bit of a lecture about frustration and working through it.

Colin had listened solemnly, then gotten to work. Now, he was flying through the knots and beyond proud of his achievements. Gabe smiled into his beer.

"Now we just need to teach you to do it underwater," Alex said from his corner of the couch, Becca curled up next to him.

With the threat of snow, Becca's mom had headed out early. Becca had convinced Monica and Colin to spend the night though, since the roads to their cabin would be worse than the roads in town. Now they were all sprawled out in various places in the living room with pie and alcoholic beverages for the adults. The women were sharing some fruity bottle of wine while Gabe and Alex stuck to beer.

Colin had groused loudly, if not earnestly, about his lame lemonade.

Gabe could admit it was nice enough, and he didn't feel quite as odd-man-out as he'd figured he would. It didn't mean he'd make it a habit by any means, but it gave him some dim hope for future holidays.

"How's tying a knot underwater any different?" Colin asked, frowning at the piece of rope.

"Well, there's water, for starters," Gabe replied dryly. "Plus, you have to do it while holding your breath."

Colin undid the knot in the piece of rope Gabe had given him and dramatically sucked in a breath and held it. Then he went about tying the knot. When he was done, he loudly blew out the breath he'd held. "Easy," he said, offering the knot up for Gabe's inspection.

Gabe shook his head. "You keep thinking it's easy."

"How old do you have to be to join the navy?"

"If your grandfather heard you asking that question…" Monica shuddered. "Bad enough your dad was an air force man."

"Grandpa must be a marine then," Gabe said.

Colin nodded. "First to fight."

Alex and Gabe exchanged an eye roll.

"But it doesn't matter. You know why?" Monica offered, smiling sweetly at Colin. "Because you're joining any military branch over my dead body."

Colin huffed. "You always say I can do whatever I want. If I get good grades and try hard and blah, blah, blah."

"Well." Monica sipped her wine. "I guess we have about eight years to figure it all out." She made a pained face, fisting her free hand at her heart. "Eight years. That sounds impossibly short."

"Yeah right. It'll take *forever*." Colin sighed gustily, holding out the rope knot for the two dogs curled by the fire. He tried to get their attention for some tug-of-war, but both Ranger and Star just stared at the boy dolefully.

Becca yawned. "I should get to cleaning up the rest of it."

"Oh, let me. I'll get Colin to bed and then do the rest. You did so much today."

Becca opened her mouth to argue, but Alex was pulling her up off the couch. "Monica's right. You did the work of ten men today. Let someone else help with cleanup."

"You're a guest," Becca said with a frown as Alex started leading her toward the stairs.

"I'm a friend," Monica replied firmly, nudging Colin with her foot. "Bedtime, little man."

"Ugh."

And then they were all heading for the stairs—Monica and Colin bickering over bedtimes, Alex and Becca sleepily arm in arm, and Gabe was left alone, seemingly forgotten, just him and the dogs.

He got up, ready to head out and ignore any of the idiotic disappointment in his chest. But bottles and glasses littered the coffee table, along with a few paper plates. He'd just grab those and throw them away, cutting down on some of the work Monica had to do. Quickly, before she came back down.

He collected the plates and a few bottles, disposing of them in the appropriate receptacles in the kitchen. Then he figured he could unload the dishwasher real quick, since he'd lived here before the bunkhouse had been ready and he knew where everything went.

Once he'd done that and added another load, he went

back to the living room. He'd just collect the remainder of the glasses and then Monica wouldn't have to do anything.

"Oh."

Gabe glanced toward the sound. Monica stood at the bottom of the stairs, and he couldn't read her expression or begin to understand what that *oh* had meant.

"Got most of it done. Just these left." He ignored the glasses he'd been going for and moved toward the door. "I was getting ready to head out though."

Monica shook her head, grabbing her glass of wine and refilling it with the last of the bottle. "Stay. Have a drink with me."

Gabe watched her suspiciously. "Why?"

She plopped herself onto the couch, staring at the fire instead of back at him. "Because otherwise I'm going to sit here and wallow about the passage of time. I'd rather bicker with you."

He'd regret it—he *knew* he'd regret it—and yet he couldn't seem to resist. Much as he hated to admit it, he wasn't tired enough to sleep instead of wallow.

He was at least smart enough to take a seat in the armchair instead of next to her on the couch. And he was not about to drink any more.

"So, why aren't you with your family?" she asked with no preamble.

Family. Funny word, that. Still, he didn't wince. He knew he'd be asked. He had his rote answers prepared. "They live all the way on the other side of the country."

"I do believe they have these things called *airplanes*."

"Really? Haven't heard of them."

Her mouth curved, and she looked different in the

flickering firelight. Fragile almost, where usually she looked impossibly sturdy and strong.

"Why aren't you with yours?"

"My parents are on a cruise celebrating their thirty-fifth wedding anniversary." She smiled fondly, but it died quickly. "Colin's other grandparents don't much care for us. Well, that isn't fair. We remind them of Dex, and they…well, I suppose they haven't fully dealt with their grief. I'm not sure I can blame them. I'm not sure all the therapist training in the world would help me if I ever lost…" She shook her head. "See? Morbid wallowing. I don't want it. Say something obnoxious."

"Marines are pussies."

She barked out a laugh, then covered her mouth, presumably since there were people sleeping upstairs.

She had a good laugh. Loud and uninhibited. Hell, he needed a beer.

"My dad is *not* a pussy," she said, sounding far more amused than offended.

Gabe shrugged. "I'm sure he doesn't think so."

Monica shook her head. She'd worn her hair down today, which she rarely did. In the firelight, it was tinged red, and *seriously*, he had to get his ass out of this chair and get a beer.

But he sat. And he watched her.

She cleared her throat, holding the wineglass with both hands, staring hard at the fire in the fireplace. The dogs had disappeared at some point when he'd been cleaning, so it really was just him and Monica.

"I know I don't owe you any explanation about how I treat my son, but…well, you're very good with him. He looks up to you. All three of you really, and it's good for him to have you three as influences in his life. But he seems to be particularly connected to *you*."

Everything in him tensed, chilled. That careful tone of voice, the way she wouldn't meet his gaze. He knew what came next. He'd been here before, hadn't he? "And you want me to stay away?"

"No, not at all." She frowned, her gaze all shock and confusion as it met his. "Why would you think that?"

Gabe looked down at his hands. He hadn't realized he'd gripped them both into tight fists, but there they were—white knuckled and clenched. He tried to come up with some explanation, but in the end, his scratchy voice just managed some lame excuse. "I'm not his dad."

"No, but he needs people of all stripes in his life, people who'll teach him different things and offer him different opportunities. He needs people to look up to because *he* feels a connection. I'll always be a shade too overprotective. I've worked through some of it, but…Dex died…"

He unclenched his fists and placed his hands on the arms of the chair, ready to push out of it. "You don't have to explain it to me."

"But I want to. I want you to understand. You're a part of Colin's life." She said it so seriously, so *baldly*. None of her usual therapist carefulness in picking the words. He knew better than to look, but he couldn't seem to help himself.

She was staring at him, emotion written all over her face. An earnestness, a hope, and, underneath all that, *love*—love for her son.

Gabe was somehow rendered speechless by that, and he was never, ever speechless.

"All of you are part of his life," she continued. "And

a part of mine. Dex's helicopter crash was a preventable accident. Someone hadn't done the right safety check, and it resulted in the crash. Because someone was careless, an accident killed my husband and my baby's father."

She paused, clearly grappling with the pain of that, staring back at the fire. Gabe looked at it, too, because he'd lost friends and brothers—more men than he cared to count. To various things. War and suicide and being in the wrong place at the wrong time.

Geiger, the other man in their vehicle when it had exploded. That man had sacrificed himself by stepping on that grenade, and somehow, the rest of them had survived.

"I was ready to lose him to war," Monica continued. "I wasn't ready to lose him to…cruel happenstance. And that's manifested itself in some unfortunate ways."

Ah, there was the therapist. The careful choosing of words. *Manifest*. *Unfortunate*. But in *this* moment, he couldn't really blame her. He figured someone who'd lived through that got to use whatever therapy words she wanted.

"So I need some people in my life who will on occasion make me let Colin cut down a tree."

He didn't say anything to that. Didn't want to. But she just kept talking.

"Thank you for today. I don't think I can adequately express how much I appreciate it."

It was enough to have Gabe finally pushing himself out of the chair. "Yeah, no problem," he grumbled, heading straight for his coat. "Have a good night."

"Happy Thanksgiving, Gabe," she murmured, and somehow those soft words haunted him all the way to the bunkhouse.

———ᨆᨆ———

At breakfast the next morning, Monica listened to Colin chatter with Becca and Alex. The couple had been up and doing chores since before dawn, yet they sat there and talked happily. Monica couldn't understand how anyone got up that early and cheerfully worked in this cold, but they seemed perfectly content. Whether it be the comfort of partnership, love for their work, or love for each other, it was sweet to witness.

And eased some of the lingering...discomfort, she supposed. She'd spent half the night tossing and turning, trying to figure out exactly *what* her reaction to her conversation with Gabe had been.

She'd wanted to thank him. Not just for the Christmas tree stuff, but for the irritating way he'd coerced her into giving Colin some freedom. She'd wanted to explain that she did need some pushes because her overprotectiveness was rooted in something real.

Then he'd thought she was going to warn him away from Colin. What was that about? The cold fury in his response that he'd blanked in the blink of an eye kept replaying in her head. Then, the way it had disappeared so quickly made her question whether she'd really seen it.

"Monica?"

Monica blinked and looked up from her mug of coffee. She smiled at Alex. "Sorry, what? Lost in pre-coffee thought. Or maybe I dozed off."

"I asked if it'd be okay if Colin comes out with me today. I doubt Jack and Rose will make it with the road conditions. I could use an extra set of hands," Alex said.

Monica forced herself to smile. "Of course."

"Finish up, then, partner. We've got some ice to break." Alex must have noticed her horrified look. "In the water tanks."

Right. Water tanks. Honestly, she was too smart a woman to always be jumping to the most dangerous possibility. Of course, that wasn't fair. She was always telling her patients that intelligence didn't have a thing to do with the emotional aftereffects of war. The smartest minds could be as easily wounded by trauma as anyone else.

She thought she'd been dealing with her trauma quite effectively, and it was daunting to realize she'd mostly been running from it, or hiding, or gently pushing it into a corner where she didn't have to deal with it.

One day at a time had come to mean considering neither future nor past. Now, she was settling in. She *had* to think about the future because she was knee-deep in helping people build a program she wanted to be involved with for a very long time.

"Everything okay?" Becca asked once Alex and Colin had disappeared from the kitchen.

Monica smiled. "Okay. Holidays are hard. End of the year is hard." *Life is hard*.

"If there's anything about the wedding stressing you—"

"Nothing about the wedding is hard. I'm having a great time helping you plan. In fact, we've got a bit of time right now, don't we? Did you want to finalize the timeline, and then I can make any confirmation phone calls next week?"

Becca drained her coffee. "You're a dream come true. Let me get the binder."

Becca disappeared from the kitchen and Monica cleared the table, rinsing the dishes so they were ready to be loaded. She'd chalk up this weird melancholy to not just the holidays, but messing with her routine.

As Becca reentered, the front door squeaked open and voices could be heard murmuring in the living room. A few seconds later, Jack and Rose appeared.

"What do you two think you're doing driving these roads?" Becca demanded.

"Heat went out at the house. It was brave the roads or freeze to death," Jack said, helping Rose shrug out of her coat.

"We would've been fine," she grumbled.

"Yes, nothing like letting a pregnant woman hang out in below-freezing temperatures in a house with no insulation."

Rose rolled her eyes and slid into a seat at the table. "I think he's being ridiculous, but since it meant I could come help with wedding stuff, I didn't argue."

"Do you mind if we stay here until we get the heating fixed?" Jack asked Becca.

"You know you're always welcome."

Alex popped in the kitchen doorway, Colin at his heels. "Didn't expect you today."

"Heat's out. We got a helper?" Jack asked, nodding at Colin.

"I don't know. He said he wants to pet the goat. Not sure I can trust him."

"You're marrying the woman in charge of that goat."

Alex grinned over at Becca. "Oh, right. Well, come on. Best get to it."

Monica watched the three depart, desperately tried to keep her mouth shut, and inevitably failed. "Bundle up," she called after Colin. "Be safe."

"Serious question," Rose demanded. "Am I going to turn into this worrywart creature once my child is born?"

"I think it depends a little bit on personality, but no matter what, you're going to worry. To the point where you feel sick half the time. Motherhood is a constant joy."

"It's not bad enough I have to push the thing out of me, now I also have to worry about it for eighteen years?"

"If you're anything like my mother, it'll be way more than eighteen years," Becca offered, grinning.

"Well, you guys suck," Rose muttered.

Becca slid a bagel slathered in cream cheese in front of Rose.

"Okay, a little less now," Rose said, pulling the plate toward her. "So," she began, her tone of voice changing and everything about her expression going far, far, far too innocent for Rose. "Jack mentioned Gabe was your little Christmas-tree-obtaining helper yesterday."

Monica kept her face bland. "Yes. I'm not an expert at cutting live Christmas trees, so the help was very welcome."

"He's very good with Colin," Becca added, also far too innocently, though Becca was better at pulling it off.

"He is. They all are. I have to say I was not expecting that when we moved here. They've been beyond anything I could have hoped for him."

Becca's smile was sweet and genuine this time. "It's nice having Colin around. Sometimes it's what the place needs. Kid's laughter. Something…light."

"Are you worried it'll be a different once the other men get here?" Rose asked, picking at her bagel. "It's definitely going to change things."

"It is," Monica agreed. "And I've certainly considered that it might change how Colin fits in here. But it's just another reason to take things slow as we build. We don't want to overextend ourselves when we're dealing with people who need a lot of help. I think starting with two is an excellent idea, and it seems like the two Becca and I selected will be really good additions."

Rose settled her hands over her slightly swelling stomach. "Well, I hope so. Jack doesn't want to say anything yet, but we've talked about him taking some time off from here when the baby is born. He's torn, I think. He wants to be able to contribute and feels guilty taking a paycheck if he's not working, but I—"

"Stop right there," Becca interrupted. "He'll damn well take time off, and he'll damn well get paid. We are a family. We'll do whatever it takes to support each other as family. That's more important than the business side of things."

"You can't risk your business at the cost of family," Rose said sternly.

"And we can't hurt our family at the cost of our business. There has to be a balance. We can't ignore the fact that we have to earn money from the cattle. But we also can't ignore that the whole purpose of this place is healing and hope. Not just for the men and women who will come here as former soldiers, but for us too." Becca settled herself at a seat in between Monica and Rose at the table. "This is me reclaiming my independence from my very sheltered life. This is Monica's opportunity to give her son and herself something she's worked long and hard for. This is as much about them as it is about us. We can't lose sight of that."

"I agree," Monica said firmly. "But there's something else we can't lose sight of."

"What's that?"

"Your wedding is in *two* weeks, and we have lots of work to do."

"Okay." Becca straightened in her seat, looking at Monica then Rose. "But first I have to say something."

"Is it going to be a sappy something? Because this baby makes me cry at the drop of a hat, and I do not cry in front of anyone."

"I never had any friends growing up," Becca continued as if Rose hadn't spoken.

"Becca, I'm warning you."

"And meeting both of you and having you be part of my life and my family has been more than I could have ever dreamed."

Rose sniffled, her dark eyes wet and wide. "I'd kick your ass if I wasn't pregnant," she muttered.

Becca grabbed Rose's hand, then Monica's. "It means the world to me that you're here and that you're going to be part of my wedding. And I'm not going to let a few tears stop me from saying that."

Rose flicked a few tears from her cheeks. "I've only ever had my sisters as friends. It means a lot that you two are also here to talk to and support me. Because God knows having a baby is the scariest thing I've ever done, and I've survived a lot of scary."

"The good news is, in my experience there's nothing scarier in the world. So once you've conquered that, you're good."

"I guess that's comforting."

"And I'll add my mush to the pile," Monica said,

squeezing Becca's hand, then reaching across the table for Rose's free one. "I've been doing this thing alone for a lot of years. I've had my parents, and they've been… I wouldn't have been able to survive without them. But there's something to be said for building your own support system, too, and doing something you love and being able to trust that your child is in the right place at the right time. It's possible because of all of you."

"And you never know when a little romance might show up at the right place at the right time," Becca offered.

Monica smiled indulgently but pulled her hands away. "And who would I meet in the middle of nowhere?"

"You know, we both managed," Rose said, nodding at Becca. "There is something to be said for a former Navy SEAL."

"If you're getting at what I think you're getting at, which is horrifying, I'll stop you right there. I'm a military therapist. I will not be getting involved with another military man." Monica didn't add that she doubted any military man in this situation would be getting involved with a therapist, but that was there as well. "It would undermine my credibility as a therapist here, which is paramount both to acting as therapist for both of your significant others as well as the foundation."

"I might agree with you if Gabe had ever been your patient."

Monica gave Becca a pointed look.

"All I'm trying to do is point out the fact you two have sparks. *Serious* sparks."

Monica laughed. "I haven't had *sparks* since I conceived my child."

"And considering how long that's been, I'd say

you're overdue for some. I did mention to Jack that Gabe needed a woman, and it might take a Christmas miracle to find him one. Well, Christmas tree, sparks..."

"Result in fire. And death and destruction."

"Wow. Who knew you were so dramatic?"

"I'm about to be dramatic about horse shit and wedding timelines," Monica returned, pulling the binder Becca had put on the table toward her. "I mean, what if the horse pulling your sleigh to the aisle poops all over the place?"

Becca laughed. "I grew up on a ranch. My life is horse poop. Why wouldn't my wedding be?"

And with that, Monica successfully changed the subject from sparks and foolishness to the very real upcoming event of two really good people joining their lives together in love and hope.

Which was not in the cards for her at all, but especially with any confusing former Navy SEALs.

Chapter 5

"Damn, it's cold," Gabe muttered, pulling his stocking cap down lower as they piled out of the utility task vehicle. They mainly relied on horses to get around in the warmer months, but that was much harder on Jack's leg, so they'd purchased the UTV. It had turned out to be quite handy this winter.

Gabe glared at the sun slowly moving higher in the sky as the morning wore on. The ball of supposed light was doing nothing to warm the air. "Whose brilliant idea was this?"

"When did you get to be such a wuss about the temperature?" Jack asked, rearranging the straw in the enclosure.

"There are pros and cons to leaving the SEALs. One of the pros is not freezing for the hell of it."

"Well, until someone invents water that doesn't freeze, get used to it. And stop complaining," Alex returned.

Gabe used the pick to break the ice that had accumulated on the top of the water tank. A few cows glanced his direction. It was strange thing, this ranch work. About six months in and he had to admit, he didn't love it. He could tell Alex loved it bone deep. Maybe that came from growing up here. The riding horses, the mountains, all that crap. To Alex, this was a kind of calling.

Gabe didn't *mind* it for as much as he liked to complain, but it wasn't his calling. He'd only ever felt that in the navy. Which was ironic, all in all, since he'd never grown up with any military aspirations.

But then again, maybe that was life. Maybe there were no callings. Maybe people just made the best of what they had. Quite frankly, that was more appealing than the idea he had to be satisfied and fulfilled all the time.

"What about you, runt?" Gabe asked, handing Colin the ice pick. "What are you going to do when you grow up?"

Colin shrugged, poking what was left of the ice with the pick. "I don't know. Firefighter would be pretty cool."

"Firefighter. You told your mom that?"

"I'm not stupid. She'd have a cow if I told her that. She wants me to go to college and be bored forever."

The three men glanced at each other. None of them could extoll the virtues of college exactly. Gabe doubted Monica would appreciate Gabe mentioning that.

"Hey, what's that?" Colin asked, pointing to a lump in the distance.

They all shaded their eyes against the sun. There off across the pasture was a lone cow, but it wasn't standing exactly. Gabe couldn't quite make out what looked wrong about it.

Alex's expression went grim. "Why don't Gabe and Colin stay here while Jack and I check it out?"

"I can go," Colin said boldly, but then some of that surety melted. "What is it?"

"Looks like a dead cow. Got caught in a drift maybe. Jack and I are going to have to dig him out, then we'll have to transport him to the composting area. It's not a fun job, Colin."

Colin chewed his bottom lip, looking out across the expanse of white.

Gabe figured Monica wouldn't care for what he was about to do, but if the boy was going to spend the next eight years on this ranch, there were some things he was going to have to learn.

"We all came out. We'll all dig it out."

Alex cleared his throat, but Gabe raised an eyebrow.

"How old were you?" Gabe asked. Alex had grown up here, and Gabe was under no impression Alex had been sheltered from ranch work.

Alex didn't respond, so Gabe turned to Jack, who might have been as new to this whole ranching thing as Gabe was, but he'd grown up on a farm, not out in the burbs. "And you?"

"Younger," Jack said, shrugging toward Alex. "Gabe's right. Gotta learn sometime."

"Gotta learn what?" Colin demanded.

Gabe looked down at the boy. "When you see a responsibility, you meet it, even if you really don't want to. Cattle ranching means sometimes cattle die, and we have to be responsible to handle it."

"What do we have to do?" Colin asked, frowning at the dead cow.

Alex went through the procedure as they all got in the UTV. The drive across the pasture was slow-moving thanks to all of last night's new-fallen snow. Which gave Gabe all sorts of time to doubt his insisting Colin be a part of this.

They worked in a grim kind of silence, digging the dead animal out of the snow, then only spoke instructions to each other as they used the UTV to drag the cow out of the pasture. It wasn't exactly gruesome work, nor was it fun work pulling a dead cow across snowy ground.

They dragged the cow all the way to the composting area at the edge of the property. Gabe, Jack, and Alex had built the area in the spring, but they hadn't had cause to use it yet. Once they got close enough, they all had to get out and pull the cow the rest of the way by hand.

Once they'd actually gotten the carcass into the area, everyone was huffing, and Gabe no longer had any complaints in him.

"Why don't you and Colin take the UTV and go get what we need to finish?" Alex said, nodding toward the vehicle.

Gabe nodded, giving Colin a nudge toward it. The kid wouldn't be making the return trip, but he didn't need to know that yet. "Let's go."

"Isn't this part of the responsibility too?" Colin asked, but his voice was scratchy and hell, the kid was only ten.

"Yeah, but sometimes a man needs a break too. Besides, if we don't get what they need, who's going to?"

Colin nodded and got into the UTV. Gabe flicked glances at him as they drove, and he couldn't help but worry he'd pushed the kid too far here. Maybe Colin *was* too young to be dealing with the basics of ranch life.

Gabe stopped the UTV at the barn, but he pointed to the house. "Let's go on up for a second. Get a few thermoses," he offered. He'd make an excuse about getting coffee or something, so he could convince Colin to stay at the house without making him feel like he wasn't man enough for the rest.

Colin got out of the UTV wordlessly, and they trudged through the snow toward the house. Gabe was tempted to wrap his arm around the boy and give him a squeeze, but it was hard to know what was appropriate with someone else's kid.

"Why... They just left the rest of them out there," Colin said softly, frowning.

"You heard Alex explain this cow was old, got caught in a bad place. Accidents happen." He thought about what Monica had said last night about how her husband had died. Gabe didn't want to draw any correlations, so that's all he said.

"But...that isn't fair."

"Life's not fair, bud. You know that better than most kids your age. We're all going to die at some point. People. Animals. It's never going to feel like the right time. It's never going to feel fair. Sometimes it's only going to give you more questions than anyone could hope to answer."

"I know I'm supposed to be sad my dad died," Colin said in that same scratchy voice, but his posture had gone defensive as they tramped across the yard. "But I was a baby. I never knew him. I know Mom's sad, but I didn't know him. He's no different to me than that cow. Except I can see the cow."

"You know, I didn't know my dad either before he died."

Colin peered up at him, clearly curious but not going to question it. Which Gabe figured meant he had to keep talking. Unfortunately. "My mom was so sad about it she didn't even want to tell me his name. So I don't miss him, since I never knew him, but that doesn't mean I can't miss the idea of him. I've wondered what might've been different in my life, and that doesn't help, but death leaves a mark even if you don't remember it."

Colin shrugged. "I'm tough. I'll be fine."

They both climbed up the stairs, but before Colin reached for the door, Gabe placed a hand on his shoulder. He knelt, winced when his hip gave a little shot of pain, then ignored it.

"Being tough isn't about ignoring the things that touch you. Being tough is about facing things that are hard. Being tough is about facing things that a lot of people wouldn't. And sometimes being tough isn't the answer. You have to be tough in the face of things that are wrong. You have to be tough in the face of your own responsibilities and the choices you make. You have to be tough in the way you protect your mom and anyone else you care about. But there are going to be times in your life when things will be hard and being tough won't be the answer."

"How do you know the difference?"

"Honestly? You probably won't always know the difference." He was a hell of a pep-talk giver, wasn't he? But he'd started this and he'd see it through. "You have to figure it out for yourself. But knowing that it's an option, that you don't have to be tough all the time, it's a good step in the right direction."

Colin stared at him like he'd just spoken gibberish. That's probably all it sounded like to the kid. With a grunt he tried to swallow, Gabe got back to his feet.

Colin frowned. "What's wrong with you? Is it why you got all those scars?"

Since they'd been swimming this summer, Colin had seen the handiwork of a grenade and a vehicle crash mapped over Gabe's upper right side. "Yup."

"How?"

"Afghanistan. While I was on patrol, someone threw

a grenade into our vehicle. The blast caused Alex to crash into an embankment. My right side got twisted and sliced to hell."

"But you lived."

"Three of us did. One of us didn't."

Colin's frown deepened at that, and Gabe tried not to picture Geiger, the friend he'd lost. Tried not to remember that day or the months of pain and healing that came after. He tried to focus on today and the cold and this little boy in front of him.

"You are tough, runt, and no one can take that away from you." Gabe patted Colin's back. "But it's a cold day, and this is complicated work. I want you to stay here."

Colin's expression went mutinous, but Gabe couldn't let that sway him. "You want to help next time, I want you to read up on disposing of deceased livestock. Alex, Jack, and I spent a lot of time learning about what we're about to do, and you'll need to as well if you want to help."

"Reading is boring."

"Then I guess you don't want to help."

Colin grumbled something under his breath as he pushed the door open, but Gabe had a feeling the kid would read up on it. Gabe had a feeling the kid would see his responsibilities through.

He didn't have any idea why that made him *proud* when Colin was nothing to him, but it was there anyway.

He decided to ignore it.

Monica never allowed herself to lead a conversation with anger. She counted to ten when she wanted to scream at Colin for being a little jerk. She breathed through hideous customer service. She'd learned to squeeze her palms together when talking with her father and wanting to throttle him.

None of those tactics seemed to be working.

Last night, Colin had woken up from a nightmare. He'd been sobbing, and he'd crawled into bed with her like he was tiny again. After she'd calmed him down, she'd finally convinced him to tell her about the dream.

It had been an especially weird one. A dead cow under the Christmas tree, a Christmas tree that had been decorated with pictures of Dex and dead cows. Monica hadn't known what to make of it until Colin had mentioned the dead cow he'd helped the Revival Ranch men move.

She hadn't slept after that, even when Colin had finally dozed at her side. She was too furious. Far too furious to approach any of them. She needed time to cool down, but as she stood next to her truck the next morning, anger started to shred her usually normal reason and rationale.

When Gabe stepped out of the bunkhouse, looking somehow as strong and rugged as all those peaks in the distance behind them, whatever small thread of control she'd had over her emotions broke.

Her *baby* had been crying and scared, and this indestructible man had caused it.

"Go inside, Colin," Monica said, deadly calm.

"Where are you going?" Colin asked, staring at her across the front of the truck.

"I'm going to…" She didn't like to lie to her kid, but she wasn't about to tell him what she was really up to. "I wanted to check on some horse stuff before Becca and I have our meeting. You head on inside."

"If the guys are there, I want to—"

Gabe was approaching, and Monica's temper was at a rare boiling point she barely even recognized. "Go inside and stay there."

Colin frowned up at her. "Why?"

"Because I am your mother and I said so. If you're not up on that porch in five seconds, you will deeply regret it."

Colin complained, loudly, but he also scurried toward the house. It gave Monica minimum satisfaction that he did.

"Morning," Gabe greeted as he approached. He tipped his hat and offered one of his meaningless, charming grins.

"Is there some place private and warm we could talk?" she asked through gritted teeth.

His eyebrows lifted, but he didn't question her. He gestured toward the bunkhouse. "That do?"

She nodded sharply and started marching toward it. It hadn't snowed again last night, but the subzero temperatures had made what snow there was slick and hard. Every time her boots crunched through it, she felt a little more righteously furious.

This man, *this man* in particular, had been the cause of her child's nightmares. She ignored the tiny little voice in her head that reminded her Alex and Jack had been there too, and she'd probably be able to handle her temper a little better around men who were her patients.

She was protecting her baby. Her life. Anger and fury were *right*, and certainly Gabe the big, strong Navy SEAL who thought he was *so* smart and that her child should wield an ax and help with removing a dead cow could handle a little of her very fair anger.

She pushed into the bunkhouse, Gabe following at a much more leisurely pace. He affected that *don't care about anything* attitude, and nothing could have riled her more, because if Gabe was going to be taking Colin places and encouraging him to do things, then he needed to care so deeply it hurt. Hurt just like this.

Slowly, Gabe closed the door, then leaned against it. "To what do I owe the pleasure?"

"What the hell is wrong with you?"

He rubbed a hand over his jaw as if contemplating it. "Depends on who you ask, I suppose. I happen to think I'm quite the prize."

"Colin is ten years old. Axes and saws were one thing, but disposing of a dead animal?"

All that easy, fake charm melted off his face until only the bitterness was left. It felt like a triumph to get under his mask.

"It's ranch work. He's part of a ranch now."

"He's *ten*. Helping you guys means riding in the UTV and petting horses, maybe shoveling some poop or helping to mend a fence. It does not mean you get to force him to face death. He has had to face that enough."

"Yeah, so have we all. But it's a part of life."

"I am *well* aware how much a part of life."

"Then I don't know why you're up my ass. Because he was the one who spotted the dead cow, and he had the option to help or not. He chose to help, because he's not afraid to stand up and do what he should."

"What he should? Were you clearing out dead animals when you were his age?"

There was a heavy beat of silence where he gave

her one of those looks she'd learned from her time in therapy never led anywhere good. Unexpected, awful.

Then he blinked, and it was gone. "So, what? Keep my distance? Never even look in your kid's direction?"

It deflated her, because it was the second time he'd made this gigantic jump to what she hadn't even considered. "Why do you always assume the worst?"

"I don't know, maybe it's all the being screeched at in private."

"I am not screeching," she said. "But I am about to be violent."

His mouth curved at that. "Try me, sweetheart."

"This is ridiculous. *You* are ridiculous." He'd somehow taken all the anger out of her and all she had left was that soft spot of hurt. "You can't know what it's like to watch your kid struggle with a nightmare. To not be able to do anything about it."

"No, I don't."

There were a million things left unsaid there, and she was tempted to slap her hands over her mouth so the questions piling up in her head didn't escape. She'd already fallen into *therapist questions* a little too easily with him, and he'd made clear again and again that he didn't appreciate it.

So she wouldn't say anything about nightmares or war or PTSD. This wasn't about *him* after all. It was about Colin. Her *child*.

"Something on your mind, Doc?" Gabe asked with that fake laziness that only ever sounded like a hard-edged bitterness to her ears.

"Nope."

He leaned forward, so close she could count the dark

eyelashes framing his dark eyes, count the whiskers he'd missed when he'd apparently shaved this morning. She could feel his breath against her cheek as he spoke.

"Ask it."

She knew he was trying to be threatening. Trying to prove a point. Trying to intimidate her so she didn't ask again. But she *hadn't* asked. He was the one putting words and questions into her mouth, so she lifted her chin and ignored the fact the last thing her body felt was *intimidated*. "Do you have nightmares?" she asked flatly, dispassionately, with none of the therapist care she usually infused into those type of questions.

He looked her right in the eye, far too close for comfort. "No," he said, enunciating it with relish.

Chapter 6

SOME TINY VOICE SOMEWHERE IN GABE'S BRAIN WAS encouraging him to back off and calm down, but Monica had stormed into *his* place and started laying accusations at his feet, and then she'd had that patented shrink reaction.

Maybe she'd kept her mouth shut, but Gabe had known what her considering look meant.

What he didn't know was why something sharp felt like it had been lodged in his gut. Something like betrayal, but that was damn stupid, and he wasn't stupid. So it had to be something else.

"Okay, no nightmares," she said, that blue gaze of hers calm and never leaving his. "Good to know. Anything else you want to demand I ask you?"

Why the hell do you think I want to hurt your kid? But he wasn't about to admit that hurt his feelings. So much so he wasn't even going to throw the fact she'd asked him to push things when she wanted to be overprotective in her face.

Hell, she hadn't just asked him—she'd *thanked* him for it.

"I gave him a choice. And we kept him away from the composting. I thought it'd be a good experience if he's spending the next eight years or so on a ranch." Why was he explaining himself to this woman so bound and determined to chew him out? But the thought of Colin having nightmares over it…

Well, maybe that's where the sharp, horrible pain in his stomach stemmed from.

All of the anger that had propelled her to stomp over here, then throw verbal darts at him, it had leaked out of her. Instead of looking like some kind of angel warrior, she looked shaken and hurt.

"I…" She sucked in a breath and let it out, all dramatic like. "I apologize."

It was too easy. Gabe didn't trust it. "Do you now?" he drawled, and he didn't move away from crowding her, no matter that there were new thoughts in his head about how she smelled like soap and syrup.

How was he supposed to keep his thoughts straight when a woman smelled like maple syrup?

"I let my anger get the best of me. I knew I shouldn't, but…" She sucked in another breath, slowly letting it out. "Well, it did anyway. This is no excuse, but I was up in the middle of the night with a crying child," she continued in that maddeningly calm voice. How Jack and Alex talked to her as a therapist, Gabe didn't understand. He wanted to shake her until he saw that fire again.

"I wanted something to blame that nightmare on, that pain, and the horrible feeling I couldn't do anything to protect him from it. That wasn't fair. Especially coming from me." She kept eye contact the whole time. It wasn't that he doubted the sincerity of her apology. It was that he didn't understand *her*.

"They teach that in shrink—"

"Would you stop saying 'shrink' all the time?" she snapped, and it was wrong that he was glad to see some of that color back in her cheeks. "I'm a therapist.

Trained and licensed and damn good at my job. I have helped both your friends deal with their problems, and at some point, you're going to have to respect that, even if you don't want it for yourself."

Fair enough. "I do." He watched the shock register and rolled his eyes. "I respect that you've helped my friends. I don't need it for myself."

She took that in without getting huffy about it, which was something of a surprise. Even more surprising was her expression going soft, almost imploring. "I'm not out to get you," she said quietly, with shiny, emotive blue eyes.

"And I'm not out to hurt your kid," he replied, more than irritated his voice sounded rusty when it should have been hard and uncompromising with no sign of weakness.

You never let the enemy see your weakness, even if they didn't feel like an enemy half the time.

She rubbed a hand over her face—that was new. He'd seen a flicker of it Thanksgiving night when she'd talked about her dead husband's accident, but she'd had that layer of therapist calm over it. This was all… Well, he recognized it. Because he'd seen it on Jack's and Alex's faces in those first few months here.

A complete lack of understanding at how the world could spin so completely out of your control.

It was where Gabe had the leg up because he'd never had any control over his life.

"I never thought you were *trying* to hurt Colin," she finally said. "Not on purpose. I tend to think other people can be careless because they're not as careful as me."

"A Navy SEAL is never careless."

He almost got a laugh out of her with that, and it

eased some of this obnoxious pressure in his chest he didn't know what to do with.

"I suppose not. But Colin isn't a Navy SEAL. Maybe it's warped, but he's all I have of Dex. Sometimes it feels like he's all I have of me." She shook her head. "You don't need to hear about all my hang-ups."

"No," he affirmed.

This time he got a real smile, even if it was rueful. "I am sorry for barging in here and letting my temper loose on you."

"I can handle it."

"You certainly have the broad shoulders to carry it."

He raised an eyebrow. The throwaway comment was interesting enough, but the blush that crept over her cheeks at his response was *very* interesting.

"You know, everyone seems to think we have..." He trailed off, stepping a little closer, watching her face intently. She met his gaze with a timidity he never would have associated with her.

"Sparks?" she supplied, and her voice was cool and calm. That smooth, in-control thing she used like a weapon.

Her eyes were a different story. Her mouth was a different story.

He smiled. He couldn't help it. "One way of putting it."

She blinked once, and then her gaze was darting anywhere but at him. "Silly, isn't it? When I was in a relationship, I wasn't quite so eager to pair my friends off as Becca and Rose are." Her voice was a little high, a lot breathless.

It made it impossible to back off even though he knew he should. He tilted his head, just a hair, so his mouth was inexcusably close to her ear. "Is that all it is, you think?"

"W-what else could it be?" She let out an awkward, forced laugh.

"Well, you stuttered. You tell me."

There was a beat of silence, as though he'd caught her completely and utterly off guard. Then she sidestepped him, putting some space between their bodies. Her arm gestures were wide and nervous. "You're…nice looking and all, but…" She cleared her throat. "We don't have much in common."

"No, nothing at all," he replied dryly.

"I mean, well, sure we have *some* things in common. Revival. Friends. But I meant personality wise. We're different."

He crossed his arms, watched her eyes drift to his *broad* shoulders, then dart away. "That doesn't usually have much to do with… How did you put it? Sparks?"

She blinked, as if taken aback. Then she edged toward the door. "Well, anyway, I have a meeting with Becca and some horses. I am sorry for…this. I mean, not *this*. That. Before. The…yelling."

"Sure."

She clasped her hands in front of her, and it seemed to center her, all those outward appearances of nerves and being flustered disappearing. "I want you to understand that I may, on occasion, take issue with how my son is handled here," she said in her usual, annoyingly calm tone. "I'll do my best not to speak in anger, but if I do, it has no bearing on… Well, you'd have to do something truly cruel for me to want to make sure Colin was never around you, and I don't think you have that kind of cruelty in you, Gabe."

"You'd be surprised what kind of cruelty people can have in them."

She stepped forward then. He wanted to look away. He wanted to fidget. When she gently placed her hand on his forearm, he wanted to scurry away.

But he didn't.

"This isn't war here. It's just life. Which means if I express a concern, even angrily, don't assume I'm out to burn it all down. I will try harder not to let my inability to keep my son Bubble-Wrapped from every horrible thing turn into anger against someone else."

Her hand just rested there on his sleeve, warm and capable, a light pressure of some kind of earnest truth he didn't want to accept.

"That more shrink talk?"

She didn't take her hand away from his arm. She didn't look away. She didn't even scowl.

"No, Gabe, that's *people* talk." She lifted her hand, patted his arm twice, then headed for the door.

Gabe stood where he was, very afraid those words would haunt him for a very long time.

This isn't war here. It's just life.

Monica was so irritated with herself. She'd acted like an idiot. And she had *zero* good reasons for acting like a silly schoolgirl.

She'd heard herself. How breathless and high-pitched she'd sounded. The horrible stuttering, and he'd just *grinned* at her as if he were in charge and the center of every female fantasy.

Well, she'd turned things around. She'd definitely

caught him off guard there at the end. As much as she knew that wasn't going to convince him therapy was a good idea, it felt like a personal triumph.

She should chastise herself for valuing a personal triumph over reaching out to help someone, except when was the last time she'd had any kind of *personal* triumph? Her life was Colin and being a therapist. If there'd ever been a strictly personal Monica aspect of her life, it had died with Dex.

And, wow, that was sad. Maybe when Colin went to stay with her parents for that week, she'd focus on herself. On finding some piece of the world that could be for her as a person, not as a mom or a therapist.

Like what?

Broad shoulders came to mind, and she firmly pushed that idea away as she stepped into the stables. Becca was already there.

"Sorry I'm late."

"No worries. Colin said you were talking to Gabe." Becca slid her a glance that had Monica affecting her best no-nonsense, let's-get-to-work expression.

"Yes, I had some things to discuss with him."

"Ah. Some things."

"Yes, a few…things. Nothing important."

Becca made a considering noise, but she went to Pal's stall and began to lead the pretty horse into the center of the stables. This past summer, they'd worked on Becca's riding hours to get her certified to lead therapeutic horsemanship, and they were close. She'd be applying for certification by January, when they brought on their first two men.

In the winter weather, they practiced the other aspect

of therapeutic horsemanship in the stables—taking care of the horses, which was good for the men, cathartic.

It was good for her, Monica could admit.

On top of that, working with someone like Becca, who needed none of Monica's actual therapy help, was a new experience. Truth be told, Monica had a bad feeling she'd lost sight of how to interact with anyone without a therapist or mom bent.

"Do you think I talk down to you?" she asked Becca.

Becca stopped what she was doing with Pal. "Huh?"

"Do I always try to make it about being a therapist or tell you what to do like I'm your mother?"

"No one tells me what to do like my mother," Becca replied wryly. "What brought this question on?"

"Nothing." Monica felt stupid for even bringing it up, but bottling up worries never did them any good. "I'm just wondering if I've forgotten how to be a human being in the past ten years of being a mom and a therapist."

"I think you're a great friend."

"Feels like there's a *but* in there."

Becca chuckled. "This is not a criticism, and I'm only saying it because you asked. Sometimes you have a habit of saying things as if that's just the way it should be. Because you know what you're talking about. I don't know if that's being a mom or a therapist, and actually, I really appreciate it. I admire the way you seem to know exactly what to say and you're sure of yourself. You don't waver. I wish I could be more like that."

"Not everyone appreciates it," Monica mumbled, thinking irritably of Gabe. But maybe he had a point. She was always trying to get a read on him, trying to devise a plan of mental health action. She felt like that was her role, but maybe…

"No. Not everyone is going to appreciate a woman who knows what needs to be done," Becca said, handing Pal's reins to Monica and giving her a meaningful look. "But if you mean Gabe…"

"I don't mean Gabe," Monica said automatically as she took the reins with too much of a tug. But that's who she had meant, and lying didn't help anyone. "Not him only. I just mean…I don't know what I mean. Ignore me."

"I will not ignore you. Because I know you wouldn't ignore me. Or anyone here. You're my friend. You're my maid of honor. You wouldn't be that if I didn't love you. So, spill. You clearly need to."

"But I don't *want* to," Monica replied, knowing she sounded petulant. She wanted a moment to be that childish, selfish thing inside of her. But as she smoothed her hand down Pal's mane, she felt calm. Working with the horses gave her that.

"You *do* want to, or you wouldn't have started talking. I've learned a few things from watching you interact with Jack and Alex. Now, go."

Monica couldn't help but be amused. Becca said what she meant and knew when she was right. She just hadn't learned to trust it completely yet. No doubt she would, and in short order.

"I don't know how to explain this thing," Monica admitted, and that was hard for a therapist to admit— that she couldn't verbalize this jumble inside of her. She was *supposed* to understand it.

But you're not supposed to beat yourself up about not understanding. You're just supposed to try. "I feel like everything is rolling out of my control," she said, hating that it boiled down to things she *knew* she couldn't control. But feelings and what you *knew* didn't always line up, no matter that she had trouble accepting it.

"Colin was upset about that cow, and I took it out on Gabe," Monica continued, stroking Pal while Becca led the second horse out of its stall. "I'm letting Colin go stay with my parents by himself for a week. The thought fills me with terror when I should be thrilled that I get a week to myself." And because Monica couldn't stand to only discuss the personal stuff and let the spotlight be on her as a person, she had to bring up the other thing that had been niggling at her. "I know the two men scheduled to arrive in January didn't express any interest in the therapeutic horsemanship."

Becca handed her a brush, and then they worked in tandem to brush down the horses. It was a rote activity that often relaxed and helped people discuss what might be plaguing them. It was a safe space to talk and discuss coping mechanisms.

But if the men didn't want this…

"No, they didn't sign up for it yet," Becca confirmed as though it wasn't a big, huge point of worry. "But that doesn't mean they won't. I think they have to get here and see it before we're going to have men really want to get into it."

"On a good day, I believe that."

"And on a bad day?"

As much as she'd wanted to wait to broach the subject until after Becca's wedding, maybe now was the best time. "I love this place, and I know I have built this program with you. But a foundation also has to operate within cost, and if no one is using my therapy services, then you are not operating in cost."

"You think we'd get rid of you because of that?" Becca demanded, forgetting her brushing and staring wide eyed at Monica. "We'd never get rid of you."

"You have to be willing to," Monica replied firmly, focusing on Pal because if she looked at Becca's horrified, green eyes, she was afraid she'd get emotional over it. "The foundation is running on grants and, hopefully at some point, charitable investments. You can't afford to have a part of your program not performing."

"You built this program. You are a part of Revival, and more, you and Colin are part of our family. On the off chance that none of these men see the value in this, we would find a different space for you. Nothing is going to make me give up on this program, and if we have to separate it from Revival, then we will. But I don't think that's going to happen."

"You've clearly considered failure, or you wouldn't have all those ideas."

Becca waved it away, turning back to brushing down the horse. "Maybe, but only because it's smart to have a backup plan. I don't think we'll need it. And you shouldn't either."

"Like I said, on a good day…"

"Why is this a bad day?" Becca asked casually, and Monica knew she was using the therapeutic strategies on her. Monica found she didn't care.

"I don't know. I just feel off and out of control, and I hate it."

"You sound like Alex."

"I think one of the reasons Alex and I make a good

therapist-patient fit is because I do understand his controlling tendencies."

"You know, I can't imagine how hard it is to be a single mom. I watched my mom do it for a lot of years. She was overprotective to the point of stifling. You're not like that."

"Because I try very hard not to be, but I've stifled him. I know I have."

"Maybe. Maybe it doesn't help, but I came to this ranch as a kid, too. It opened up a world to me I never would've dreamed for myself. If it had just been me and my mom, she would have locked me in the house and never let me out, but I had my stepdad and he let me run free. Let me do things my mother never would've approved of. It's a good experience to have someone who... Well, we're here too. If you feel like you're stifling, you can trust some people around you to show him what else is out there."

"So, I need to let the guys take Colin out on excursions that I would never approve of? Don't even answer that, because I know the answer. The most horrible part of today is that I thanked Gabe for the whole Christmas tree thing. I sat there Thanksgiving night, and I thanked him for doing something for my son that I know I would never have let him do. But...it's all these layers. I want Colin to be safe, and I always want to double-check everything and follow every safety rule known to man. If someone had been diligent enough to do that, my husband would not have died in that crash. But the emotional stuff? My son crying or being scared? There aren't any safety rules for that. So I lost it at Gabe after I'd just thanked him for the same, and I'm sure it doesn't make any sense to him, but it makes sense to me."

"And if it were Jack or Alex saying those things to you, what would you say to them?"

"I've been giving you too many therapeutic horsemanship lessons if you're turning things around on me," Monica grumbled, working down the length of Pal's large body.

"What would you say to them, Monica?"

She blew out an annoyed breath. "I'd say that emotions are normal and nothing to be scared of. We all have to experience them, and it's even good that we do. Good for us as human beings to be sad and scared and happy. You know what the difference is?"

"What?"

"Colin is *my kid*. Reasonable or not, I don't want him to hurt or be sad ever. We've had so much of that already—so much hurt, and I know life isn't fair, but I want it to be for my kid, even when I know it can't be."

"That's what makes you a really good mom. Because you want those things for him, and I think somewhere deep down, you know you can't make it happen or you wouldn't be conflicted. You wouldn't be upset."

"And I wouldn't be taking things out on Gabe that have nothing to do with him."

"Maybe you take things out on Gabe because you want to be around Gabe?"

"You're as subtle as a sledgehammer, Becca."

She grinned over her horse. "I know. But let me tell you something. When the guys first got here, and it was just me and them, I liked Gabe the best. He's the most charming, the most personable. Alex was so hard and so different than I remembered him, and Jack was downright surly. Gabe smiled. He was nice to me. There were a few interactions that got a little dicey, but the point is, over something like nine months of being around them, getting to know them, and understand them as best as I can, I think I know the least about Gabe."

"He uses his charm as armor."

Becca nodded. "Exactly. He uses that smile and that politeness and that kindness to hide whatever is going on underneath all that. Much like Alex and Jack, some of his behavior suggests he's getting worse instead of better. Gabe hides it differently than Jack and Alex did. I think he needs something different than Alex and Jack do. There's something separate about him, and I think he sees you as a threat to that separateness."

"I can't make him get therapy." She didn't like to accept that simple fact, but it *was* a fact—she couldn't force anyone. They had to want it on some level.

"That's what I'm saying. Maybe Gabe doesn't need therapy. At least not the way Alex and Jack did. If he's separate and different, maybe we need a completely different approach."

"Like what? Because that's one very annoying question that I don't have a clue what the answer is."

"I don't know either." Becca moved so she was hidden behind her horse. "Sex is always an option."

Monica screeched a laugh. "Becca Denton."

"Well, I'm just saying. I mean, don't get me wrong. You helped Alex immeasurably, but sex was some good therapy, too. It got him to a place where he was ready to get the therapy."

"*Love* did that. Not sex."

"Eh, I think it was both."

Monica laughed again. "Well, because you've got both, I wouldn't suggest you have sex with Gabe."

Becca appeared at her horse's tail. "You know I didn't mean me."

"Then who?" Monica asked innocently, focusing on brushing Pal's tail.

"Don't play dumb. It doesn't suit you."

Monica straightened her shoulders. If she couldn't play dumb, she'd play her other roles. "I'm a mother and a therapist. I'm not just going to go *hook up* with some guy. Especially some guy I have to work with."

"But you said yourself you're worried about only being a mom and a therapist. You should be a woman too. A great place to find your inner woman is in a guy's pants."

Monica tossed her brush at Becca, and Becca jumped out of the way, laughing.

"This wedding of yours has made you lose your mind," Monica said, pointing an accusatory finger toward the sleigh in the back.

"Sex was only a suggestion. I guess you could also take up knitting."

"There has to be some middle ground between ill-advised sex and *knitting*."

"Maybe. Although Montana is pretty isolated. I'm not sure what middle ground you're going to find."

Well, she'd find *some*. Because sex with Gabe was not an answer to any of her problems. Or his. Ever.

If she was picturing broad shoulders again—this time shirtless, like she'd seen them this summer—well, no one had to be the wiser.

Chapter 7

"IF YOU DON'T STOP MAKING OUT WITH YOUR DAMN fiancée, I'm leaving without you," Gabe announced, probably more irritably than he should have and for no good reason.

"You can't leave without me. I'm the bachelor in the bachelor party," Alex called from where he and Becca were huddled in the next room, doing who knew what.

"I don't think Pioneer Spirit is going to close down before we get there," Jack said, seated all cozy with Rose on the couch.

Gabe narrowly resisted scowling at the both of them.

"I want a full report," Rose said, since she owned Pioneer Spirit. She'd taken a leave of absence, letting her head waitress run things while she was pregnant. "Crowd size. How's the new hire doing. If anyone is hassling my waitresses," Rose said.

"Why are you asking me for a report? He's your lapdog," Gabe said, gesturing at Jack.

"You were just down there this morning," Jack said. "I think Tonya warned you that any more checking in would result in you being bodily blocked from the bar until the baby is six months old."

"I am the boss, not Tonya." Rose crossed her arms over her chest and scowled, but Gabe had a feeling she'd be dealing without any reports.

The front door swung open, and Colin bolted inside,

Monica following at his heels with a box in her hands. She leaned back on the door, clearly struggling with the weight in her arms.

Gabe scowled, marched over, and took the box from her. Christ, it was heavy.

"Thanks," she offered. "Just some supplies for our little party," she said, unwinding the scarf from around her neck.

Since he didn't want to watch the staticky strands of blond hair swirl around her face as she took off her winter gear, he peered in the box. "Are those *board* games?"

Becca and Alex finally emerged from the other room.

"We're having an old-fashioned sleepover. So don't you three dare stumble in here drunk later. It's the bunkhouse for you."

"I hope someone won't be stumbling drunk," Monica offered, hanging up Colin's already shed winter gear along with her own.

"I'm the designated driver," Jack said, unwinding himself from Rose and getting to his feet. "I took the nine-month alcohol-free pledge."

"You've got him so whipped, I don't know how you live with yourself."

"I guess the same way you live with that piss-poor attitude of yours," Rose replied sweetly. "Maybe a little whipping would do you some good, Gabe."

Gabe just grunted.

"Do I really have to stay with the girls?" Colin whined, looking hopefully up at Gabe.

Gabe patted his dark head. "Sorry, kid, twenty-one and over for this party. But do me a favor and play with the dogs. They'll be needing some male companionship."

Colin grumbled, but soon enough, he was sprawled out

on the rug with the two ranch dogs, happily scratching their stomachs while Jack and Alex pulled on their winter coats.

"Be safe, you three," Becca said sternly, slipping Alex's hat on his head.

"No bar fights or you're paying me damages," Rose added.

The couples exchanged kisses, and Monica and Gabe stood awkwardly, pretending like they didn't notice they were the two singles in the room.

Then, thank Christ, they were out the door and on the way to the bar. Finally. Gabe hadn't had a decent drinking night in *weeks*.

Alex and Jack talked about the fixes they'd done to the furnace at Jack and Rose's place on the way to the bar, and Gabe mainly nodded along, pretending to listen. Montana was dark and stark outside the truck's window, and Gabe appreciated that lack of red-and-green Christmas lights out here in the middle of nowhere.

Of course, once they got to Blue Valley proper, it was all lit-up storefronts, wreaths on doors, and those obnoxious pieces of tinsel and garland strung from streetlights on one side of the road to the other.

Even Pioneer Spirit was decked out in twinkling lights and ribbons. "The one hope I had for this town was its total lack of holiday charm."

Alex laughed. "Everyone loves Christmastime, Gabe. Even Blue Valley. Perhaps even you, deep down." He parked in the small gravel lot next to Pioneer Spirit's somewhat shabby exterior, somehow made to look inviting by the red, white, and green lights decorating the storefront.

"Don't confuse me with the Grinch. This cold, black heart ain't ever growing three sizes."

Jack snorted, sliding out of the truck in time with Alex. "Yeah, you're a real hard-ass. That kid is terrified of you."

Gabe stepped out of the truck, wincing at the cold and the pain in his hip, which was made worse by the temperature and the gravel beneath his feet. "Whatever, Captain Whipped America."

They razzed each other as they made the short trek to the bar entrance, then stepped into the dim warmth of the bar. Alex and Gabe grabbed a table while Jack went and ordered them a round.

Finally, they all sat at the table, uncomfortably like old times that felt even older than they should. Because during old times their lives had been the three of them. Now it was more like couples and one solitary Gabe. Gabe raised his glass and did his best to pretend this was all *fantastic*. "A toast to the last days of the single man."

"I think it's supposed to be a happy toast, Gabe," Jack replied. "Not one that sounds like a funeral."

"It *is* a death of sorts. At least for the guy downstairs."

Alex shook his head. "The guy downstairs has no complaints."

"Well, that is something to toast to." They all clinked glasses, and Gabe ignored the way his chest tightened. It *was* the end of something. Jack and Alex wanted to pretend like time wasn't marching on, but Gabe knew what marriages and babies did. They separated people. Gave you new people to love, and the old people didn't fit in anymore.

He drank deeply. "So, when are we going to toast you?" he said to Jack. "Make an honest woman of that girl you knocked up?"

"As if I haven't tried. Rose has a timeline of her own, and I'm just following it."

Alex shook his head. "You should put your foot down."

Jack gave Alex a doleful look. "Since I like my foot, and Rose would chop it off if I tried to 'put it down' anywhere near her, I'll stick to her timeline."

That earned a laugh from both Alex and Gabe. Gabe couldn't say he would've predicted either woman for his two best friends. Shy, skittish Becca, who'd come into her own and was nearly as much of a military leader as Alex himself. She had a softness to her, and it was good for all of Alex's tightly controlled edges.

Then there was snarky, tattooed, take-no-shit Rose and Captain America Jack. As opposite as night and day, but it worked. Clicked. And because they were his best friends, the men he'd become a man with, a SEAL with, he was *glad* for them and what they'd found.

But he also recognized their trio was coming to an end. Everything would change. Marriage and babies and families. No matter how hard Alex and Jack tried, Gabe would be the odd man out. The one who didn't fit. It was a place he was so used to it was somewhat of a shock to be hurt by the change.

"Before we really start celebrating, there is something I want to talk to you about, Gabe."

Gabe sipped his whiskey suspiciously. "Is it a discussion I'll need more alcohol for?"

"We just wanted you to know that if you need to take some time off and go back to New Jersey to visit your family for Christmas, we can make that happen."

Gabe stiffened. It was quite the ambush, and one he certainly hadn't seen coming. He'd been friends with and deployed with Alex for nearly fifteen years, Jack for more than ten. Alex had asked about his family a few times, but Gabe had never answered in any meaningful way. He'd thought both Alex and Jack had accepted long ago that Gabe didn't have a family.

"You're not going home," Gabe said, nodding toward Jack. Deflection was always the best way to not have to answer a question.

"No, we didn't think Rose would be up for the trip. Since my family just visited this summer, it didn't seem imperative, especially with Rose's family so close. I imagine next Christmas, we'll find some time to go there, or they'll find some time to come up here."

Alex leaned forward, resting his elbows on the table. They hadn't been Navy SEALs for two years now. But during that time, they'd given Alex a lot of grief for still acting like the leader, and yet sometimes, that was comforting—to watch Alex put on that suit of armor and be prepared to fight for something.

It was not comforting when they were talking about this.

"I've never pushed on your family business, and I know you appreciate that, but I have to push now. Afterward, we can get drunk and forget it ever happened, but for a few seconds, we're going to be straight. I don't know what your deal is with your family. You've made sure never to tell us. And that's your prerogative. I just know I missed a lot of Christmases at home on purpose, without even really being aware of what I was doing. When my dad died, I realized I'd missed out on all these things. I let something subconscious build and cause me to miss something, and I'll always regret it. I don't want you to go through the same thing."

Gabe leaned back in his chair, trying to put on his best mask of a smile. But he couldn't. He couldn't muster it with this lump in his throat or this awful constriction in his chest. He couldn't smile and brush it off. He couldn't laugh and say something flippant like, "The difference between you and me, Alex, is that your family gave a shit."

He had to find a way to end this conversation without making it seem like a bigger deal than it was. Without giving it an emotional weight it didn't need.

"I don't need to go home for Christmas. That's not something I'm going to regret." He said it decisively, and he didn't let it show that it nearly cut him in half to say it. Not because it was a lie, but because it was simply the truth.

"Okay, answer me one question and then we'll move on."

Gabe looked at Jack with as much blankness and unaffectedness he could manage. He had the sinking suspicion he didn't fool his friends all.

"Will you not regret it because you think you don't want to deal with it, or will you not regret it because there's a mutual break?"

The bitterness was so thick he could barely curve his mouth into a smile. "Trust me, it's very mutual. They want as little to do with me as I want to do with them. That's the way it's been for fifteen years. No deaths will change my mind. I'm exactly where I want to be. And I don't plan on going anywhere else."

"Good," Alex said firmly. "Because we don't want you going anywhere else. You're family. Our brother. This is where you belong."

"Just don't sleep with my fiancée, please. So far that's my only experience with brothers."

The fact Jack could make a joke about his ex-fiancée's previous infidelity showed just how far the man had come. And Alex saying *brothers* without mentioning *Navy SEALs* showed just how far he'd come. These men had grown and changed and embraced civilian life. They'd found women who were somehow exactly right for them.

They were leaving Gabe behind.

Gabe raised his glass. "To building your families," he said. Because that's what Alex and Jack were doing. That was the thing Gabe was never going to do.

So he downed his glass and got to the very familiar work of getting drunk as a skunk.

"The fact you own Mall Madness is the greatest damn joy of my life," Rose said as Monica cleaned up the game. They'd spent something like hours playing board games and getting Becca drunk.

Monica had never been to a bachelorette party—she hadn't even had one. She'd known Becca wouldn't appreciate penis paraphernalia, and Becca hadn't had many friends growing up, so Monica had decided to go for sleepovers and nostalgia.

They'd overdosed on junk food, wine for her and Becca, board games, and lots of laughter, while Colin sulked with the dogs. He was sleeping next to one as Monica finished cleaning the game up.

"You can thank my parents, who saved all my childhood toys, and my son, who had no interest and thus did not destroy them. What's next?"

"I'm sorry, Becca. I love you, but I'm not playing another round of Monopoly. Mall Madness was awesome, but I'm board-gamed out." Rose linked her hands over her expanding stomach.

"You're just mad that you landed on Broadway with the hotel."

"No, I'm mad that I'm pregnant and can't get blisteringly drunk while we do this horror show masquerading as a bachelorette party. Where's the penis talk? We could have had strippers *while* playing Mall Madness."

"Rose," Monica admonished. "My ten-year-old is *right* there."

"Oh please. He's out like a light and he should probably know that women talk about penis just as much as men talk about—"

"Don't you dare finish that sentence," Monica hissed as Becca giggled uncontrollably. "I don't want him knowing what men *or* women talk about."

"Just so you know, after I get married and then have this baby, we're having a retroactive bachelorette party for me, where we will actually do things you do at a bachelorette party. *Fun* things."

"I thought the future bride was supposed to have a bachelorette party *she* thought was fun."

"Well, drunk Becca *is* fun." Rose moved to face Becca. "All right. Spill some sex stuff."

"I am taking this boy upstairs before he wakes up and is scarred for life," Monica said, moving toward her sleeping child. "Then you can have as much sex talk as you please, Rose."

"Thank God." She bounced on the couch, grinning. "I want to hear about girth."

Monica groaned trying to pull Colin out of his prone sleeping position on the floor without waking him up. He grumbled something, but she managed to lift him. He was tall but all gangly limbs instead of heavy bulk.

Monica managed to carry him up the stairs and into one of the extra bedrooms. She laid him down on the bed and pulled the covers over his shoulders. Part of her was tempted to stay here with him. Keep an eye on him. She didn't want him to feel like he was alone.

But there was another part of her, probably the part aided by a glass or two of wine, that wanted to hear about girth.

When she returned to the living room, Becca was laughing so hard she had tears streaming down her cheeks. Her face was fire-engine red and Rose looked pleased as punch.

"If you don't fill me in because I took my son to bed, I'm excommunicating you both from my friendship."

Monica plopped herself down on the empty cushion of the couch, picking up the glass of wine she'd been sipping on earlier. She might regret a few more glasses, but it would be fun and something she hadn't done in forever. It wasn't irresponsible to get a little tipsy because Rose was here and sober, and could handle any problems that cropped up.

Monica deserved a tiny bit of fun for once, a little girl time. She hadn't had that in… Well, she'd never had drunk, talk-about-actual-sex girl time. She'd gotten married at nineteen, had her son at twenty, and spent the past ten years raising him and building her career.

"Rose has decided…" Becca dissolved into another

fit of giggles. "How... Well..." Becca made awkward hand gestures as she laughed.

"What?" Monica demanded.

"I was just saying that I've determined the size of our three fine Navy SEALs by, you know, months of dedicated research."

"Does Jack know you've been researching the size of the other two?" Monica asked, happily amused both by Rose's conversation and Becca's scandalized laughing.

Rose waved her away. "Oh, I'm talking about before Jack and I got together. When those boys first walked into my bar all Navy SEAL sure of themselves with just a hint of an edge to make them interesting, let's just say I scoped out the landscape."

"So who wins?"

Rose smiled slyly at Becca. "Depends on what you're looking for. Length. Girth. Stamina."

"You cannot judge stamina by looking!" Monica said, giving her a light slap across the arm.

"*I* can. It's like a sixth sense."

"A penile sixth sense. Maybe you're the eighth wonder of the world."

"Now, it isn't fair to share *all* I've surmised considering I'm sleeping with one, and you're sleeping with the other," Rose said, nodding toward Becca. That all-too-satisfied look slid to Monica. "And technically I can't prove my theories until someone takes a gander at Gabe *without* clothes."

"I nominate Monica."

Monica glared at Becca. "You need to stop obsessing about me getting into Gabe's pants."

"It's not so much an obsession as *my* sixth sense. I

think you and Gabe complement each other. Besides, Rose and I are taken. You're all that's left."

"Well, I only believe in penile sixth senses, so your complementary sixth sense can bite me."

Both Rose and Becca dissolved into fits of giggles, and Monica couldn't help but follow. The discussion then ranged from Rose's sex talk, to Revival, to first times. The more Monica drank, the more she felt a little bit like crying at how nice this all was.

When a thump sounded loud somewhere out by the porch, Monica frowned. Her first thought was Colin had woken up, but it wasn't right above them, like it should have been for that.

"Oh no," Becca said, looking at where the thumping had come from.

"What? What is it?" Rose asked, wide eyed.

"Ron Swanson's on the roof."

Monica groaned. "Not the goat. Please, not the goat."

"That's what that sound is. He's up there." Becca looked imploringly at Monica. "You have to get Rasputin." Becca's rooster was the only thing that could ever get Ron off the roof. "I mean, I could get him, but I'd need someone to hold me upright, as the world's kind of spinning."

Monica wasn't exactly steady on her feet, but she wasn't going to send a pregnant woman or a completely loaded woman to do the job. Which meant it fell to her. She pushed to her feet. "Rose, I hope your retroactive bachelorette party doesn't involve goats or roosters."

"From your lips to God's ears," Rose returned as Monica pulled on her winter gear. She lost her balance a bit but caught herself by leaning against the wall as she pulled on her second boot.

"You okay there, champ?" Rose asked with some concern.

"I think a little drunk is necessary for me to even attempt to touch that rooster." Monica pulled on her hat. "If I'm not back in twenty, send a search party after me. I imagine the rooster has pecked my eyes out."

"Rasputin wouldn't do that. Not both eyes anyway."

"Uh-huh. I'll be back." Monica stepped out into the icy night. As she stepped off the porch, she looked up at the dazzling sky above. Stars twinkled everywhere, and the moon's light bathed the snowy ranch in silver. Becca had strung Christmas lights all over the house and barn, so red and green cut through all that white.

Monica took a deep breath. Oh, it was beautiful. How lucky she was to have come here, to get to experience this.

Then she remembered herself and turned to look up at the roof. And there was a goat, munching on a wreath, while red and green lights sparkled around him. She doubted very much that many people got to experience this.

She pulled her phone out and took a picture of Ron Swanson on the roof, chuckling to herself. Before she could head for the barn to get Rasputin, she heard a truck rumble in the distance, then saw headlights cutting through the dark.

When the truck came to a stop, Jack slid out of the driver's seat and glared up at the roof. "Damn goat."

"I'm on my way to get Rasputin. Unless, as the only sober one, you want to handle that for me." Monica smiled winsomely.

Jack grimaced. "Oh, fine, but keep an eye on those two. They're going to need help getting to the bunkhouse. Just keep them inside the truck till I'm back."

"Sure."

Jack strode to the barn and Monica peered into the truck. She thought both Gabe and Alex were passed out, until the back door swung open.

Monica jumped, taken aback as Gabe stumbled down from the truck. Monica waved a hand in front of her face as the smell of alcohol and bar hit her like a punch. "Dear Lord, how much did you have to drink?"

"S-still conscious s'apparently not 'nough," he said, falling to a knee, then getting back to his feet and brushing the snow off his pants.

"Jack said you're supposed to stay in the truck."

"Jack ain't never been my commanding officer, and he's not starting now." Gabe took a step toward her, stumbled again, and she reached forward to try and help keep him upright. Except then they were both somehow in the snow, Gabe something like half on top of her.

He didn't get up, and she was shocked enough to just lie there in the cold, icy snow with his dark eyes assessing her.

"You smell pretty."

Monica laughed in spite of herself. "You need to work on your drunk compliments." She pushed at his chest. "Get off me." Good Lord, it was a hard chest. Even under his coat and heavy shirt, she could feel the strength of him.

But Gabe rolled off her and got to his feet. He held out a gloved hand, and she let him pull her to her feet. But then he pulled her closer, not letting go of her hand. His head tilted down to her ear, much like it had in the bunkhouse the other day.

"I doubt you want to hear my other compliments, s-sweetheart."

It was a slur more than a stutter, and he was falling-down drunk and foolish, so she did not shudder at that. Not at all. "Don't let alcohol put words in your mouth, Gabe."

He kept his grip on her hand, pulling her so close their bodies touched. It shouldn't have mattered. They were both wearing enough layers to ward off the cold of a Montana winter night. She didn't feel cold. Shivery maybe, but not cold.

"Oh, I have those words when I'm sober too. I've just got enough sense to keep them to myself." His lips barely touched her ear as she spoke. "Sparks, remember?"

She could only stare at him, and she didn't feel all the icy wetness on her back or the frigid chill of the air around them. She only felt his big hand holding on to hers and, somehow, all that heat emanating off him. "I remember."

He leaned closer, so close his cheek actually pressed to hers. Everything inside of her rioted to some sparkling life. A feeling so long forgotten it was almost foreign, centering itself low in her belly.

"Drunk enough to make a bad decision?" he asked in a low, rough voice.

She paused. Even knowing it should be an automatic no, there was that foreign part of her *tempted*. A bad decision with him sounded *enticing* instead of wrong. Something she deserved instead of something she should avoid.

But he was drunk. *She* was a little too. That was all that foreign part was. The loss of sense and control, and she'd never let herself give in to that. "N-no."

He grinned, pulling back, all wolfish in the silvery light of the moon. "Too bad." Then he was striding... well, stumbling, toward the bunkhouse.

Jack returned with Rasputin and used the rooster to coerce Ron Swanson off the roof. Monica could only watch, thinking a little too hard about that foreign part of herself and how much she wanted to make it a lot less foreign.

Chapter 8

HANGOVERS WERE A BITCH. HANGOVERS WHILE women were fluttering around talking about weddings were an extra bitch.

"We need to have as much set up in the barn as we can," Monica was saying, looking over Becca's wedding binder while Becca banged around the kitchen. "Then tomorrow everything has to be set up before noon, so we have time to get dressed and ready and take pictures."

"Do you think we should send one of the boys to pick up the floral arrangements? I'm worried about weather and the roads," Becca offered.

"I'll do it," Gabe piped up, because, God, it would get him out of here and this.

"I'll call the florist and see if that works for her," Monica said, making a note in the binder. "But you aren't worried about the food and cake getting up here?"

"Mom's church ladies will *build* a road here for that. She's probably with them now with eighteen hundred backup plans. Besides, the guest list is so small, if we end up having to eat sandwiches and Twinkies, I'll live."

The women were banging around louder now. Jack had taken Colin out on a ride, and Rose was still asleep, something about pregnant women getting a pass. But these two were making enough noise for ten men.

Gabe placed his head on the table and tried to cover

his ears with his arms, while Alex groaned. "Why aren't you hungover?" Alex asked his soon-to-be bride.

"I *am* hungover," Becca replied. "I'm just tougher than you."

"Of that I have no doubt," Gabe muttered. "Can't I just get out of here and get those flowers?" The inside of a truck would be quiet. No banging. No chattering.

"This'll help," Becca offered, sliding a plate full of eggs and toast in front of him.

Gabe smiled up at her. "You sure you don't want to marry me?"

"Sorry, Hannibal doesn't like you."

"How do you know? I've never seen this mysterious cat you claim to have."

"That's how I know," Becca replied happily. She set another plate in front of Alex before going back to the toaster and adding more bread. "Why doesn't Monica call the florist, and if they give the okay, you two can head out there?"

"Two?" Gabe said, jerking his head toward Becca and immediately regretting it as his stomach roiled.

"I need someone there who knows what the flowers are supposed to look like. And if you're going to transport them all, it's probably a two-person job."

Gabe wanted to withdraw his offer, but he knew what that would look like, so he focused on eating. Becca and Monica blah-blah-blahed while he and Alex sluggishly ate their breakfast.

In the end, the florist gave the okay, so Gabe spent the remainder of the day dreading the car ride to get the flowers with Monica.

At least there was work to do, even if it was

wedding-prep work. The small number of guests would be seated in the barn on a variety of chairs and benches they were pulling from the house. There'd be rented portable heaters, decorations, and then a reception in the same spot.

That afternoon, Gabe had been given sweeping duty, though it was currently giving his shoulder a hell of an ache. Still, he wasn't about to admit that. Jack was scrubbing down chairs, and Alex was alternating between washing windows and hanging more Christmas lights up around them. Rose was inside, putting together a playlist for the reception, and Becca was apparently practicing with Ron Swanson for his flower goat duties.

Flower. Goat.

Sometimes Gabe couldn't help but wonder if Revival Ranch was some weird dream world that only existed in his head.

He swept the pile of straw bits and dirt into the industrial-size dustpan, then headed for the trash bin outside. It was nice and cold out here. Inside was some mix between too cold to take off a coat and too warm to leave one on. Besides, it was quiet out here instead of the low strains of music Jack had cruelly insisted they put on.

Most of the hangover had receded after lunch, but he still wasn't one hundred percent. So he gave himself a moment to cool off, look at the gray sky and heavy winter around him, and breathe.

Except soon enough, the world around him wasn't gray—at least not solely. Instead, a bright blob of red was headed toward him, blond hair wisping out from underneath her green hat.

She looked like a Christmas postcard. Which was *not*

appealing. Last night and the foolish offer he'd made had been a *joke*.

He kept trying to make himself believe it.

Monica crossed the yard, overly wrapped up in coats and hats, her hands shoved deep into her pockets.

"Hey," he greeted, because he wasn't about to let her know he felt uncomfortable over the events of last night. Or that they stuck in his mind in glaring detail—wide, blue eyes, the way there'd been a moment of considering as they'd stood oh so damn close, and then the stuttering, shuddery way she'd turned him down.

His body did *not* tighten at the thought. He wouldn't let it.

"Hey. Listen, I know it's an inconvenience, but I was hoping we could run a few errands before we pick up the flowers. It's hard to find the time to get into town, and I have a few Christmas things I need to pick up for my parents and Colin. If I'm unloading flowers right when I get back, I can hide the Colin stuff where he can't snoop."

Gabe scowled. He didn't want extra time with this woman, but how could he argue with that? "Does he still believe in Santa?"

Monica's mouth turned into something he might have labeled a pout on any other woman. On her it just made him think about, well… He wouldn't let his mind go there.

"No. Some jerk-off in his kindergarten class spilled the beans and I couldn't repair the damage. But I still like to pretend, especially because he gets to pretend to be *so* over it while practically screaming with joy over things."

Gabe couldn't help but smile. "Well, I'm driving."

"Are you expecting me to argue? I hate driving up here. Why do you think I make Colin ride the bus?"

"Who's going to pick him up?"

"The Lanes. Their daughter gets off at the same stop, and I think Colin has a little crush on her. They had to do a school project together, so he's been over to their house a few times. Summer Lane is the sister of the man Rose's sister is married to and whose cabin I'm renting."

"I didn't follow that."

Monica waved a hand. "Doesn't matter. Would you be up to leaving now?"

"And get out of sweeping duty? Yeah, let's hit the road." He might not want to spend quiet time in a truck with Monica, but his shoulder was screaming, and this was a way of getting out of the work without admitting that.

"So," Monica began, studying him out of the corner of her eye as they headed for where the Revival Ranch truck was parked. "Feeling better?"

"Sure."

"You certainly had a lot to drink."

When he looked at her, he noticed that despite all those layers, he could see her cheeks were pink and her blue eyes were shifty.

This wasn't about therapist stuff, which pleased him way more than it should have. "If this is your shitty way of asking if I remember last night, let me answer you plain. I remember everything."

"Everything," she echoed, staring at her feet as they stepped one after the other into the heavy snow.

He tried to fight off a grin. "Yeah, especially the way you threw yourself at me and I so politely declined."

She stopped in her tracks and the sound that came out of her mouth was some amazing mix of outraged screech and threatening growl.

It really shouldn't turn him on.

"*I* turned *you* down," she said through clenched teeth, glaring up at him.

"Oh, right." Gabe stroked his chin with his gloved hand as if he was going back over it in his head. Then he flashed her a grin he hoped would make her turn even more red. "Regret it yet?"

She stared at him openmouthed and then shook her head, something like a laugh escaping her mouth. "You are something else."

"Doesn't answer my question."

She stood there, staring at him too hard and too long, to the point he felt a little…lost in it all. Blue eyes and a mouth he desperately wanted to taste.

You do not want the shrink.

Except, he did. He *did* want this woman, no matter what she was. The only way he was going to do the *sane* thing was to admit it to himself. Pretending it wasn't there wasn't going to eradicate that want. He had to face it. Head-on.

Just not his…head. On anything.

"Maybe I don't know the answer to your question," she said quietly, damn near solemnly, those blue eyes of hers staring up at him as if he'd have any clue what to do with that.

They stood like that, in the cold that felt somehow like heat, eyes seemingly incapable of looking away.

Finally, she cleared her throat and gestured toward the truck. "We should head out."

"Yup." Yup. Head out of crazy town. ASAP.

Monica sat in the passenger side of the ranch truck trying not to relive the horror of saying *Maybe I don't know the answer to your question.*

What on God's green earth had she been thinking? And there was no alcohol to blame for that gigantic lapse in judgment.

There might be some teeny, tiny, idiotic, worthy-of-scrutiny part of her that *did* regret turning down Gabe's "offer." She might have dreamed of his voice, low and somehow seductive even *drunk*, which wasn't possible.

She was hard up and losing her mind. Even camels needed water at *some* point, and boy, was she a sex camel. Gabe was the first offer of water she'd had in a long time. Didn't mean the water was safe to drink.

Right. *Right.*

"So, where to first?" Gabe asked.

Monica rattled off her list as Gabe navigated what little traffic there was in Bozeman. It was the closest town with a box store, and while she'd ordered most of Colin's gifts off the internet to be shipped and delivered while he was at her parents, she still needed a few odds and ends for stockings and the like.

She grabbed a cart as they entered and figured Gabe would go off on his own, but he merely followed her.

"Are you done with your Christmas shopping?" she asked, hoping he'd take the hint and vamoose.

"Gift cards aren't complicated."

She frowned at him as she wheeled her way to the video game aisle. "You did not get your family gift cards."

"I didn't get my family anything. I got my Revival family gift cards. Well, I got Becca a llama bottle opener and a gift card. Yours is to the liquor store. Colin's is to that video game shop in Merriton. Merry Christmas."

She opened her mouth. He'd gotten her and Colin gifts? She hadn't…considered that. Of course, she'd planned gifts for everyone at Revival, but it hadn't occurred to her they'd buy anything for Colin, or anything that might be a personally tailored sort of gift rather than just a rote thing you gave coworkers.

"What do you get from your family?" he asked, squinting at some display as if trying to figure out the trial video game, while Monica considered a scarf with Colin's favorite video game villain on it.

"My mom will get me clothes. Maybe winter gear, since I'm always complaining about the cold. I shouldn't say 'my mom.' It'll be from both my parents."

"And Colin?"

"Oh." She pretended to study the price tag. "Well, depends."

"On?"

"If they made something in school and he remembers to bring it home." Which she shouldn't have to defend. He was ten, and what would be the point of buying something for herself and having him give it to her? She glared at Gabe where he was still fiddling with the game system. "We're not big on gifts," she said imperiously.

"But gift cards are a travesty, huh?"

"He's ten." She threw the scarf in the cart. "Now, I need to get my parents books."

"Somehow less of a travesty than a gift card?"

"Yes. Picking out a book for someone shows that you know them, and you have some *clue* as to what they like. It shows you're paying attention, and that you like them."

"So, what book are you going to get me?"

She tapped her chin, pretending to ponder it. "Maybe I'll find one on the great art of narcissism."

He chuckled good-naturedly.

"You can stay here and play your video games."

"Nah, I'll look at books."

So they walked over to the book section of the store, and Monica tried very hard to concentrate on finding a book that her mother would like, and then her father. It was admittedly hard to concentrate with six-foot-something of former Navy SEAL just...lurking.

Which was silly. She was used to tough military men in her life. She'd been *raised* with one, then married to one, and none of that lurking had ever affected her. Not like this.

Sex camel. Sex camel. Only one cure for a sex camel.

"Hell," she muttered.

"What's that?"

"Nothing. Nothing. I think I'm going to have to order something for my dad. None of this really works. Besides, it's nearly five, and we should head over to the florist."

"Here. Try this one." He handed her a book.

She took the heavy, dry-looking tome. She wrinkled her nose at the black-and-white picture on the front. It was some complicated-looking nonfiction book about the role of presidents during wars of the twentieth century.

Damn Gabe Cortez.

"How did you know he'd like this?" she demanded.

Gabe shrugged, taking it upon himself to push the cart toward the front of the store while she trailed behind.

"Marines are all the same. Like all that bullshit about politics and war. Like it's complicated and not always a dick-measuring contest."

"Is that all war is?"

"Is to me."

"I don't believe that." He looked sharply over his shoulder at her, but she simply held his gaze. "You don't join the military if you think that."

"First of all, you don't know the first thing about why I joined the military. Second, a lot of guys think it once they've been through one. Because you don't come out unscathed from that. You either double down on what you believe, or you realize it's all a bunch of bullshit."

"So, you're the enlightened, I suppose."

"No, it's not enlightened. It's just how you deal. One way's not better than the other."

He always managed to surprise her. She was used to uncompromising military men, and there was an element of that to him. But it was somehow…open-minded. There was a lack of judgment. Gabe seemed to believe in survival however you managed it. Considering that was at the heart of her therapy mission, it was impossible not to admire him for it.

"So why did you join the military?" she asked, unable to resist. It wasn't a therapist's question either. No, this was a Monica question. *She* wanted to know, as a person, about his person.

She wasn't sure what to do with that, but he smiled. Not those bitter ones meant to push her back a few paces, but one of his charming smiles. The ones he flashed her before he said something…suggestive. Her cheeks heated against her will and that foreign flutter from last night was back in full force.

"Sorry, sweetheart. That's not a question I answer for just anybody."

"Oh," she said, trying to sound calm and not at all affected as she started putting her items on the conveyer belt of the checkout line. "What would an anybody have to do to become a somebody?" She steeled all her courage and calm and self-possession and looked pointedly at him.

But that grin didn't change any, except maybe turn the air a little hotter. Which was impossible. All this *heat* was a figment of her over-wintered imagination.

"I'm not sure. No one ever has. But you're more than welcome to take on the challenge."

That word wound though her. *Challenge.* She never, ever backed down from a challenge. It was one of those things her parents had insisted she learn to do: face any challenge, any hardship, any responsibility.

And she had. Over and over again. But this was different, because she had a bad feeling his challenge would involve nakedness.

Oh, remember male nakedness? That was nice. His would be very, very nice.

The cashier cleared her throat and Monica blushed even deeper. "Sorry," she mumbled, fumbling to pull her credit card out of her purse. She centered herself with the rote actions of sliding the card through the reader and taking the receipt as Gabe loaded up the cart with her bags.

As they walked out of the store, side by side, Monica kept her gaze forward. "I might take that challenge," she said hastily as they reached the truck.

"You might fail."

She looked up at him and gave him a very carefully blank smile. She knew it irritated him by the way his lips firmed and his jaw tightened.

"I might," she agreed, validated somehow when he was the one to break eye contact and finish loading the bags into the truck bed. "But I also might not," she added, heading for the passenger side door.

The fact that Gabe didn't slide into the driver's seat for another minute or so was very validating indeed.

Chapter 9

GABE PULLED AT THE COLLAR OF HIS SHIRT AS HE, JACK, and Alex were lined up by a very overzealous friend of Becca's mother. The barn had been transformed, the pastor from Sandra's church was calm and ready, and the guests were all seated.

Gabe felt like a monkey on parade. "I hate suits," he grumbled, trying not to scowl at the small group of people in attendance.

"You hate everything," Jack replied, giving him a slight nudge as the woman arranging them glared in his direction.

It was fair enough. He also hated weddings, but he'd kept that one to himself because he was a good friend, after all.

Alex didn't say anything. He stood, still as a statue, beside the pastor, his eyes glued to the barn doors, which would be opened when it was time to start.

"Nervous, big guy?" Gabe asked.

"No."

"You sure look it."

Some of Alex's blank stoicism firmed into irritation, which may have been Gabe's plan. If Alex was irritated, he wouldn't be overthinking the next fifteen minutes or planning for every possible disaster as he often did.

But the doors began to open, Hick doing the honors, looking like a completely different person in his suit.

The grizzled ranch hand Alex's father had employed for years was now a suave, well-dressed gentleman.

The doors opened. Christmas lights and luminaries had been put along the aisle runner and now lit up the outdoors.

Becca had said something about their entrance being like *White Christmas* and the reference had gone way over Gabe's head, but snow was softly falling outside. Gabe knew that would give Becca a thrill.

He might hate weddings, but this one wasn't so bad.

A sleigh appeared, pulled by Pal. The horse was decked out in a big wreath of flowers around his neck, all dark reds and bright whites with evergreen holding it all together.

"Maybe a little nervous," Alex muttered as Hick helped Colin out of the sleigh and handed him a leash decorated with greenery and pinecones. Colin was in a suit and looked quite proud to be doing his job of leading the flower goat down the aisle.

Colin made it to the end and handed the leash to Jack. Because yes, Ron Swanson the goat was going to stand up at the front of the wedding with the groomsmen.

Rose was next, wearing a long, flowing, red dress with a fluffy, white wrap. She held a bouquet that matched all the rest of the floral stuff that was about. She smiled at Alex and gave him a wink, but then her gaze was all for Jack.

Monica slid out of the sleigh, tall and willowy in some dark-green contraption that looked soft and silky. Her blond hair was all pulled back in intricate braid things and her lips were a deep, fantasy-worthy red.

Gabe looked down at the goat. It was a better focus, all in all. Besides, Ron might start chewing shoelaces if someone wasn't diligent. But the goat stood there, happily creepy as all get out in his Christmas-themed sweater.

Next to Gabe, Alex swallowed. Very audibly.

"You'll be fine," Gabe said quietly, glancing up. Becca was now stepping out of the sleigh, pretty as a picture and sweet as candy all dolled up in her simple, white dress, something like holly tangled up in her fancy hairdo. She flashed the widest, brightest smile down the aisle, and even Gabe had to admit it gave his cold, black heart a little spark of warmth.

"Yeah. Sure." Alex took a deep breath and let it out. "We've been through worse."

"You sure as hell haven't been through better," Gabe said in a moment of emotional honesty he couldn't say he was comfortable with.

Becca hugged Hick as the music for her procession began to drift through the barn. Sandra met her at the beginning of the aisle runner and began to walk her daughter down it.

Gabe felt the goat brush his pants leg, Ron's mouth getting perilously close to his shoes. "God, we could do without the goat." He nudged the thing away.

"I'd take a million goats," Alex said, his voice suspiciously hoarse, his eyes on nothing and no one but Becca.

"Don't let her know you said that," Gabe replied, but he had no more smart quips after that because she looked beautiful. Perfect. So damn happy it hurt.

Alex had been through hell, before and after war. Seen the worst humanity had to offer, and sometimes the best in the face of it. Together, they had lost friends, good men, honorable men who'd left families behind.

In this moment, there was nothing but joy and love and hope. A universe-deep goodness as Sandra handed

Becca to Alex. As Alex and Becca grinned at each other, shiny-eyed. As they pledged to love each other for the rest of their lives, scratchy-voiced and committed. To each other. To love and hope.

They said I do. The small crowd cheered, and they kissed an inappropriately long time that had a few of Sandra's friends whispering behind their hands.

Gabe's heart did not grow three sizes, as he'd assured Jack and Alex it never would.

But in that moment, it might have grown one.

Monica sat on a long wooden bench, very happy the snow hadn't gotten bad enough that the cake hadn't made it. Because real wedding cake was hard to beat, especially when the alternative was Twinkies.

Most of the couples in attendance were dancing. Alex and Becca, happy and oblivious. Rose's sweet little baby bump between her and Jack reminded Monica a little too much what that was like. So much promise in the spark of a tiny life inside you, and a man who looked at you like you were carrying the world.

Almost ten years had dulled that sharp pang of loss, so these days it was just a dull ache. More generic than specific to Dex. But it still made her a little misty, and mostly she wanted to be happy. Happy for her friends and happy she got to witness it.

Besides, she had Colin. He was in the corner playing with his handheld video game since there was no one even near his age to talk to, and he'd behaved so well. He'd talked with people—mostly Gabe—but had been sociable and polite with other adults for the duration of the wedding and half the reception before she'd given him the video game go-ahead.

Monica finished her cake, looking around the room. It was only when her gaze landed on Gabe that she realized she'd been searching for him.

Her stomach did that obnoxious swoop that reminded her of being an innocent, clueless teenager. She had given herself quite the inner lecture when it had done that as she'd glanced at him as she'd walked up the aisle, but apparently, the lecture hadn't taken root.

She felt shaky and like she didn't know what to do with her hands. She looked away, knowing her cheeks were getting warm. Could she be any more of a *doofus*?

She pushed the plate onto the table, trying to casually look back over the room around her. She should focus on Colin. Remind herself she was a grown up. An in-charge, adult woman. Who could flirtatiously banter with an all-too-attractive former SEAL and come out on top.

Except, *on top* only sounded sexual, and God, sex was one thing she was definitely not on top of.

Get yourself together.

She felt someone approach her, but she faked interest in the last vestiges of frosting on her plate. Then a hand thrust into her vision. A very large hand with a white scar across the knuckles.

"Come on," Gabe said gruffly.

She frowned at his outstretched hand, then up at him, steeling herself against the swoony-stomach feeling. "Come on what?"

"We're going to dance."

She laughed, but he didn't drop his hand or laugh along with her.

"You're joking," she said. Not a question. He *had* to be joking. She couldn't…she couldn't *dance* with him. Dancing was intimate. It meant bodies touching and moving together. She was smart enough to know where her brain would go and how much that would be written all over her face.

A woman did not win a challenge when *lust* was written all over her face. She had to apply some tactical advantage here and there. Gabe in a suit and that obnoxious dimple she could see so clearly on his completely clean-shaven face had the tactical advantage.

"Not joking. Dance with me."

"Why?" She just didn't trust that. Besides, he wasn't *asking*. He was demanding, and she was not prone to following other people's demands.

"Want to know the truth?"

"Pretty much always."

Gabe nodded toward Colin. "Put me up to it."

She frowned at that, glancing at where Colin was face down in his video game. "Why would he do that?"

"He said, and I quote, 'I don't want my mom to be the loser who didn't dance at all.'"

Her jaw dropped. "He did not say that!"

"Okay, he didn't say *that*, but it was the gist. Him worried you were…" He shifted a little bit, that apathetic charm slipping for just a second. "Lonely," he finished, not meeting her gaze.

Something sharp and sad wound around her chest. *Lonely.* Such a strange word. She didn't feel lonely. She had friends. Family. A job she valued and a son to care for. Her days were filled with human interaction.

But *lonely* wrapped around her, a truth she'd been refusing to acknowledge. *Lonely.* Yes, she was. A part of her anyway. The *Monica* part of her she wasn't so sure existed anymore. Except, that little pang seemed to suggest it did.

"Come on." This time, he took her hand. Just took it like it was his to take and pulled her to her feet. She could have stopped him. It wasn't like he was *dragging* her, but her feet were moving along at the pace he set toward the dance floor.

Then he just pulled her into him, like it was natural or normal to feel his body brush hers. To have the hand not holding hers on the small of her back while an instrumental version of "I'll Be Home for Christmas" filled the barn.

She wasn't a tiny woman by any means. She'd inherited her father's height and breadth, but somehow Gabe's hand still seemed to take up the entirety of the small of her back. Somehow, he still had some inches on her even though she was in low heels.

But the mix of Gabe and the pretty, silky, feminine dress she was wearing reminded every last cell of her body that she was a woman, and she hadn't been touched like this in *quite* a long time.

"I *hate* Christmas music," he muttered.

It steadied her some. That grumpy complaint. So *him*. She might find him attractive, but she had for months, and she'd kept a certain professional distance. But you couldn't exactly be a therapist to a guy you'd pictured naked. It didn't mean she had to give in to the nerves and flutters though.

Even if she was slowly opening herself up to the possibility… Well, it *was* a possibility, wasn't it? If he could get over his hatred of her profession, and she could learn to treat someone like a person, not a patient.

Talk about your slim possibilities.

She shook away that pessimistic thought and smiled sweetly up at him. "You know what I'd love to know, Gabe. What *is* something you like?"

"What do I like?" he said as if considering all the possible things he might like. He didn't say anything more than that, but his body was just a centimeter closer to hers, so that her breasts brushed against his chest. So that she could feel his breath on her neck, so that his cheek glanced hers.

Something like a shudder wound through her, then held deep in her belly. Everywhere they touched felt like something between a featherlight caress and static electricity.

There was nothing unintentional about any of it, she realized. The pause, the closeness. Suddenly she could imagine all the things he might like, and she had no doubt that was his intention.

"I like whiskey," he offered, his voice so low she involuntarily leaned her ear closer to his mouth to hear it better. "I like baseball. Go Yankees."

"Ew."

"Oh, don't be one of those obnoxious Yankee haters."

"Don't be one of those obnoxious Yankee fans," she retorted. It was odd. Feeling like an out-of-control, hormone-driven teenager and then moments of adulthood clarity was…weird. But not off-putting. In fact, there was something oddly exhilarating about it.

"Why are you a Yankees fan?"

"Why wouldn't I be?"

"You're very good at deflecting questions. When you

deflect innocuous ones, it only makes me wonder what you're trying to hide."

"That the therapist in you?"

She tensed, the fluttery warmth evaporating. This was what he thought of her. Therapist only.

She wanted to be mad or even irritated, but it merely deflated her. It was how she'd thought of herself for so long—therapist and mom. She couldn't expect people to view her differently than she viewed herself.

But if she wanted to change, if she wanted to explore this unknown part of her that might not exist under any label except *Monica*, then she had to start making strides. Not just beating herself up about it.

"Do you believe in New Year's resolutions?"

"No."

She smiled a little at that. She did appreciate Gabe's straightforward answers that he never attempted to explain away or apologize for. She wanted to find some of that for herself. "That doesn't surprise me. You don't seem like the type. But I do believe in them—in setting goals for yourself. It's never occurred to me to try and just be me. I think I'm going to change that."

"We are what we are. Sometimes the things we do define us, and that isn't a bad thing."

"Sometimes," she acknowledged, intrigued by the way his body tensed. "But these are things that won't last forever. Oh, I'll always be Colin's mother, but he won't always need me the way he does now. At some point, I'll retire from being a therapist. So, what's left when those things are gone?" She looked up at him, but he was staring hard at the closed barn doors. Jaw tight and eyes blank.

"I know you've had to deal with that," she said gently.

His gaze flicked to hers. He opened his mouth and she just knew it was going to be some scathing thing about being a shrink, so she released his hand and placed hers over his mouth. "Whatever nasty thing you have to say, I don't want to hear it. I wasn't speaking as a *shrink*. I was speaking as a person who understands how hard it must be to lose the things that defined you. Which you brought up, I might add."

His dark eyes held hers, and he lifted an eyebrow. Belatedly, she realized her hand was still over his mouth. It was like a match striking, realizing she was touching him now, not just shushing him. His lips were against her palm, and her fingers were pressed to the firm line of his smooth jaw.

She jerked her hand away, then felt like an idiot for having such an overreaction.

"Maybe you'll consider some advice from me then," he said, back to soft and smirky, like he knew some deep secret about her.

That mask, because he expected her to argue. To scoff at his advice. She didn't think Gabe suffered from any low opinion of himself, but he did think the worst of people sometimes. It shouldn't hurt. It probably stemmed from the horrible things he'd seen.

"What you don't understand is that being a therapist doesn't mean I think my patients are less. I don't think I'm above them, morally or psychologically. My job is to help, not think they don't know what they're doing. So, yes, I'd love to hear some advice from you."

"I'm not your patient."

"And I'm not your therapist, so the belligerent act is getting old."

His mouth quirked at that. "All right. Don't wait for New Year's."

"But it's only a few weeks away."

"And in those few weeks, you're going to be alone in a cabin without your son and probably without your work. Why wait some arbitrary number of weeks? Seize the moment because you never know when you'll have another one."

She thought about that in a few different ways. One being that she would be alone. Colin would be gone, and she wouldn't have any sessions with Alex or Jack. She wouldn't be working with Becca, because Becca and Alex were taking a week off foundation work for their stay-at-home honeymoon.

It would just be her. No masks and no protections. Nothing to distract her from herself.

She'd known that, and yet she hadn't really let it sink in. "What do you do with all the time?" she asked, something like panic making her throat feel too tight.

"What time?" Gabe replied gruffly.

She swallowed, looking up at him imploringly, hoping he understood why she needed to know. Hoping he would take this question seriously when he took so little seriously. "What do you do in the in-between times? When there's no work to do and you're in that bunkhouse by yourself? What do you do?"

He stared at her for the longest time. She couldn't read that expression, except she was pretty sure there was at least a moderate amount of compassion hidden there. If that compassion was a figment of her own imagination, well, so be it.

"I work. I sleep. It's not that complicated. Not that

different from the navy, all in all, except I don't have to worry about explosives anymore."

"Isn't it lonely?"

He hardened. "Sometimes it's better to be lonely."

"Why?"

"Because people aren't predictable. Life isn't. You never know who or what you'll lose. What will change."

"Yes, I am intimately acquainted with that. But if I'd embraced lonely, I wouldn't be here. Not standing up as a friend's maid of honor. Not laughing at Hick's corny jokes or giving Rose advice on labor. And you're no different than me. You're in the thick of things too. They're your friends. They're part of your life."

His gaze slid to where Becca and Alex were dancing, if one could call it that. It was really more like a swaying tangle at this point.

"For now," Gabe said, so flat and final, it felt like a crack in her own heart. Where did all that bitterness stem from? That lack of *trust* in people? It had to come from something.

And as you said yourself, you're not his therapist, so maybe it's none of your business.

Maybe, but she was desperately curious. Desperately fascinated by this man in front of her who had such a hard shell, and yet there were pockets of all this warmth. How good he was with Colin. Gentle with the horses. Kind and honorable in all his actions.

But he fixed that blank, charming smile on his face and looked down at her. "Well, duty's done. I'm going to go get myself a drink." He dropped his hand from her back and walked off the dance floor.

Chapter 10

GABE POURED A SINGLE SHOT OF WHISKEY INTO A plastic cup and sipped. Gabe had been in charge of stocking the self-serve area this afternoon, so it offered one of those rare things he liked. Whiskey.

He wished he had less sense of decorum because that would have been very convenient under almost any other circumstance. But he wasn't about to get drunk at his best friend's wedding. He'd just needed an excuse to get off the dance floor.

Monica's conversation had sounded an awful lot like shrink talk on the surface, but he hadn't been able to take it like that. Not with the vulnerable warmth in her eyes or the cast of worry to her pretty, red-painted mouth.

It brought up the uncomfortable realization that she was a person, not just a shrink. He'd known that in an abstract sort of way. He was attracted to her after all. It wasn't like he didn't understand that she was more than just her job.

But it was a lot nicer to be able to put that between them. Having to look at Monica as though she might be vulnerable, as though she might have concerns and worries just like his…

Flirting with her was one thing when she blushed and stuttered, then got herself together and acted like she was going to take the bait when he had no doubt she never would. That was easy, even fun.

There was nothing fun or easy about that conversation, about giving advice when she seemed to need it. Nothing good would come from reaching out and offering something to her.

She wanted something that would take away the loneliness when what she really needed to understand was that loneliness was a way of life. When you stopped fighting it, that was when a lot more things made sense.

Someone slapped Gabe's back, and he looked over to find Alex grinning at him.

"You okay there, big guy?" he asked, repeating Gabe's words from before the ceremony.

Gabe lifted his glass. "Why wouldn't I be?"

"You sure ended that dance with Monica awfully quickly. Quick enough she was standing there, staring after you like you'd slapped her."

"Interesting interpretation," Gabe replied, offering Alex a plastic cup. Alex took it, then nodded when Gabe held up the whiskey. Gabe poured.

"What's your interpretation?" Alex asked, turning around to survey the barn around him, leaning back on his elbows.

Gabe felt he had to do the same, so he mirrored Alex's pose. "Danced with her because the kid asked me to, then decided to get a drink. No quickly. No slap. Just a dance, and then not."

"Never knew you were so altruistic."

"Guess you don't know everything about me."

Alex sipped his drink thoughtfully. "You know, I'm starting to realize how true that is." He slid Gabe an all-too-perceptive glance considering the guy had just gotten married and should be wrapped up in his new wife. "And how purposeful."

Gabe nodded toward Becca. "Don't you have a wife to pay attention to?"

Alex looked at Becca, everything in his expression visibly softening. Which proved Gabe's point. Alex didn't belong over here quizzing him.

"I do have a wife to pay attention to." His smile widened. "Wife. Hell, that's weird."

"She's going to have you on the baby wagon so fast your head'll spin. Once Rose pops that baby out? You're toast."

Alex sipped again, and none of that smile left his face. "I'll probably live."

"Just wait till you tell the kids you were stepsiblings once."

Alex only laughed good-naturedly.

Gabe's gut churned with an awful mix of happiness and something akin to jealousy. Except that wasn't the right word. He didn't want Alex's life. Didn't want Becca or babies. He didn't want anything.

So he didn't know what that hurt was, and he'd be damned if he examined it here and now.

"I didn't come over here to talk about babies."

"But when you came over here, I decided to talk about things that made you a little green behind the gills." Even though Alex wasn't in the slightest. Still, it sounded good.

"I came over here," Alex continued as if Gabe hadn't spoken at all, "because my friend looked a little miserable."

"You misread me, Alex."

Alex shrugged philosophically. "Maybe. Maybe I

do. But regardless, I came over here to tell you I like Monica a lot. She's got a nice pragmatism to her that's hard to find. She's good with people. You're so wrapped up in that kid of hers you can barely see straight. There isn't a reason in the world that *I* know of you shouldn't be over there dancing with her again."

"You're seriously trying to play matchmaker at your own wedding reception?"

"I'm trying to figure out why my best friend looks like he's miserable at my wedding reception."

"I'm not. I'm not miserable." Misery wasn't the right word. Not that he knew what was. And he didn't want Alex to think it was misery, so he'd give a little, and then he wouldn't have to dig into the rest. "I've never been so happy to see two people married. Never been so happy to be able to be there for something good and right. We deserve that good. You deserve that good."

"*Deserve* is a funny word. I'm not sure we ever get what we deserve out of life. Good or bad."

Gabe laughed a little bitterly at that. God knew there were people in his family who hadn't gotten what they'd deserved. He'd been kicked out, forced to abandon everything all for lies. After he'd done everything to fit the part, to give them what they'd wanted. What had it gotten them? He was alone, and they were together.

He downed the remainder of his paltry drink and pushed those thoughts away. His family had no place here. What they deserved or didn't, it didn't matter to him because he wasn't a part of it anyway. He was here. In this *good* place.

His gaze found Monica across the room. Colin stood in front of her, and she had her arms around him. She was talking to Hick with that bright smile on her face as though the conversation about being lonely had never happened.

Except it *had* happened, and she'd put to words things that would haunt him for days or weeks.

"Once upon a time, when I was stomping around quite resolute in not getting mixed up with Becca—"

Gabe snorted. "The stomping is incredibly accurate."

"Jack said something that stuck with me. Changed my mind or my life or some damn thing."

"And what is this nugget of wisdom?"

"That he cared as much about my future and happiness as I cared about his. That he wanted what was *best* for me, that you both did."

"You got your best," Gabe returned, nodding at Becca. He understood what Alex was getting at, but Gabe was different. He didn't know how or why. He only knew that no one had ever loved him. Maybe he'd never really loved anyone in return. Maybe he wasn't capable.

But here was Alex, the man he'd spent the last fifteen years with, through a hell he'd never imagined, even when his home life had felt like hell. Alex Maguire was his brother, if not by blood, then by everything else. Because that's what fighting a war side by side did to men—turned them into brothers. Gave them the capacity to love someone outside of their family. Outside of their duty.

"If I had any clue what was best, I'd have it. If I had any idea what I was afraid of, I'd fight it," Gabe said, more baldly than he'd planned.

"We fought a lot of enemies we didn't know."

"That was a different life, Alex. A life that is long gone." Like so many of the lives he'd lived and lost.

So many lives and people who'd been blown out from under him.

"It's been years since we lost that life. And in those years, we've started building new ones. A family. A foundation. You can keep yourself separate from those things because you think that's what you need to do or whatever it is that keeps you trapped behind this wall. But we are your family. We are here, and we are part of that foundation and that life. No matter what. Forever."

"So you're suggesting I sleep with your shrink?" Gabe asked, because the emotion was getting too thick, too hard to fight through, and he couldn't. He just couldn't.

Alex shook his head and shoved away from the bar. "I'm suggesting you think about building instead of protecting. I'm suggesting you reach out instead of push away. I'm suggesting you give *and* receive. And I'm telling you that even if you don't, even if you're not ready, we will all be standing here waiting. Loving you and wanting the best for you the whole time."

Gabe tightened his jaw against not just this moment, but the whole of the day. Something a little too close to tears. It was too big and too much. This kind of emotion did terrible things to people. It made them believe. It made them hope.

But belief and hope always died, at least for him, and he couldn't let himself fall into the trap of believing it.

<hr>

As the crowd began to disperse, Monica insisted Jack and Rose head home. Both argued that they should help clean up as originally planned, but Monica could tell

Rose was drooping about as hard as Colin was. Colin could sleep anywhere. The pregnant woman could not.

But it wasn't until Gabe stepped in, a few well-placed sarcastic quips and that easygoing smile that was such complete and utter crap, that they agreed to be on their way.

So it was just her and him. And Colin trying desperately not to fall asleep on a hay bale decoration where he'd curled up to keep playing his game.

"Um." She winced at the *um* considering how much time she'd spent working on speaking without hesitations. *Um* did not inspire confidence in her patients.

Gabe wasn't her patient. Colin, Becca, Rose, Hick— this list of people who did not look at her to be their therapist. She could say *um*. She could be *wrong*.

"We left all the stuff in the bunkhouse. I mean, like… clothes. I need to change my…clothes." She maybe *could* be wrong, but good God, she could at least be coherent.

"So I can expect lots of lacy female stuff all over my man cave?"

It surprised a laugh out of her. "Yeah, we're quite the lacy female trio. Just give me a few minutes to head over there and change and—"

"You can go home."

Monica looked around the barn. It wasn't trashed or anything, but there was plenty to put away. And there was Ron Swanson, munching happily on the flower crown he'd finally managed to get off.

"I can't leave you with a mess and a goat."

Gabe grimaced at the animal. "Sometimes I think I like the rooster better. At least he doesn't have those demon eyes." But his gaze slid to Colin. "Get him home. I can handle this."

It didn't feel right, and she couldn't help but wonder if this had to do with their conversation earlier. He didn't want to be around her. He didn't want to hear about loneliness. He'd rather *run away*, and he'd probably faced men with guns and bombs and stuff.

She was that big of a mess. Yikes.

But she was also not going to run away from herself. She was not a coward, and she was up for the challenge of…something. She wouldn't find out if she didn't keep moving.

"How about this? I'll clean up some of the easy stuff that won't ruin my dress, and then we'll head out. That way I didn't just dump an entire wedding's mess on you."

Gabe shrugged. "Suit yourself."

Yes, she would suit herself. She passed Colin, who'd finally fallen asleep and was snoring faintly. She slipped the handheld device out of his hands and stashed it in her bag.

"Impressive, really."

"He's always been a good sleeper. Can sleep anywhere. Anytime. My mom used to get so irritated by it." Monica smiled at the memory. "Apparently, *I* was a terrible baby, and how dare I get such an easy one."

"You didn't have anyone's help. Probably deserved one."

"I had her for help. And my dad. When I was a baby, even though my dad was alive, he was deployed. Mom lived on the base far away from her family."

"Doesn't base life come with a built-in support system?"

"Sometimes. But you have to be willing to open yourself up to it, and my mom isn't one for asking for help."

"Gee, that doesn't sound familiar."

She glared at him as she tossed some napkins and plastic cups into the trash. "I had a lot of help in the early years."

"Then what?"

"Then I wanted… Well, it felt necessary to do some things on my own. I finished school. Colin started school. I was an adult and I'd been through a lot, but it had all been with my parents. After Dex died, I moved into their house. I lived with them until Colin was five. Suddenly I was twenty-five and I'd only lived for little over a year without them. It seemed…important to stand on my own two feet."

He didn't say anything to that, so she glanced his way as she pulled tablecloths off the handful of tables in the corner. He'd taken off his suit jacket a while ago, since the heaters kept the barn suitably warm. Now he had his sleeves rolled up as he folded chairs and stacked them.

She watched him for a moment, because there was an effortless grace in the way he moved. There was a mesmerizing quality to the way his forearms flexed when he picked up a chair and relaxed when he moved for the next. And comparing and contrasting the arm without a scar and the one with a jagged one down to his wrist was damn near irresistible.

"Want me to flex a little? Give you a real show?" He angled his head to meet her gaze and grinned.

"I was looking at your scars," she said as haughtily as she could manage with the heat stealing into her cheeks.

"That crash did quite the number on this canvas of human perfection, I have to say."

She rolled her eyes and turned back to her work folding and stacking tablecloths. When she glanced over at him again, he was carefully rolling up the aisle runner. A big man, rough and tumble, in a suit, rolling up a pretty little scrap of fabric. And yet the way he crouched as he did the chore was so *military*.

She was reminded of their conversation last night. He didn't just let anyone know why he'd joined the military, and she said she'd take the challenge to be a somebody. Well, here was her chance.

"Your father was military."

He frowned and looked up at her. "Huh?"

"I'm trying to figure out what made you join. Following in your father's footsteps is my first guess."

He shook his head and finished rolling up the runner. "Only thing I know about my father's footsteps is they were Dominican, and I inherited his double crown." Gabe rubbed a hand over his close-cropped hair.

"You joined to pay for college."

He shrugged and placed the rolled-up runner across a line of chairs that didn't fold. "Didn't go."

"You joined to get *away* from your family."

There was the slightest moment where he tensed and hesitated, and she knew if not exactly it, she was close. "You know, you should be mad at me."

She blinked, trying to understand him at *all*. "Mad at you? Why?"

"Because if you weren't a therapist, just a regular woman—"

"I *am* a regular woman," she interrupted between clenched teeth.

"—you would've been mad I ditched you on the dance floor. And you'd make me pay for it. Instead, you're trying to figure me out. You should be mad.

You know, if you're learning how to be Monica or whatever."

Oh, she *was* mad. Now. She tapped her chin, affecting her best "shrink" voice. "No father at home, but someone mentioned you had a big family. So, your mother must have remarried."

"Because let me guarantee you, a woman not trying to play therapist would be pretty irritated—"

"And you didn't get along with your stepfather?"

"—to the point where she would have taken off when I told her I didn't need help cleaning."

"If I had to guess, as both a mental health profession and a damn real woman, I'd say your mother had children with your stepfather and you felt left out."

He stopped working then, and she didn't see any of the fury she'd expected. No, it was like he gathered himself up into *soldier* mode. So stoic and tense and menacing simply because he somehow changed the air around them, not because his expression was threatening.

Slowly, he crossed his arms over his chest. "We seem to be talking at cross purposes."

Which sounded like something she would say. That calmness was supposed to be her, and it made her all the angrier that he was employing it. So she decided to take the Gabe role. She smiled. "Is that SEAL talk?"

His expression flickered from stoicism to something dangerous. Her heart kicked against her ribs and nerves fluttered in her chest, and yet she stepped toward him. She wanted to dive into that *dangerous*. Poke it until something got through his stoicism or fake charm.

She wanted to poke at him until the mask came off. Until she got behind the barriers. She wanted to reach whatever genuine *man* existed under that facade. She *knew* it existed because he was a kind, good man in action.

She just needed him to express that goodness in words, too. Why? She hadn't really figured that out, but maybe if she provoked him enough, she would.

His eyes still glittered, but she watched as he very purposefully relaxed his shoulders, his jaw. A grin curved his mouth. "You know, I bet we can find a purpose not to cross on." His gaze flicked to Colin's sleeping form. "If we were alone."

"You like to throw your innuendo around an awful lot, but you've never once acted on it."

He was suddenly so much closer, and she wasn't sure how he'd done it so fast, so quiet. He was looming over her, all sharp edges and so many emotions she couldn't sort through them all.

She didn't want to. She wanted to absorb them rather than dissect them. Reach out and stand through the storm with him.

"Is that a dare, Monica?" he asked in that silky, dark voice that slithered along her skin. Part nervous fear, and then deeper, a kind of want she didn't know what to do with. Except move away from it.

"N-no."

He cocked his head as if he'd scored some point. "Then what is it?" he asked all innocence and utter bullshit.

She lifted her chin. Maybe she'd blush or stutter, but she wouldn't slink away like a coward. "An observation."

"You haven't taken me up on any of my innuendo, Monica. Why would I act on it if you didn't want me to? Because I've routinely asked if you want me to, and your answer is always no. So, until it's yes…"

He shrugged, and it was as if the smart, rational part of herself died—or at the very least passed out completely—because she moved forward. As close as they'd been when they'd been dancing, and she tilted her head, so she could meet his dark, glittering gaze, and she said the craziest word she'd likely ever said in her life.

"Yes."

Chapter 11

A simple, one-syllable word, and it cracked through him like an explosive.

Yes.

He wanted to taste the *S* sound on her mouth, wanted to hear that *yes* a few more hundred times, and he wanted her.

But her kid was *there*, and she'd guessed too much with all her obnoxious questions. She'd brought up old ghosts, no matter how half-formed, and there was some awful, dark piece of him that wanted her to hurt the way that he did.

"You think I'm going to make you a real girl?"

She didn't wilt or wither. She held his gaze, and though the color was still high on her cheeks, everything about that expression was a shade too close to patronizing for his peace of mind.

"I said yes, Gabe. What's the excuse now? First it was my profession, then it was my consent. So, what's the next one?"

He could use the kid. Probably effectively too. Colin might be the soundest sleeper in the world, but what mom wanted her kid to accidentally wake up in the middle of anything, well... But she was making his excuses—even valid ones like Colin—feel cowardly.

He wouldn't let her turn him into a coward. He wanted her, and maybe there were a million reasons not to have her, but what did they matter? She was close and challenging and, hell, something like a kiss might even get this whole needling, persistent *want* out of his system.

Seemed like a long shot, but sometimes long shots worked out.

He reached out to take one of those flyaway strands of hair between his fingers, and her breath caught. He forgot all about caution or cowardice or long shots. There was only the silky feel of her hair between his fingers, the reddish tint to her mouth, the way the dark green of her silky dress made her skin look like untouchable marble.

He was so tired of all the things in his life he wasn't supposed to touch, to get.

So he touched. His fingers tracing the line of her neck, up to that stubborn jaw that somehow haunted him even before he'd admitted to himself he could be haunted.

Her shuddery sigh washed over him like an order. *Carry on.* Which was a command not to rush, but to continue the job you were doing. Right and thoroughly. He brushed his thumb across her lower lip, lingered there in the corner of her mouth as his body tightened and whispered, *More. Now.*

But he knew a little something about delayed gratification, about withstanding the worst kind of bodily torture. He'd withstood the sea, pushing his body to every possible limit. He'd withstand this *pleasant* torture, the one that promised sweet release.

He let go of her hair slowly. He curled his fingers around her waist, so he could pull her flush against him. His hand, right there, felt as if it belonged against her waist, his fingers printed with some perfect code that unlocked her, and everything clicked into place.

Them together.

"This dress is torture," he muttered, because it was all smooth silk, like he imagined her skin would be underneath.

"T-torture. How?" she asked, just enough breathless to make him grin.

He dragged his fingers from her mouth, down her jaw and neck, until they brushed against the silky strap of her dress. Then he traced the line of the dress, down her chest, to the center drop. Modest, really, but she made a sound, close to a squeak but softer.

He hadn't thought anything in his body could get tighter, harder, and yet that sound moved everything a notch closer to a breaking moment. Still he stood there, holding her against him, nothing more than featherlight touches and the feel of her chest moving against his when she took a deep, hitching breath.

There was some twisted part of him that missed this challenge, this painful, bruising assault of holding yourself in an uncomfortable position for an impossible amount of time.

So he lowered his head only incrementally, memorizing the way dark and light blue threaded through the irises of her eyes, the tiny mole she had just at the top of her cheekbone, the way her chin nearly formed a sharp point. Until their mouths were only a whisper apart. He wasn't sure a piece of paper could fit in that tiny, minuscule separation. He reveled in the want and need and anticipation of that separation.

"Oh, for heaven's sake," she muttered before closing that last speck of distance herself.

He might have grinned at that, but her mouth was on

his. Soft and insistent, sweet and perfect. She wrapped her arms around his neck, drawing him closer, and she became the world. A softer world than he thought existed.

Her mouth was like the silk under his palms, her taste sweeter than summer honey. Everything centered here, at the slide of her tongue and the heat of her mouth and her arms banded around his neck as if she'd never let go.

It spiraled through him, desire, need. Hers. His. All mixed into a million things he didn't usually let himself feel, let alone swamp him. He pulled her bottom lip between his teeth until she moaned against him and... *hell. Hell.*

It wasn't enough. It wouldn't possibly ever be enough, and he wanted to drown in the sweet torture of that knowledge.

But there was just enough reason somewhere inside him to remember Colin was around here, sleeping or not, and hiking up Monica's skirt was very off-limits as long as that was the case.

He didn't let her go, didn't try to unwind himself from the tight grip of her arms, but he did edge his mouth away from hers.

"W-wow," she breathed against his cheek.

He grinned, because if he didn't, she might see the way she'd flipped his world on its very axis. "Did you just say wow?"

She pulled her arms away from him, stepping out of the circle of his embrace. It was like watching her come back to herself. "No. No. I did not... No." She shook her head, though she pressed her fingertips to her mouth.

Sometimes he liked every damn thing about her. "Oh, you said wow."

She dropped her hand, smoothing it over her dress, but there was a slight upward curve to her mouth. "I most certainly did not. I was just breathing."

"Breathing *wow*."

She glared at him, but that glare was undercut by her failure to scowl. "Fine. Maybe I was."

He rubbed a hand over his jaw. "It was a little wow."

"A little." She scoffed. "Well, maybe for you. Maybe you always go around kissing women like that," she muttered.

"I don't." Which he hadn't precisely meant to say. There was something to be said for a little mystery, for a woman to think you weren't quite as impressed as you were. But he couldn't force that kind of lie with Monica.

She blinked once, then looked down at her clasped hands. "Well." She looked all too pleased, and he wanted to gather her up and tell her a million more things that would put that look on her face and...

Well, he needed to get his shit together. *Clearly*.

She cleared her throat, those hands still clasped, but when she looked up at him, she was all calm, cool Monica. "I just need to make one thing clear."

"Yeah?"

"I know you're not interested in therapy—"

It was a sledgehammer to all the warm, soft feelings he should have known better than to have. "Christ, Monica."

"But, just so you know, this means even if you changed your mind, I wouldn't be available for that."

He stared down at her, and maybe he shouldn't be shocked or hurt. Maybe he should have expected that.

But he hadn't.

———◆———

Monica had known he wouldn't love that, but well, this *was* complicated, and some things needed to be clear. Just so they could… Well, she wasn't sure what the next step was after kissing.

Oh, you know. Except it was hard to imagine *more* than that kiss when it still had her unsteady on her feet and her lips were practically throbbing from the attention. Years. Nearly a decade since someone had kissed her like that, and back then she'd been too young and dumb to really appreciate it.

But, oh, all these years later, she could appreciate it. She could damn near cry over how good it felt and how much *more* she wanted. Not here and now, certainly not with Colin sleeping right in the same room, but maybe this was a step toward…

Except Gabe was standing there, his expression morphing from confusion, to shock, to fury. And then to that distanced blankness she'd never seen anyone have perfected so well as he did.

This was not good.

"You should go," he said flatly.

Clearly, she hadn't said it right. Or maybe she needed to explain more. Yes, just a few more words, and he'd see. "Don't be irritated with me. That *is* my role here. It's not an insult to you or anything. It's my job. I just had to say that, so it was clear."

"Oh, it's clear," he said bitterly, turning away from her. "I can carry Colin to your truck."

"Gabe." But he was striding over to Colin's sleeping form, then easing the boy gently off the bale.

"Gabe," she repeated, but he kept moving, and she found she didn't have any more words. She didn't understand this. Didn't understand him.

As though Colin weighed nothing, Gabe held him with one arm and grabbed his coat from the peg near the door. Then without any gentleness, he tossed hers at her.

She glared at him as he draped Colin's coat over his shoulders. Colin yawned sleepily into Gabe's shoulder and that…hurt somehow. Dug deep and hard in painful places she didn't want to go.

"We should talk about this."

"You made yourself clear, Monica. So very clear. What's there to talk about?" With that, he opened the barn door and stepped out into night. She hurried after him, grabbing her purse before she followed him outside. His long strides in the snow made it hard to catch up. She grabbed the hem of her dress and held it up, so it wouldn't drag through the snow.

It was freezing, but Gabe walked the distance to her truck as though coatless in Montana in the middle of December was anywhere near sensible or comfortable.

"Unlock," he ordered.

She wanted to be contrary, but it was too cold to. She hit the unlock button on her key chain.

He opened the door and deposited Colin in the passenger seat. Colin blinked blearily at Gabe and yawned.

"Night, runt," he muttered before gently closing the door.

Monica shoved her arms into the sleeves of her coat, letting the dress fall. "You misunderstood something if you're acting like this," she said. "I only meant—"

"I know what you meant, Monica," he said so damn

dismissively. "You meant, *Crap, I kissed the poor sap who needs therapy. Better explain to him how—*"

"I don't think you, any of you, are poor saps. I respect you. All of you. I told you that."

"Well, why don't you tell me that when you're ready for your actions to back up those words?"

"Well, why don't you tell me when you're ready to have an adult conversation instead of a knee-jerk, worst-case scenario reaction to every damn thing I say?"

He gave her a little mock salute. "Will do, Doc."

Oh, she could just punch him. But it wouldn't do any damage, so she whirled around and stomped to the driver's side of her truck. "Fuck you, Gabe."

He had no retort to that, but then again, he was already halfway back to the barn and might not have even heard her. She thought of yelling it after him, but from a look into the truck, where the dome light was on from her opening the driver's side door, she could see Colin's concerned expression.

Crap.

Fixing a bland expression on her face, she slid into the driver's seat. She started the car, urging the heater to fire up, urging her boiling temper to calm.

Great, amazing, soul-flipping kiss followed by irritating, purposeful misunderstanding argument. It was so very Gabe Cortez, all in all, why should she be surprised?

"Mom?"

"What?"

Colin was silent for a while. "You said the f-word."

"Yes, I did." She let out a sigh and glanced over at Colin. It was not the gleeful pointing out of swearing he usually did when she slipped up. He was concerned. Worried. And he was looking back in the direction of Revival.

She pushed the truck into drive and started down the hill. It was only a short drive home to their cabin over on Shaw property, so she didn't have time to really think things through. But she had to reassure Colin that nothing he'd witnessed was going to alter his life.

"I'm sorry you had to witness Gabe and me fight," she said sincerely, because she was. She hated that she'd let anger and hurt and who knew what all take over when Colin was within witnessing distance. "We both let our tempers get the better of us. I'm sure we'll work things out so we're friendly again." She wasn't that sure, but she'd at least pretend for Colin's sake, and Gabe probably would too. "Nothing Gabe and I argue about will change *your* relationship with him. I will always find a way to be friends with him for you."

Because as much as she wanted to throttle him, he was a good man, and Colin had developed an attachment. She wouldn't end that for Colin no matter what she felt.

Maybe Gabe was right. Maybe they had the same exact problem. Her actions didn't back up her words, and neither did his.

She wasn't particularly proud of that, and if she analyzed it closely, which she'd been avoiding doing for something like months, she realized far too late what that was.

Not a mask, not a boundary, but a deflection. A protection. He'd kissed her, and she'd felt utterly powerless, so she'd used her position to get some of that power back. She'd used it to protect herself and the weakness she'd felt in allowing it to happen.

That was wrong. Utterly wrong. But how did you right a thing you hadn't even been aware you'd been doing? And for how long?

Colin yawned, leaning his head against the door. "I like Gabe," he murmured sleepily. "I wish he was around us more."

Monica stared hard at the road, ignoring the tears stinging her eyes. "I like Gabe, too," she replied.

But she didn't know how to navigate him, and she didn't know how to let herself go enough to let there be no navigation.

Chapter 12

GABE DID HIS REGULAR CHORES THE FOLLOWING morning, and for the first time since winter had struck hard and vicious, he was glad for the icy bite. The relentless, stinging discomfort of it all. It felt right. So did swinging the little pickax and breaking the ice of the water tanks.

He'd decided to shovel out around the tanks too. It wasn't expressly necessary, but he needed the hard kind of physical labor involved in chipping away at inches of trodden snow and ice.

When Jack appeared sometime around lunch looking happy as a damn clam, Gabe realized the morning of hard labor hadn't done a whole lot to work him out of his mood.

He parked the UTV in the stables and glared at Jack's approaching form.

"Where've you been?"

Jack frowned and stepped into the stables with him. "Doctor's appointment. I told you that yesterday. Rose and I found out the sex of the baby this morning."

A bunch of words he didn't want to think too deeply on. "Oh. Right. Well, I chopped the ice, fed all these guys. Probably going to need to hay the north pasture, then I might take on the roof patching here."

When Jack didn't say anything, Gabe glanced over at him.

"Not curious about the baby?" Jack said in a *what the hell* tone that had Gabe wincing.

"Ah, right, yeah. Baby. So, what's it going to be?"

Jack dug something out of his coat pocket. One of those black-and-white ultrasound things people were supposed to *ooh* and *aah* over. Mom had shoved three in his face, and Gabe hadn't known what to do back then when he'd been a lonely, isolated teen. He really didn't know what to do about them now.

"A girl," Jack said, foisting the picture at him. "We're having a girl."

Gabe took the proffered picture, though it looked mostly like blobs with a little arrow at something that was supposed to be proof of a girl.

A little baby girl. Jack and Rose's baby girl. Blob or not, those words certainly made it all so real. Too real. Time marching on. People moving on. Building things and lives, and here he was doing what exactly?

Hiding from all that. What else was there to do? Face it? How did you face that kind of promise? That kind of possibility?

He handed Jack the picture and grinned. "Let me be the first to suggest the name Gabriella." He went to grab the pitchfork he'd need to loosen up the hay.

"We talked about it."

Gabe nearly dropped the pitchfork as he whirled to face Jack, because Jack was not joking. That voice was all serious, and Jack just wasn't that good of an actor.

"Gabriella Alexandra Armstrong has a nice enough ring. Rose can't name her after any of her sisters because it'd only be confusing or someone would get jealous, so she said. She suggested this."

Gabe swallowed. His chest felt tight as panic settled in, heavy and solid. "You can't…"

Jack raised his eyebrows. "Can't what?"

"You can't name your kid after me, man." He tried to laugh. Tried to do anything other than breathe a little too hard.

"Why not? Way I see it, you're half the reason I'm alive and here and maybe even with Rose. So. You get the first name. Alex'll be the godfather and the middle name."

"Jack…"

But Jack just stood there as if it was a done deal. There'd be some little girl out there in the world named after *him*.

"I really didn't know how you'd react, but I have to say, this wasn't what I expected."

"Never had a kid named after me."

"Here's a tip, act excited or interested or something not like I've lobbed a grenade at you."

It felt a little bit like that grenade. The moment of impact. The heat, the burn, the panic. The way time slowed down, sped up, slowed back down. But Jack was standing there through it all, looking calm and patient. But not in that old soldier way that might have given Gabe some ounce of comfort.

He looked like a man. Like any man. Bundled up against the cold, ultrasound picture in his hand, a handful of years ahead of him to build a family and a life that had nothing to do with uniforms, grenades or old SEAL brothers.

Except that ultrasound picture was unbelievably going to carry some version of Gabe's name, as if he was a part of it all—that future and that family.

"Thank you," he managed to croak out.

"I'm not doing it for you. I'm doing it because of you. But you're welcome."

They both stood there, and Gabe wasn't sure how long that moment of silence stretched. He wasn't sure how to be *normal* after that, and he didn't have any asshole comments or distancing jokes. All he had was this too-much feeling.

"If I told you something," Gabe began, having no clue why he was doing this, but the words tumbled out, "could you promise not to tell anyone? Including the nosy ass mother of your child?"

Jack considered. "I guess it would depend on the secret and if it would affect her in any way."

"It's got nothing to do with anyone. Except me. And…well, Monica."

"Okay, I won't tell anyone," Jack said quickly. Too quickly.

Gabe frowned. "You changed your mind awfully fast."

"Rose would be far angrier with me if I didn't find out the secret than if I kept it from her."

Sounded about right. Gabe grabbed the pitchfork, hit it against the ground a few times. "Kissed her."

"That so?" Jack rubbed his chin. "That all you did?"

"Yeah."

"And you wanted to tell me because?"

Hell if he knew. Or if he knew anything he was doing. It had just been sitting there, and he'd needed to say it out loud for some unknown reason he wished he could poke to death with his pitchfork.

"Didn't end well," he muttered.

"Why not?"

"She started talking about shrink shit, and I wasn't too keen on it, and I let her know."

"You got a real hang-up about that *shrink shit*."

"Yeah, so?"

"So maybe you should tell her why," Jack said as if that was some reasonable answer.

Tell Monica why he thought shrinks were full of it? Gabe snorted. "No." He already knew what she'd say. She'd have to defend her precious profession. She'd throw every damn excuse at him, and he didn't want to hear it.

"Why not? You're not a liar, Gabe. I don't know why you couldn't just tell her the truth," Jack said so reasonably. But Jack didn't know the truth. No one did, and no one needed to.

"Because it's none of her business."

"So you don't like her. You're just attracted to her?"

He thumped the pitchfork against the ground again, but it did nothing to ease this band of discomfort. "I didn't say that."

"Well, if you like her on top of sharing a kiss or more, I don't see why explaining to her why you hate therapists isn't her business. Sounds like a lot of her business."

"Rose knows everything you ever went through?" Gabe demanded.

"Maybe not everything, but anything that's come up. I don't lie to her. I don't keep things from her, though I'll honor my promise not to tell her you kissed Monica. Luckily, we aren't in high school."

Gabe flipped him off, but he couldn't let it all go like he knew he should. "Why do you tell her everything?"

"Because that's how you build a life."

Gabe turned, ready to load up the pitchfork and head out to do some more hard work in the bitter cold. "I'm not building shit."

"But you're telling me about a kiss," Jack pointed out, still so equitable and reasonable.

"And it was a mistake. As was that kiss. A bunch of mistakes I won't be repeating."

"If you say so."

He did. He definitely said so. Because the alternative was facing up to the fact Jack was probably right. The only way past this was explaining to Monica why he couldn't trust her job or people like her.

No way in hell.

"Well, here we are." Monica smiled nervously at the man in the passenger seat. She'd picked up her parents at the Bozeman airport this morning, and they'd be staying the night to see Revival and meet her colleagues. Then they'd head back to Denver with Colin in tow, and she would stay behind until the twenty-third, when she'd head to Denver and spend the night and have a family Christmas before heading back to Montana with Colin on Christmas Eve.

She'd parked in the Revival lot, which gave quite an impressive view of the house, the stables, the barn.

Her father looked stoic as ever.

"Isn't it gorgeous?" Mom said enthusiastically from where she sat with Colin in the back. "I can see why you'd want to move here."

Dad grunted.

She'd been nervous all day, from the morning airport pickup, to this. Alex and Becca had had their week of staycation honeymoon solitude, so Monica had been scarce. So scarce she hadn't talked to anyone since the wedding night.

Well, she'd had a phone conversation with Becca and Rose. But none of the men, and maybe there'd been a purposeful avoiding when it came to Gabe. Which meant she was going to introduce him to her parents after their hostile parting.

The only way out was through though. She pushed out of the truck and her family followed. "Since it's afternoon, everyone is going to be out and about. We could always go to the cabin first and settle in a bit and do this lat—"

"Show us around," Dad said.

Ordered more like. But Monica smiled and tramped through the snow, leading them toward the stables. "The house is something of a home base. Becca and Alex live there."

"The newlyweds, right?" Mom asked.

"Yes. Then Gabe lives in the bunkhouse there, and that's where the new men will stay. We've got two coming in January, and we'll slowly determine how many we can keep on at one time from there. Luckily, with a ranch this size, there's plenty of work to go around."

"Hard work is good," Dad said.

Monica warmed a bit at that. Her father could be hard, and that was probably as close to a compliment as she was going to get. But it *was* a compliment coming from him.

"You hear that, Colin?" Dad asked, motioning Colin to hurry up and come walk by his side.

"Yeah, Gramps. Hard work."

He ruffled Colin's hair and that warmed Monica, too. He was still not a particularly effusive man, but he'd softened a lot. He never would have ruffled her hair growing up. She liked seeing him be more demonstrative with her son.

Mom linked an arm with her as they made it to the stables. "It's a postcard," Mom said happily. "I didn't think it could be that much different than Denver, but... well, it's beautiful."

Monica squeezed her mom's arm. "I know. Just wait till tonight. We've got so many Christmas lights the whole places blazes. It makes my heart happy."

They stepped into the stables, and Becca had the horses out.

"Oh, hi!" Becca smiled warmly. "You made it. Roads weren't too bad?"

"Not too." Monica made the appropriate introductions, then they talked a bit about the therapeutic horsemanship. It was fun to watch her father's skepticism melt in the face of Becca's exuberance and knowledge.

"How many horses do you have?"

"We've got six right now," Becca said, nodding to the stables. "The goal will always be to be able to have enough horses for all the men if its financially feasible. We do a lot of work with tractors and utility task vehicles now, with winter in full swing."

"Quite the operation. Quite," Dad said, nodding thoughtfully.

It was possibly one of the biggest compliments Monica had ever heard him give, and she might have ridden that giddy pride all the way into tomorrow—except Gabe stepped into the stables.

"Hey, Bec. I—" He stopped abruptly when he saw there was more than just Becca in the stables. "Oh."

Monica cleared her throat. "Mom. Dad. This is Gabe Cortez. Gabe, these are my parents. Martin and Lorraine." Monica tried to smile, tried not to look nervous or still mad at him or any of the confusing things she felt.

You've kissed that man. His tongue has been in your mouth and his hands on your ass.

Yeah, she really wished she could ignore all that, but she felt like it was imprinted on her forehead. A bright-red, shining beacon of embarrassment.

But Gabe was smooth and charming as ever, shaking both her mother's and father's hands with one of those easygoing smiles that hid everything. *Everything*.

But he didn't make eye contact with Monica herself, so she'd consider that some sign he wasn't as *easy* as he appeared.

"Nice to meet you both. Hope you're enjoying your tour of Revival."

"Quite a place," Dad offered, giving Gabe a very obvious once-over.

"Gabe was a Navy SEAL," Colin said excitedly, aiming his comment at her father.

Dad huffed a little at that.

"Got hurt and everything," Colin said, practically jumping from foot to foot. "All these big scars on his arm and leg. *Huge* scars."

Gabe's mouth quirked. "You're really selling it, kid."

"Middle East?" Dad demanded.

Gabe nodded. "Afghanistan."

Dad nodded.

Silence descended.

Monica glanced at her mother helplessly. Mom rolled her eyes and muttered, "Men."

"I'd love to see the cows," Mom offered brightly. "Can we do that?"

"Gabe can take you out in the bigger UTV," Becca offered cheerfully. "You were going out there anyway, weren't you?"

Monica almost, *almost* laughed at the deer-in-headlights look on Gabe's face before he smoothed it out.

"Sure. Yeah, just have to walk over to the barn." He gestured in the direction of the barn.

Colin immediately scampered outside. "I'll show you the way guys!" Then he took off for the barn, Mom and Dad walking after him arm in arm.

Gabe followed, then Monica had no choice but to walk toward the barn side by side with him.

"Didn't know your parents were coming," he offered conversationally.

"Why would you?" When his expression didn't change, when nothing about him changed or reacted, she sighed. "They're taking Colin back with them tomorrow."

"Should be fun for him."

"Yup."

"And you'll get all that alone time you're looking so forward to."

She wanted to scowl at him. Instead, she smiled sweetly. "I'm sure the time will just fly by. I've planned so many activities." Like baking to within an inch of her life, then eating as much as she could until she felt sick.

"That's good. Idle hands are the devil's workshop and all that."

She wrinkled her nose. "You sound like my father."

"The marine," Gabe said with an edge of scoff to his voice, reminding her what he'd once said about marines.

"I dare you to say it to his face," she said quietly.

That rare true grin split his face. None of the blank

charm meant to put her off. Just true enjoyment, and she hated herself for wishing she could see that more. Make him do it more. She wanted to be the reason and the cause, and oh, she was pathetic.

"I think I'll pass."

"Coward."

"There's a difference between a coward and a man who knows when to tactfully retreat."

"So which are you being with me?" she asked, unable to stop herself. She nearly held her breath over the answer. But he walked, mulling it over, until she had to blow out the breath.

"Hell if I know," he muttered.

Chapter 13

GABE WASN'T GOING TO DO IT. THERE WAS NO WAY he was going to be this stupid.

But he was sitting in his truck, wasn't he? Cold and dark as he watched the night sky out the windshield. Clouds were rolling in, but pockets of winter stars still peeked through.

He wasn't going to do it. This was a moment of insanity, and he was going to break it and go back to the bunkhouse where he belonged.

Even if the word *coward* haunted him. And her question about tactical retreats and the difference between them. What did it matter what she thought he was doing? What did it matter what *he* thought he was doing? All that mattered was the doing.

And he was not doing *this*.

The porch light of the house turned on, and hell if Gabe was going to explain sitting in a truck in the middle of a winter night without having turned the damn thing on.

He started the truck. He'd go to Pioneer Spirit. Get drunk. Of course, there'd be no way to get home, since Jack was no longer his bar partner.

Didn't matter. That was a problem for future Gabe. And this was current Gabe, and he was not going to Monica's little cabin where she'd be home alone.

Alone. All alone.

If he was going to have a discussion with her about that kiss, it would be on safe, neutral ground. That wasn't cowardly. That was smart. It was strategic.

They probably didn't even need to have a discussion. It wasn't like he was going to be building any relationships. He knew how that sort of thing went, and it was fine enough for someone like Becca and Alex or Jack and Rose, but Gabe knew far better than to give anyone that kind of power over him.

Monica wasn't the type of woman who'd be interested in something casual or temporary. Even if something between them was possible, it wasn't possible.

But as he drove down the road, he couldn't help but slow down at the turnoff that would take him to the Shaw ranch. Which would take him to Monica's cabin.

Why wouldn't he go talk to her now? When they had some privacy to air it all out? They would talk like two rational adults who didn't have to worry about prying, friendly eyes or impressionable, youthful ears.

Find a way to be around each other without being awkward. He might be involved with the cattle, and she might be involved with the therapeutic horsemanship, but there were still areas in the foundation where they'd both have to give their opinions and suggestions without things being…weird.

That kiss couldn't linger between them every time they had a business conversation. It would be a distraction and a problem. So he'd go tell her it was a mistake, that it had meant nothing.

He turned onto the road. It was the right thing to do. It wasn't like she was going to fall into bed with him. Certainly not if he made it clear that there was nothing to start. She wasn't going to agree to something temporary and superficial. She didn't have that mind-set.

That was that, and all he had to do was make it clear. No hard feelings. He was an expert at no hard feelings, wasn't he?

He followed the road that curved up the rise. Moonlight shone down through a clearing in the clouds on the path of icy, glittery snow. Maybe it was some sort of positive sign all in all, a beacon of light leading him to exactly what he needed to do at the right exact time.

No other symbolism beyond that.

When the drive forked, Gabe took the snowy path of tire tracks that would lead him to the cabin. It was out of sight of the main house, so he didn't have to worry about his headlights raising any questions.

He parked his truck next to hers in front of the warm, cozy-looking cabin, shining bright with both lamplight from inside and twinkling Christmas lights all over the front of the house.

Gabe stepped out of his truck and stared at hers. She'd bought it with Alex's help and advice, and wouldn't that be weird? Taking advice from someone you were...

Gabe didn't even know how to put it. What Monica was doing for Alex by being his therapist. Jack and Alex discussed it enough for Gabe to know it wasn't anything like his experience with therapists. It was all about coping mechanisms and working through thinking patterns.

His experience had been all about his feelings and them being wrong, no matter what feelings he offered.

But Alex and Jack were working through a specific disorder. Anxiety and nightmares. Gabe had just been *wrong*.

And now, he had no nightmares, few anxieties. War didn't plague him in the least. He was fine.

In those moments with Jack and Alex discussing what Monica did for them, Gabe had to wonder why he was the odd man out. The one who didn't need help. It was almost like being back in that therapist's office, being told he was all wrong, all bad.

A good man would need help, because Alex and Jack were the best men he knew.

What the hell was he doing standing out here, freezing his balls off, thinking about that? Gabe marched himself across the yard. He was here on something of a business mission really—clear the air so they could work together normally. Without bringing it back up again.

Maybe he needed to prove to himself that he was no coward. Because he could face these types of things. He wasn't going to skitter away from her the rest of his life. No. His runaway days were over. No one got to intimidate, warp, or threaten him anymore.

He raised his fist and knocked hard on the front door. He could hear the strains of music from behind the door. Christmas music. He grimaced.

The door swung open, and Monica came into view. She'd clearly looked out the window to see who was there, but she still looked shocked at his appearance.

Shocked and too beautiful. Her blond hair was a little wild, her cheeks a little flushed. All that tense anger that had been coiling inside of him loosened somehow.

"White Christmas" blared from somewhere inside, and the smell of cookies was almost overwhelming. Monica had white smudges all over her shirt, and for one blinding, stupid second, all he wanted to do was push her inside and take her mouth with his.

But he was not here for that. He was here to have a conversation that would put them on even, solid ground.

"Hi. What…what are you doing here?" she asked, smiling, but it didn't hide the nerves.

"I thought we should talk."

"Oh. Um…" Something beeped from the direction of the kitchen. "Come in."

He stepped inside, closing the door behind him and trying not to notice the way she clasped her hands together and then released them.

"Just give me a second to get the cookies out. And then…we can, we can…we can talk. Right. Talk."

He shouldn't get any pleasure from her stuttering or the way she scurried off to the kitchen clearly trying to find some center of calm, but he *liked* getting to her.

You are not here to get to anything.

Gabe stepped into the living area. The interior of the cabin was mostly open. The small living room was filled with couch, TV, and fireplace, and the only thing that separated that room from the kitchen was a small counter.

Monica had the fireplace blazing, so Gabe shrugged out of his coat and placed it over the arm of the couch. When he glanced over at Monica, she was bent over the stove.

He attempted to remind himself he could resist anything. Including the desire to have his hands on her ass. Including the way his body tightened at just the sight of her.

"Um, want a cookie? They're chocolate crinkles."

"What's a crinkle?" he found himself asking, moving toward the kitchen even as something in his gut told him *not* to move. As a man who listened to his gut in all things, it was disconcerting to find how easily and quickly it could be overruled.

"Chocolate. Powdered sugar. If you haven't had one before, I'm going to have to insist, since that'd be a travesty." She held out the messy-looking cookie.

Gabe shrugged and took it, lifting it to his lips. He bit into it, and somehow their eyes locked over that, and she watched his mouth as the cookie disappeared into it. She exhaled, a little shuddery and overloud.

Well, this was a mistake, that was for sure.

~~~

Monica turned away quickly, almost knocking over the pan of cookies she'd just taken out and all but burning herself in the process.

Good Lord, get a grip.

But he was *here*. In her *cabin*. They were *alone*, and, oh God, all she could think about was sex. Which was wrong. So, so, so wrong. She was not going to have sex with him. They couldn't even kiss without getting into a fight. My God, what would they do after sex?

Stop. Thinking. About. Sex.

"What did you want to talk about?" Was that her, sounding high-pitched and panicked? She needed to employ some of her usual office calm. Except that was half the reason they *had* a problem—she couldn't seem to learn how to separate things.

"The other night."

"Oh." Oh. She focused on scraping the cookies off the pan and lining them up on a cooling rack.

"We should clear the air. We do have to work together after all."

He sounded so calm and rational, damn him. If they'd been having this conversation anywhere else, she might have had the wherewithal to put those masks she wore so well in place.

But he was *here*. Where she lived. Where she slept and showered and had maybe had a few inappropriate thoughts about the man standing in her kitchen.

More than a few, if she was honest. She hadn't exactly done benign imagining either. Oh *God*, she could not think about *that* when he was standing right there. In her house. Her house.

"Monica?"

"What?"

He tilted his head, studying her all too closely. "You okay? Your face is all red."

"Oh, just…the stove. Heat." She gestured stupidly. "The heat from the stove."

"Are you okay?"

"I'm great. Great." She shoved a cookie in her mouth. "Great," she repeated between chewing.

"You're acting really weird."

"You're in my *house*."

"So?"

"So? So." She swallowed her cookie. "I don't know. It's weird."

"Why?"

"I don't know!"

He grinned at that, and it was not fair. Not fair he could grin like that and her whole stomach would drop and parts of her body she'd thought long since dead would spring to thrumming life.

"I don't know how you want to clear the air, Gabe.

I... You think I'm out to get you or something, and I'm not. But nothing I say can convince you of that because you've decided actions speak louder than words. Well, Gabe, words and actions aren't that simple. People aren't that simple. Sometimes people say and do things that don't make sense to someone else, and sometimes... you say and do things to protect yourself, purposefully or just instinctually."

"What are you protecting yourself from?" he asked, his grin gone, arms crossed over his chest. He looked so intimidating, closed off. Funny, that wasn't what she was protecting herself from.

But it was a fair question, and in that fair question, she found a little bit of her courage. What *was* she afraid of? A man? One she might be attracted to? It was silly, but it also made sense.

She took a deep breath and then went ahead and blurted it out. "I haven't been with anyone since my husband."

His eyebrows shot up, but that was his only reaction. She swallowed, encouraging herself to keep talking. Clear the air? Well, that was good and healthy. So that's what she'd do.

"I was twenty when he died. I was basically a child myself, even though I had a child. So, I didn't...date or anything. At first it was grief and Colin, then it was a time issue, and it just spiraled until... Well, you know, I don't think I'd had a sexual thought in about five years or something."

He muttered something that sounded a lot like *Jesus*, but she kept going.

"I *am* attracted to you, which is a first since all that. And the thing is...being a therapist has become armor

I get to hide behind. I used it when I was still sad about Dex. Told people everything was great because I was going to school and I was going to help people. I used it to talk myself out of my Colin anxiety. Oh, it's normal after a tragedy to have certain worries, but if I acknowledge them, it's totally fine. I'm mentally healthy because I am a mental health professional."

She paused because everything inside of her brain was screaming at her to shut up. Why was she giving up all her secrets? All the things she only allowed herself to think about in the middle of the night? Why was she giving him that kind of power?

But underneath all that fear was an easing. She didn't feel like there was the same weight on her chest.

"I'm attracted to you. I didn't and don't know what to do with that. It has been knee jerk sometimes to revert to that armor. The role of therapist. I think you're the only one in my life who noticed or who it bothered, I guess."

He stood there like a statue. Blank faced and still, so very still. In her kitchen. As though he belonged there.

But he didn't. Truths didn't make someone belong. Being vulnerable didn't change the world. But it was good for the soul and for the mental health, so she'd go with that.

She fixed him with her therapist smile before she realized she was doing it. Then she shook her head. No blank, placid smiles. Though God knew what she was supposed to do with her face. But it didn't matter. She'd said her piece.

She nodded firmly then. "So, if you want to clear the air, you weren't wrong. I'm not sure you were one hundred percent right, but you weren't wrong. I pull out the 'shrink' stuff when I need to, when it suits me, when it might create a barrier between what I'm feeling and the person I'm feeling it toward."

She didn't know how long they stood there with only the strands of "Blue Christmas" in the background, Gabe not moving, and her a little scared to.

Finally, *finally* he inhaled with enough force for her to see the action move through his body. He cleared his throat. "I don't have PTSD," he said. Firm and clear. Just…said it.

"W-what?"

"I do not suffer from PTSD," he said, decisive and certain.

She softened a little bit at that. "I know you want to believe that you're strong enough to—"

"Monica." He stepped forward, curling his fingers around her upper arms. It wasn't a tight grip, but it stilled her nonetheless. "Listen to me. I don't have PTSD. I let the guys think I do because it makes them feel better, but I don't have any of the symptoms. No nightmares, no shakes. None of the anxiety or depression or difficulty sleeping. There isn't one symptom that I have with any sort of regularity."

She tried to work through that. He let the guys think… "You let them think that because you think it makes them feel better?"

He released her arms, turning away. There'd been some flicker of emotion on his face, but he made sure to hide it. "No one wants to be the only guy who's dealing with something. No one wants to be left out, even if the group is a shitty group to belong to."

Something inside her chest cracked, hard and painful. She reached out even though his back was to her. She pressed her fingers to his shoulder. "But you are left out. You are the only guy."

So much crystalized for her in that moment. The things Becca had said about Gabe being the nicest to her, but the one she knew the least about. Gabe kept himself separate, and oh, the man was lonely. But he seemed to think he needed to be. He didn't seem to know how *not* to be.

It near broke her heart.

But he stepped away from her hand, and when he faced her again, he was all stoic blankness. "I appreciate you explaining all that to me," he said, gesturing toward the stove as if *all that* encompassed all she'd discussed. "So I wanted to make it clear I don't need that kind of help anyway. Maybe that's why I'm touchy about it."

She smiled sadly. "I wish I could believe that, but you don't build that kind of righteous fury without incident, Gabe. Something else about therapy or therapists eats at you."

His mouth went hard. She didn't want to turn this into a fight though, so she didn't let the smile fade off her face. "But you don't have to tell me. It's not pertinent. Hopefully explaining my stuff to you will make it easier for us to navigate each other."

"Navigate each other," he echoed, his gaze dropping to her mouth, then lower, as if slowly drinking every last inch of her in.

Suddenly, *navigate* seemed to take on all new meaning. And, oh, wouldn't that be nice? She let her gaze take the same tour of Gabe that his was taking of her.

Way more than nice.

"I should go," he said, his voice sounding suspiciously...strangled.

She swallowed, reminding herself she was an adult. An adult who got to choose. An adult who could, in fact, make a few mistakes here and there, most especially when her son was out of town and she hadn't had sex in something like a decade.

"Or you could stay," she squeaked.

Chapter 14

GABE KNEW HE'D HEARD HER EXACTLY RIGHT. No matter that her voice had cracked, no matter that she looked like a panicked bird, he knew exactly what she had said.

Much more than that, he understood that she meant it. It was certainly no secret at this point that they wanted each other. The problem was in the complications. Unfortunately, when it came to complications, he couldn't let his dick lead.

"Bad idea," he managed to say, though his voice was still as strangled as it had been when he'd made the first attempt to leave. As though his throat were fighting against everything his brain needed it to do.

"Why? I know you're not naive enough to misread my invitation. I thought it was against guy code to turn down sex with an unattached, willing woman."

"Monica, I'm…I'm a bad bet."

Her eyebrows drew together, and she studied him. Maybe because of everything she'd said earlier, or maybe because he was *this* close to having all of her, he didn't see it as he usually did. Not a predatory, under-the-microscope analysis so she could unravel his psyche. Simply a woman trying to understand a man's cryptic statement.

He was probably losing it.

"I guess that depends on what the bet is," she said softly.

All that softness was way too tempting. "Look."

He swallowed because he needed a moment to remind himself why he was being noble here. He wasn't a particularly noble guy. Not like Alex. Not like Jack. If he'd had a noble impulse in him, it had been eradicated long before he'd joined the navy. Though he supposed the military had given him a certain sense of what was right and what was wrong.

Hurting Monica would be wrong and, more, he wasn't sure he could live with himself if he did hurt her.

"Look," he repeated, finding his voice again. "Obviously I'm attracted to you and would like to…" Jesus. He'd never had trouble talking frankly. Why was he now? "Stay," he finished lamely. "But there are a million complications and even if I had the wherewithal to work through them, the bottom line is: I'm not like Jack or Alex. I'm not looking for my happily ever after. I don't want to settle down. I don't want to have kids. I don't want to build some…life. I don't want those things, and I figure someone like you probably will."

"I guess I wouldn't rule it out," she said slowly, as if mulling that all over very carefully. "But I can't say I've ever spent much time hoping for those things. I *did* settle down, and I did have kids. I've loved and lost, and I can't say I'm too keen to do it again. But even if I wanted to want those things or started wanting those things, I couldn't go after them. At least not with you."

It was on the tip of his tongue to demand what the hell was wrong with him that she wouldn't, but that was stupid, considering he'd just told her he didn't want those things.

"In a couple weeks, we are going to have two former soldiers here," she continued. "My job is to be an on-site therapist. I can't be in a relationship with you. Do you have any idea how bad that would look? What kind of respect could they possibly have for me if I was sleeping with another former soldier working here? I know how men think. Even if I didn't… The point is, I'm not looking for something permanent. I'm not looking for settling down. I like my life. I love my job. I haven't had sex in a decade, and I'm attracted to you, and here you are in my house. So I don't know why, for the next week or so, we couldn't…you know, do that."

"That," he repeated.

"Yes, that. In fact, keep your gift card. Sex will be our Christmas gifts to each other."

It shocked a laugh out of him. Why it did or that she could was beyond him, but he laughed nonetheless, and enjoyed the pleased expression on her face far too much. Which at least sobered him some. "You don't think it'll be a little awkward to go back to the way things were after we've seen each other naked?"

"Of course it'll be awkward," she said with a hand gesture and a pretty pink blush staining her cheeks. "It'll be painfully awkward in every way. But you already kissed me. Either you're a much better person than me or you've gone ahead and pictured me naked. So, awkward no matter what. Why not get something out of it? It's been an awful long time since I've gotten something for me out of anything."

"So, you're suggesting we have sex. No strings attached, temporary sex."

"Yes. In fact, Christmas can be the cut-off date. We won't have any physical contact after Christmas. It will be out of our system, and should anything linger, well, there's always next Christmas."

"You're proposing a Christmas sex deal."

She lifted her chin, and though her expression was serious, there was a certain mocking curve to her mouth. "I am. Are you accepting the Christmas sex deal?"

"On one condition."

"What's that?"

"We stop saying 'Christmas sex deal.'"

She laughed, and he'd have been lying to himself if he didn't admit that sound did something to him. Not a sexual something—a deeper and far more dangerous something. He wanted to make her laugh again and again, and he couldn't let himself fall for that kind of bullshit fantasy.

She held out her hand between them. "Deal?"

He looked at her outstretched hand. She had long, elegant fingers, but there were bits of flour and dough stuck in the lines of her hand. He wasn't sure why he noticed it or why that flipped over in his chest like something important. So he denied it. He slipped his hand into hers and then gave her arm a little jerk so that she stumbled forward and into him.

She looked up at him, big, blue eyes swirling with surprise and desire. Much like the other night, he wanted to stretch out the moment where she was something like at his mercy. Looking up and waiting for him to make the move. Where he was in control of every breath she took.

"I-I don't think anyone should know," she stammered.

It hurt. No matter that it shouldn't. "I don't keep secrets from Alex or Jack."

That shock and stuttery nervousness faded into something soft. "Oh, Gabe. You keep secrets from everyone."

Somehow that hurt more—that she could see it. That

she didn't seem angry or put out about it, just sad. He didn't know what to do with sad. He didn't know what to do with the truth. So he did what he always did. Went on the offensive.

"Any more silly rules you want to lay down?" he asked with one of his too-sharp smiles that had him coming to the uncomfortable realization that he might use his charm and irritation as his own armor. A barrier between people and his heart and the truth because he didn't know what to do with either. Even less with the people who might be able to see them.

But it was too uncomfortable a thought when Monica's hand was in his and her body was so near. This woman wanted to have sex with him. Temporarily.

What did feelings matter? What did truths matter? He wanted her, and he was going to have her.

"Just one. I don't want you to lie to me. You have your secrets, Gabe, and I won't press on those. But I won't have your lies."

"I'm not a liar," he returned stiffly.

"Everyone's a little bit of a liar. Whether we know it or not. We lie to protect ourselves, and we lie to make the world around us makes sense. You can lie to yourself any way you want. You can lie to everyone in the world. But for the next week, I need you to tell me the truth. No matter how uncomfortable the truth is."

There was a split second where he actually considered walking away. He didn't want to promise her anything. He didn't want anyone even mentioning his secrets. Most of all, he didn't want the earnestness in those pretty blue eyes of hers. The way the vulnerability seemed to leak out of her when she let go.

He'd only ruin that. Hurt it. He always hurt vulnerable things.

But she moved onto her toes and brushed her soft mouth against his, a quick, light touch. Then the moment was gone, and all he could think about was her, naked beneath him. Finally getting her any which way she chose.

"So, are you staying?" she asked, as though there was a question.

"I'm staying."

———

Monica wanted to laugh. Hysterically. Not because it was funny, but because she was giddy at the prospect. His big hand still held hers, and it was scarred and calloused and rough. It would be on *her*. Naked her. And he would be naked.

Jeez.

"I bought condoms," she blurted out.

She got another one of those eyebrow-raised looks where he didn't say anything, just stared at her in surprise. Why she got such a kick out of surprising him was beyond her. Maybe it was because she was so used to not surprising *anyone* with anything other than her insights into their life, which were never as impressive as the person seemed to think. She wasn't magic. She just paid attention.

"Planned this, did you?"

"Well, I didn't plan you coming *here*. I was just alone in a store. You'll never understand the sheer joy of a mother being alone in a store. No kid whining or begging or complaining. And suddenly I was in the condom aisle."

"Suddenly?"

"Well, technically I was buying tampons, if you really want to know." When he grimaced, she laughed. "Men are so predictable. Anyway, it seemed like a smart thing to have. Along with the ingredients to make ten different kinds of Christmas cookies on the off chance I lost my nerve and didn't use said condoms."

"You know, I can't figure you out. You seem like a reasonable, rational person and then I come to your house that looks like Christmas threw up everywhere and you wax poetic about being alone in a store."

She would have fisted her hands on her hips, but he was still holding her hand, holding her close. Much like that moment in the barn the other night. The way he'd stretched out those seconds of thrumming attraction until she hadn't been able to take it anymore.

She liked that—the way the anticipation wound so hard and so tight it felt like she'd explode. But she had to admit she was a little ready to explode.

She stepped even closer, so their knees and chests brushed, so she had to tip her head back a smidge to maintain eye contact. "And how would you decorate for Christmas?"

His eyes were dark and fathomless, and that wide, expressive mouth of his curved. "I wouldn't."

"Even if you had a little boy you were in charge of?"

"Okay, throw a Christmas tree in the corner. Voila. Christmas."

She sighed disapprovingly and shook her head, and still they stood too close and too far apart all at the same time. That dark gaze of his studied her as if looking for some magic key to something, and she had the sad, silly thought she wanted to find it for him.

"You sure about this?"

"Do I strike you as the type of woman who buys condoms and has sex on a whim?" She cocked her head, angling her mouth closer to his jaw. "Are *you* sure about this?"

For a man who seemed solitary, alone, and maybe even a little sad sometimes, he had a dozen different smiles. That was his own armor, she supposed, but she liked this smile. The one that wasn't blank underneath, and the only sharpness to it was intent. The rest was enjoyment, and she wanted to be the source of that for reasons she hadn't worked out yet.

But the want was there, and he was here. His mouth touched hers, and *Lord*, he was a patient man. All gentle pressure, the slowest releasing of her hand before his found her waist, found her neck, drew her closer and closer a millimeter at a time.

She sighed against his mouth, and he took the opportunity to draw his tongue across her lower lip. It exploded through her, hot and bright and a little scary—but the kind of scary a person could never quite resist.

"Hell," he muttered. And then it was like the world ignited. Nothing but heat and the soaring notes to "O Holy Night," which might have been sacrilegious, but she didn't care. Not when Gabe's mouth streaked across hers, not when his arms banded around her, holding her so close she could feel every flex of every impressive muscle in his body. Arms, abs, thighs.

Hell was right. Because how could she do anything but give into this and him, and she was not used to *giving in*. It was like leaping off a cliff and free-falling, having no idea when and if she'd land, and how many broken bones she might suffer if she survived at all.

But underneath all that fear was the steady thrum of a pleasure so big and wide she didn't care about the landing. She only cared that she got *more* of it.

She managed to create enough distance between their bodies to slide her palms up his stomach and find all that hard, rangy muscle. He scraped his teeth against her lips, and her legs nearly buckled at how much *more* she wanted than this.

Then his arms were loosening, and somehow his mouth was off hers. She let out a sound of protest, but she swiftly swallowed it when he reached behind his head and pulled his T-shirt off.

"Oh."

"Was that another wow?" he asked with that razor-sharp grin that she wanted to taste, then learn how to soften.

"I said *'oh'* this time," she replied primly. Or as prim as she could be with her cheeks on fire and a low pulse of *oh, please, God* thrumming deep inside of her.

"So…" He moved close to her again, his fingers curling under the edge of her flour-dusted T-shirt. "You admit you said wow when we kissed the other night?" he murmured right next to her ear.

She very nearly giggled, but she covered it up by clearing her throat. "Maybe."

He pulled her shirt up slowly, that obnoxiously wonderful patience he had where it seemed like minutes before it was over her head and she was standing in front of him in her plain, serviceable bra. She might have wished for lace if not for the way his eyes raked over her like she was some sort of prize. As though when he looked at her it affected him just as much as her looking at him affected her.

He reached out, those big hands enveloping her shoulders, then moving down her arms, trailing goose bumps in their wake. Her breathing was too quick and too shallow, but she couldn't get her brain to send the *chill* message to her lungs.

Colin hugged her so rarely these days, and Mom and Dad were so far away and just not super demonstrative, and it was such an aching *thing* to be reminded how much she missed being touched. A hug. A caress. A kiss. For so incredibly long, she'd just had to do without, and she probably would again after Christmas.

But for here and now, there was a man who wanted to share his body with her, and she wouldn't *cry*, she wouldn't ruin this precious time. She would indulge in every last aspect of it, memorize it maybe, and it would get her through the next.

She launched herself at him. Wrapped her arms around him, kissed him as deep and wild as she could. She arched against him, desperate for more, and he groaned into her mouth, the sound rumbling through her like an earthquake.

"Which way?" he asked breathlessly.

It took her a few moments to figure out what he meant. "Oh, well. I sleep on the couch."

"You…what?"

"It pulls out."

He frowned down at her. "You sleep on a pullout couch?"

"It's a one-bedroom cabin. I figured since I was the

one who made him move here, Colin could have his own bedroom."

"And you sleep on a pullout couch."

"It's practical. Who are you to talk? You sleep in bunk beds."

"I do *not* sleep in bunk beds. I sleep in a bunk*house*."

"That is filled with bunk beds."

"Okay. Fine. We both have ridiculous sleeping situations." He stalked over to the couch and started tossing the cushions off. "We can discuss it later."

Monica crossed to the couch, pulling the handle so that the bed unfolded into the space of the living room.

She undid the button of her jeans and started to push them down her legs. "We'll discuss it *much* later."

He grinned, doing the same. "Much."

Chapter 15

SHE WAS TOO BEAUTIFUL, GABE THOUGHT. IT SEEMED some great cosmic mix-up he even got to look at her. Acres of pale skin he wanted to bare completely and taste, and he in no way deserved any of that.

But he'd take it.

Then there was this ridiculous bed, with gingerbread-man-printed sheets. A mix of the ridiculous and the practical, which seemed so very *her* it just about hurt. He didn't understand her, didn't want to, but something about her caused this horrible ache inside of him he couldn't trust.

But he was here. In this pullout couch bed because she slept in the living room, so her kid could have his own room. It was a kind of sacrifice he'd stopped thinking existed. Not outside of war and famine anyway.

It swamped him with such feeling he was almost afraid to touch her, to move forward. She didn't know what she was doing, dirtying herself with him.

"Oh, let me go get the condoms." She blushed just saying the word, but she shook her hair back, sailing toward the dark little hallway. "You should be naked when I get back," she said firmly, an order.

He wasn't big on taking orders, but he had no problem with naked. No problem ignoring all the shit in his head and focusing on what they were doing. Sex. Naked together. The rest didn't matter. He could self-flagellate all he wanted tomorrow, but first he was going to get something out of it.

He pushed off his boxers and slid onto her bed. There was a gingerbread man smiling up at him from the sheets, its creepy gumdrop eyes and grotesquely smiling, frosting-painted mouth repeating over and over in pattern.

"You're going to be scarred for life, buddy," he muttered, trying to focus on something that wasn't the sheets. But everywhere he looked, Christmas paraphernalia glowed or smiled or downright creeped him out.

It wasn't nerves. He had sex. Maybe not, you know, a *lot*, and maybe not with women who were most decidedly in his life, but this was still temporary. A scratching of itches that would have no bearing on the future.

He wasn't sure he really believed that, but he wanted Monica enough to pretend for the time being.

She returned to the living room and placed the condom on the end table next to the couch. She still had her underwear on, but she'd pulled her hair out of its band and the flyaway strands of blond somehow made her look younger, more…innocent.

Gabe couldn't say he cared for that. The reminder she hadn't been with anyone since her husband, that this might be important even if she didn't want it to be. That they might be only a few years apart in age, but they were ages apart in experience and cynicism and—

"Do they hurt?" she asked, hovering there, studying his body. Not the kind of excited perusal he would have welcomed, but the careful, concerned study of the web of scars over his body. A few lines on his leg and hip, a web of marks on his shoulder, including the burns he'd sustained from the grenade blast that had exploded behind him.

He tried not to tense, worked on looking almost bored and relaxed lying naked on her gingerbread man sheets. "The scars themselves? Not so much these days."

"But the injuries do?"

He shrugged, trying not to let irritation simmer through him. "Sometimes they ache a bit. Winter seems to make that more the case, but it's bearable."

She nodded, then looked at him solemnly. "I should probably be very, very gentle with you," she said, and he might have fallen for that serious tone if her mouth hadn't curved up at the end.

He grinned and crossed his arms behind his head. "Oh, baby, I was a Navy SEAL. We don't do gentle."

She laughed as he'd hoped she would. Then she bit her lip and reached behind her. Her bra went slack, then she let it fall to the ground.

She was...perfect somehow. More perfect than he could have imagined in his most detailed fantasies. It was so close to too much, but he was selfish enough not to care what he deserved and what he didn't.

"It's amazing how fantasy never quite measures up to real life," he murmured, content for these few humming seconds to just watch her. To let it ratchet the anticipation higher and higher till it was almost painful.

He didn't mind pain, not when it came in the most beautiful of packages.

She laughed, just the slightest hint of nerves edging it, so he got to his knees, drawing her closer to the edge of the bed. He ignored the sharp stab of pain in his hip and pressed a kiss to her chest, between her breasts, then her belly, slowly edging her panties down her legs.

She was impossibly soft, impossibly sweet. Every time she sucked in a shallow breath or let it shakily out, that tight edge of desire scraped sharper, and still he was slow, patient, careful. He moved his calloused hands over her hips, her thighs. He soaked up that rough against smooth slide until his body felt as though it was throbbing from the inside out.

Then in a smooth move he'd pat himself on the back for later, he flipped her onto her back on the bed.

She let out a surprised squeak, and then a laugh. "Is that a special Navy SEAL sex move?"

"Of course." Positioned on his side, he enjoyed a few seconds of just taking her in. Long and lean, and he barely even noticed she was sprawled out on a gingerbread-man-printed nightmare. He leaned down and kissed the tip of her tightened nipple and she squeaked again, so he licked, sucked, lost himself there in the sweet softness of her breasts until she was panting his name.

Then he moved lower, tasting and nibbling down her torso, carefully maneuvering her until he'd positioned himself between her legs, tasting the sweet velvet of her thighs.

She gave his shoulders a little push. "O-oh, no. No, you-you can't."

He glanced up, raised an eyebrow at her. "Why not?"

"B-because. Because. *Because*." She gave his shoulders another ineffective shrug. "I cannot speak coherently when you are... You're..."

"Who asked you to speak coherently?" He kissed higher on her thigh, letting his breath trail over the center of her as he moved to the other leg. "You don't like it?"

She let out a sound he thought was maybe supposed to be a laugh, and the thing was he wasn't the one holding her legs open. He certainly wasn't the one shaking and watching him with intense, wide eyes.

"W-we have to look each other in the eye after this is all over. I can't… You'll…"

He grinned up at her over that gorgeous body. "If you think this will make you incapable of looking me in the eye, we probably shouldn't have sex."

"Oh God, we *have* to have sex."

He laughed at that, then went ahead and tasted her. She nearly jolted off the bed.

"Want me to stop?" he asked, looping his arms around her thighs to keep her on the bed. There was the longest pause, and when she finally answered, it was on a whisper.

"No."

She couldn't quite admit to him that no one had ever… *well*. She'd been so young and naive when she'd been married, and *this* had always seemed too…intimate. She hadn't had years with Dex to get beyond that either.

In retrospect, that was stupid. But that was retrospect, and now she was thirty years old, and this could quite possibly be the last time she had sex ever. She'd experience it. Enjoy it. Savor it.

"Eep." If she could stop squeaking every time his tongue touched her. But it was like electricity. A shock that jolted, but only pleasure was left after. A pleasure that seemed to wave bigger and bigger as Gabe's mouth explored her.

She squirmed, unable to stop herself, but Gabe held her firm and still and she had to grab on to the sheets to stop from…something. Something.

"Gabe…"

But he didn't stop. If anything, he only focused harder until that last wave seemed to break, a spiraling crash of a million sensations she could only let roll over her, a perfect kind of drowning.

"Okay," she managed, her voice a scratchy thing as she tried to stop panting. "This time I am going to definitely and without reservation say *wow*."

He laughed, dragging the sound and feel of it against her body as he moved up until she was completely covered by six-foot-a-lot of former Navy SEAL. She sighed happily, winding her arms around him.

He nuzzled into her neck, as though content to simply lie there as her heartbeat and breathing slowly came back to normal. She could tell certain parts of him were *not* content, were hard against her, and yet he made no move for himself.

She trailed her fingers over the soft bristle of his short hair, down the surprisingly smooth skin of his neck, to the scarred shoulder.

She traced the outline of a tattoo that must have predated his scars. "It's a bird," she murmured, angling her head to get a better look.

"Mm."

"What's it mean?"

"That I sailed a lot," he said, his voice muffled against her neck.

"Really?"

"More or less."

"But why not an anchor or rope or some other such thing? A boat? One of those captain wheel things?" She traced the outline of the bird, the slash of a scar through its wing and a blotch of pale skin as though part of the tattoo had simply been burned off.

The idea made her gut clench. Even knowing about the accident that Gabe had been a part of, seeing it marked across his body when they were naked together was something completely different.

"I might have been a sailor, but I like the idea of being free to fly wherever." His hand slid down her side, slow and gentle, a sensuous glide at odds with the way those words seemed so emotionally honest it took her breath away.

"Gabe," she whispered.

"Hmm?"

"Get the condom."

The expediency with which he followed that order was truly something to behold. He had the package open and the latex rolled on before she could scarcely blink.

Then he simply paused, hovering over her. This beautiful specimen of a man. Muscles and scars and that wicked mouth. It might all have been enough. If she'd been desperate and wanting to experience something she'd denied herself for a decade, she might have seen him in a bar and needed only that smile, that body. Maybe it was possible to want this when only looks were involved.

But the feeling inside of her, the *need* inside of her, was tied up in Gabe's big heart. *That* was what made it possible to give this piece of herself to him, to take a piece from him. The muscles certainly didn't hurt. The way he looked at her like she was some precious gift didn't hurt at all. But it was the whole—the attraction *and* the heart.

It was in this moment, more than the rest, that she knew things were going to be so much trickier than she'd given them credit for. She didn't know anything about sex without love, but she didn't think it felt like this. Like her chest would burst with anticipation and it would be worth it. Like she wanted to live in the moment forever, just him naked and hovering over her. Beautiful and sweet.

Too many emotions swirled around her—new feelings and old familiar ones she was afraid to give any room to. Too many worries and too much confusion lived in those old feelings showing up here and now. Because there was no part of her that wanted to stop. No retreat. She wanted him and this more than she wanted or was able to listen to any reasonable thought in her head.

"You okay?" he asked gruffly, positioned there between her thighs, gorgeous and more than ready.

"I'm amazing. And very much enjoying the view." Her voice was scratchy, and maybe her somewhat-teary eyes gave her away, but he acted as though he didn't notice.

He grinned. "The view from here isn't so bad either."

She reached out and touched his face. It was supposed to be sex. It was supposed to be simply about attraction and acting upon it, and yet even with a new blaze of fiery passion igniting inside of her, she touched him with all the gentleness inside of her. All the sweetness.

So much about Gabe was hard and sharp, and she wondered if he had any gentleness in his life at all. She wanted to be the source of it. All of it. Selfishly, she wanted to be the only one who gave him that.

She traced his jaw with her fingers, and he leaned forward, into the contact. His palms were planted next to her shoulders, and he held himself above her, but his eyelids fluttered closed as she continued to trace the lines of his face. She sighed over the prickly scrape of his whiskers against the pads of her fingers.

He lowered his mouth to her shoulder, pressing a kiss there. Unbearably sweet. But with that unbearably sweet motion, he positioned himself at her entrance, slowly nudging inside.

She'd forgotten what this felt like. The slow invasion of someone else becoming a part of her. That feeling of being full and connected, physically and more. The way it ignited sparks of pleasure and desire. She had forgotten *all* that, and even as it swept over her, as *he* swept over her, she couldn't remember what sex had ever been like before.

There was only this. There was only Gabe. He was all that existed—in this room, around her, inside her.

She simply let herself go. She didn't worry about control or what he was feeling, she just let herself be a part of it. The sweet, slick slide of desire. The giddy pride over being the source of his ragged breath against her skin. The way the pleasure and the need for release could coil deep inside of her again, almost sharper and harder this time because he was so deep inside of her.

Each stroke was a slow, agonizing glimpse of what she was after. That edge, that fall, all the release that awaited her after this buildup.

She whispered his name against his mouth before

kissing him softly, and it broke something inside of him. His kiss became fierce. Teeth and growls. His grip on her hip was now an iron-hard band that might leave marks.

And she loved it. Reveled in it. Wanted more of this rough, untethered side of him.

"More," she urged. She deserved so much more. She deserved it all, every which way she could get it. She'd been alone so long, and now she wasn't. Maybe this was temporary, but she would take every last second and everything she wanted out of it.

"More. More."

On the third *more*, she found herself being maneuvered, somehow flipped over and splayed on top of him. She blinked at his chest, shocked beyond words he was still deep inside of her.

"You want more," he said, his voice and its dark, dangerous edge. "Take more."

It took a few seconds to truly have those words penetrate. To understand what he meant. What he was offering.

Gabe fancied himself something of a broken, selfish man, but he was none of those things. Even in this temporary get-it-out-of-our-systems moment, he was offering what *she* wanted. *She* needed. He would enjoy it too, but it wasn't the same as just going after whatever he wanted.

She placed her palms on his chest and moved into a sitting position. His eyes glittered, and his hands came to her hips, clamping there again. She moved her body forward, and he hissed out a breath.

She was affecting him, torturing him maybe, and there was such an amazing power in that. It gave her a patience she didn't know she was capable of—and maybe she only had it because he employed it on her.

She'd absorbed his ability to draw out a moment until it nearly hurt, until you thought you would break.

And then you did.

She moved slow, so slow she nearly hated herself, but every time he gasped, as his breath went from shallow to panting, something new and brighter sparkled to life inside of her.

"Monica," he murmured, hushed and holy, like a prayer. Then he mumbled something that sounded like a *please*. It crackled through her like lightning. Like power.

She leaned forward, breasts brushing his chest, mouth going to his ear. "Are you begging me?" she whispered.

He laughed so dark and edgy, it sent a shudder of anticipation through her. The kind of shudder that felt almost like fear, except she was too excited, too far gone to ever be afraid.

"Baby, I never beg." He held her hips hard and tight, moving himself slow and deep inside of her. "But you might be a first," he said on a loud exhale.

The power, no matter how much of a lie it might have been, coursed through her at his words. Almost as if he'd known it would eradicate all the patience she'd been using.

She moved against him, faster and faster, chasing her own pleasure as though it were the answer to all of life's problems. When the orgasm rushed over her, hard and shuddering, she barely noticed Gabe's fingers digging tighter into her hips as he arched up into her, growling low and feral.

She collapsed forward on the wide, hard expanse of his chest. Remembering the way he'd covered her before, she attempted to do the same to him. She stretched out and then pressed her nose into his neck and kissed the underside of his jaw.

"I guess it's my turn to say wow," he offered, his hand gently brushing up and down her back.

She managed to chuckle. "You damn well better."

She wanted to lie here for possibly ever. Happily sated and warm and in Gabe's arms. On top of him as if she had bested him in some way. No, she didn't want to leave this place.

But he was probably uncomfortable and maybe she shouldn't be a needy post-sex cuddler. She didn't know what casual sex was like. As the lingering edge of her orgasm began to wear off, anxiety crept in. They did have to spend a lot of their future lives dealing with each other, and she didn't want to be the silly, desperate-for-more-of-him woman.

But as she made a move to get off of him, his arms only tightened around her so that she couldn't move.

Her body immediately relaxed. It wouldn't last. It couldn't last. But for right now, in this moment, he wanted her there, and she wanted to be there. She was going to let that be comfort enough.

Chapter 16

GABE HAD NO IDEA WHAT HAD POSSESSED HIM TO hold her there. Sure, she felt amazing on top of him. Like heaven. Like one million things he hadn't had in forever. Or forever period.

He had to let her go. Partly because this was all too much and partly because he wanted more than he could ever allow himself to have.

Still he didn't let her go. How could he when she sighed happily into his neck? When her fingers traced gentle, soothing patterns over his arms. She had no qualms about touching his scars or his burn marks. He hadn't been with all that many women since he'd gotten them, and most of his partners had avoided them. Because sex then had just been…sex.

He squeezed his eyes shut and finally allowed his arms around her to loosen. "I should take care of the condom."

She rolled off him fast as a shot. As though the words had broken her from some trance. Some trance he wished she would've stayed in.

"Bathroom's in the hallway. You can't miss it," she said, weirdly overbright about the whereabouts of her bathroom.

He nodded and slid out of bed. He didn't bother for clothes at this point. The fire was high and crackling, he was warmed all over, and she'd seen it all.

He entered the hall and the first doorway was open

but dark. Still, he could make out a window, maybe the corner of some furniture. Definitely not a bathroom.

Colin's bedroom—a stark reminder of so many things. Because he liked the kid, but he knew what being the kid of a single mother was like. He was aware of all the complications that came with your mom having relationships. If Colin ever found out about this…

Gabe couldn't even let himself think about it. How it might sour Colin's opinion of him. How it might change everything.

One of the things he liked so much about Monica was that she was a good mom. She would never, ever make Colin feel like a second-class citizen in his own home, but it could still change how Colin saw Gabe.

If Gabe was stupid enough to think this could go somewhere, he would be the second-class citizen. Yet again. Colin would always be first.

Which was right and good. It amazed him there was a mother out there like that. He hadn't believed it.

Gabe couldn't live that kind of life again, second fiddle to everyone else. It broke too many things, and he couldn't bring himself to pretzel into a million pieces trying to fill those cracks only to lose. He would always lose.

Gabe forced himself away from Colin's bedroom and found the bathroom. He got rid of the condom, trying not to dwell on the sex any more than he had just dwelled on idiot thoughts and what-ifs.

But the thoughts came at him anyway. How sex with Monica was somehow different than any other sex he'd had. He'd known on a kind of mental level that sex could be different. After all, there had to be some reason Alex and Becca wanted to be married to each other for the rest of their lives. Jack wanted to similarly shackle himself to Rose. Gabe understood there had to be *something* special about a relationship, even if he never wanted one.

But now he understood all that on a visceral level. Sex might be the same act regardless, but it didn't involve the same feelings. It didn't involve the same tangle of emotions afterward. When it was with someone you didn't really care about, it was all transaction. You got what you wanted—and that was nice.

But it wasn't like *this*. It didn't fulfill or light up the world. It didn't infuse hope where hope had no business being.

Gabe caught his reflection in the mirror. He could see the panic in his own expression and knew he had to get a handle on it before he returned to Monica. This was supposed to be a casual thing. There were no other options beyond getting sex out of their systems.

Getting it out of his system was never actually going to happen. She'd gone on about how they'd already kissed and how could the wondering be worse than the doing.

Oh. It was worse. So much worse.

He had to get a handle on his shit. There was no way he was going to let her see what a mess he was. How this had worked through him and changed him somehow. He felt like a different man. He didn't like this new man. He wanted nothing to do with this vulnerable sad sack.

He looked away from the mirror and mechanically turned off the light. He counted the steps from the bathroom back to the living room, finding a center in the numbers.

She was snuggled under those ridiculous gingerbread man sheets, her hair a tangled mess, golden and youthful. She had this self-satisfied smile on her face that unwound all of the crazy emotions inside of him.

At least until she aimed it at him.

"I should probably go." It sounded overloud in the quiet room, even with the crackling of the fire and the faint sounds of Christmas music still playing. "All I Want for Christmas Is You."

He grimaced.

She didn't say anything to his proclamation. In fact, nothing about her changed exactly. She was lying there still.

He felt as though he needed to defend himself against something, which was stupid because he should go. That was the deal. Sex. Not sleeping together. "They're going to ask where I was if I don't get back tonight. You didn't want anyone knowing about this."

"No, I didn't," she said slowly, carefully.

What the hell was she being careful about? He didn't want to know. "So, I should go." He moved stiffly for his clothes. She just lay there, watching him, and he didn't know what to say, so he got dressed. Avoiding eye contact.

Like a pussy.

"This was fun," he offered. Lamely.

"It was fun." She moved up onto her elbows. "We should, uh, do it again. You know, before Christmas. Just to ensure we do the things we, uh, didn't get to."

This side of her, unsure but braving through things anyway, utterly undid him. He found her completely irresistible even in the midst of his own slight break with sanity.

"Well, you've got me curious. What kind of things?"

She raised that chin as primly as a woman wrapped up in gingerbread men could be. "You know what kind of things far better than I do."

"You sound like you have a few ideas in your head of other things we could do."

She tried to scowl at him, but it failed, curving up at the edges. That always undid him too, little glimpses at her humor.

Every single cell in his body wanted to shuck his clothes and get back in that bed and do all those things tonight, all night long. He couldn't imagine that being good for either of them. He had to go.

"How about tomorrow night?"

She nodded, smiling. "I'll be here, so just whenever."

"Will there be more cookies?"

"Undoubtedly," she returned with mock seriousness.

"I'll be here then." He moved for his boots, and he watched her out of the corner of his eye as she grabbed her clothes and got dressed.

"I don't have any nicer underwear. Just FYI."

Gabe had no idea where that remark could have come from, and he tried not to look at her like she was crazy. "I don't really care much about your underwear, Monica. I'm far more interested in what's under it."

"Well, that's…good. I just… You know, when you're a single mom, there's no reason for pretty, lacy underwear. Except this kind of reason, and I don't usually have this kind of reason, so—"

"I don't care about your underwear. Period."

She gave him a sharp nod. "Got it." She tried to smile, but it was all twisted, and somehow that twisted him. An aching, awful thing.

He couldn't give in to that. He found his coat and shrugged it on and considered for a second giving her a goodbye kiss. Except he wasn't strong enough to touch his lips to hers, then walk away. It'd have to wait. Until tomorrow. He walked to the door and grabbed the knob.

"Gabe?"

He didn't dare look back. "Yeah?"

She paused for the longest time, this endless series of minutes where his heart beat hard against his ribs and a hope for something he couldn't possibly allow himself to have tried to overtake his body, his brain, his heart.

"Good night," she finally said.

"Good night," he repeated, wrenching the door open.

And then he nearly fell over something. Something cold and... Snow. The light from the cabin spilled outside, and all he saw was white. In the air, on the ground. Everything was a swirling, nearly indistinguishable white. They'd been supposed to get a blizzard tomorrow, but tomorrow wasn't *tonight*. There had to be a foot of snow on the ground if not more. There was no way...

"I think that's what they call a whiteout," Monica said, her voice blank and completely unreadable.

"That would make sense," he said, staring at the white emptiness in front of him. It was loud and eerie and—

"I guess you're stuck with me."

He glanced over at her then and tried not to feel the panic that was bubbling inside of him. Panic. That's what it was. Not joy. Not anticipation. This was sheer and utter panic.

She grinned the kind of grin she must have copied from him. "We can probably find something to do."

Panic or joy, it didn't matter, because he was stuck,

and she was here, this gorgeous, sweet woman he couldn't have.

Later, in the future, he couldn't have. But tonight, for as long as they were stuck in this storm, he could have her.

Gabe closed the door. "I guess we could."

———*~~~*———

Monica woke up the next morning sure she was dreaming. Because the cabin smelled like coffee and she was sore in ways she wasn't sure she'd ever been sore and something in her bed smelled like a man.

Not a boy. A man.

Her eyes flew open in a second of alarm before the night's previous activities rushed over her. Her face went hot, and she pulled the sheets a little closer to her chin.

She was naked. Asleep and naked and her cabin smelled like *coffee*.

She hadn't woken up to coffee already made since she'd lived with her parents. She hadn't woken up naked in far longer than that, if ever. She had never, ever woken up to the smell of a man in her bed who wasn't a man she was married to.

She blew out a breath, daring herself to open her eyes. She tried to take in her surroundings by only moving her eyes. She didn't know why, but she didn't want Gabe to know she was awake until she knew where he was. Until she saw him and could determine…

Something.

"Morning," he said casually.

She whipped her head toward the kitchen, where he was standing, back to her. She frowned at it. Military men. She should have known. He probably sensed it the moment she woke up in that weird, dizzying second of panic. "Morning," she returned, peering over the bed to see if her clothes were within reach.

"Made coffee," he said as she pawed the ground for her discarded T-shirt. "Didn't see any breakfast food."

"Cookies," she said, pulling the shirt over her head.

"You can't eat cookies for breakfast."

She glanced at him again, and this time he'd turned to face her. His brown eyes dark and mysterious, his clothes the same as last night—jeans and a rumpled henley that hugged all those impressive muscles and the breadth of his shoulders. But he wasn't wearing his boots, just socks. As if he were a normal man who would walk around anywhere in socks. Plain white socks.

She swallowed, because now she was staring at his socks and that was weird. She forced her gaze to move back up his body and tried not to catalogue every inch of him. Or think about how much she would have liked to have woken up with him naked next to her.

She cleared her throat. "Of course you can have cookies for breakfast. It's no different than a donut or a muffin or a cinnamon roll."

"All terrible choices for breakfast. Breakfast is supposed to have protein. It is the point of breakfast."

Surely, she had something smart or arch to say to that, but she could only stare at him in her kitchen. There was a too-handsome-for-words man in her *kitchen*. She'd had sex with this man. *Sex*. She'd touched his naked body and welcomed him inside her naked body, and it was so surreal to stand here and just have to exist in that knowledge.

His mouth quirked as if he found her silence funny.

She sniffed daintily. "You've got a lot of opinions on breakfast food. I'd invite you to eat breakfast elsewhere, but I have a feeling that isn't an option."

He nodded toward the window. "Have a look."

She was still mostly naked, and she knew her T-shirt wouldn't even begin to be long enough to cover her if she got out from under the sheets. With her shirt now on, she could crane her neck a little farther out. Somehow her jeans were, well, not within reaching distance.

It was silly. She should slide out of bed and grab them. Hell, she should get out of bed and walk calmly and proudly half-naked to her room and change into sweats or something.

But this was the light of day. She could wrap the sheet around her, but that felt childish. As though she were ashamed to be naked in front of a man she'd already had sex with.

Well, ashamed wasn't the right word. Nervous. She walked a lot, and only around Christmas did she indulge in cookies for breakfast, but she didn't work out or anything. She was all soft, jiggly bits—jiggly bits that had once grown a child inside of her. He was honed muscle and perfection, day or night.

Then he was exiting her small kitchen and walking right toward her, and all she could think about was she finally knew what all that *man* looked like underneath his clothes. She knew what it felt to be skin to skin and breath to breath with him. She knew what it was like to feel him surge inside her and—

She seriously needed to get a grip.

He bent over a few paces from the bed and picked her

jeans up off the floor. He held them out toward her, but just before her fingers grasped the material, he pulled them back and held them farther away. She couldn't reach them without getting off the bed, and though it was more than possible to pull the sheet with her, she couldn't get over the idea that it seemed rather cowardly. Somehow more cowardly than staying put on the bed.

So she held out her hand and donned her most imperious voice. "George Bailey, give me my robe." He looked at her as if she'd grown a head, and she sighed gustily. "*It's a Wonderful Life?*"

"What's wonderful about it?"

"You've had to have heard of *It's a Wonderful Life*." He shrugged.

"You really are a grinch," she muttered.

"The grinch I'm familiar with. George Bayfield—"

"Bailey."

"Sure, whatever. Never heard of him."

"That does it."

"Does what?"

"We're going to make the couch, and then we're going to get a big plate of cookies, and then we are going to watch *It's a Wonderful Life*."

"I was planning on digging myself a tunnel out of here."

"Sorry. No shovel." She smiled sweetly up at him. "You're stuck in the hellish depths of Christmas doom."

"God save me," he muttered, tossing the pair of jeans at her.

She caught them easily, cheered by the prospect of breakfast cookies and company to watch her favorite Christmas movie. She'd tried to force Colin into a viewing last year, and he'd complained so long and so loud about it being black and white that she'd finally shoved his handheld video game at him.

Monica shimmied into her jeans under the sheet. "God can't save you here, Gabe." She slid out of bed, then patted his cheek. "But if you're a good boy, Santa might bring you a very, very nice present."

He didn't move, arms crossed over his chest, staring down at her with one of those unreadable expressions she'd never stop wanting to figure out.

"That sounds suspiciously dirty," he said, some tiny hint of humor in his voice if not his face.

"There's only one way to find out how dirty." She walked over to the TV stand, where she had all her Christmas DVDs piled up. She pulled *It's a Wonderful Life* off the top and held it up so he could see it.

"Oh, God, black and white? I'm not sure it's worth it."

"Just be thankful I didn't make a *White Christmas* joke. You don't strike me as the musical type."

Gabe grimaced. "That would definitely not be worth it."

She raised an eyebrow at him until his mouth curved.

"Maybe," he amended.

She had to turn away from that smile because she didn't know how to react to it. There were too many big, warm, smooshy, and oh-so-vulnerable feelings fluttering around her chest, and he would see them. Probably squash them if he could.

Squashing might be best, but she wanted to revel in some smooshy feelings before she had to go back to being Monica Finley, therapist and mother…and sexless automaton.

She began to strip the bed, something to occupy her thoughts with. Strip the bed, fold up the bed, make it a couch and a living room again, and not think of all *that* symbolism.

"Well, if I'm stuck here for the foreseeable future, at least I can rest easy in the fact the Christmas-themed sheets are gone."

"Don't be silly," Monica replied. "I'll replace these with candy cane ones."

"Well, at least those don't have faces."

She looked at him over her shoulder, affecting her most serious face. "Oh, no. They do."

Their gazes held for the longest time, till it turned hot and heavy. Till the room seemed to shrink into this little pinpoint of vision between them. She suddenly felt as if she'd run a mile, and still they stood frozen, staring at each other.

"Monica," he said, slow and sure and some dark, edgy thing in his voice.

"What?" she said, her voice a silly, breathless whisper.

"Don't take off the sheets."

Chapter 17

THE MOVIE WAS HORRIBLE. ABSOLUTELY, horrendously awful. Gabe kept telling himself to talk her out of her clothes again, make her forget about the relentless tragedy of George Bailey's life. But he never could find the words, the moves, and the movie trudged endlessly on until a whole crowd of people were singing "Auld Lang Syne" and Gabe wanted to scream.

No man is a failure who has friends. What utter bullshit. All the crap about a man's life touching too many to count? He supposed it made some sense Monica was all sniffly over it. She had a soft heart for all her pragmatism. More, she *did* actually help people, loath as he was to admit it.

She sighed happily as the movie ended, and Gabe figured he should pretend it was fine. He should definitely ignore the claustrophobic feeling that the cabin walls were closing in on him. That the air was too heavy to breathe and everything…

"Isn't it the best movie?" Monica sighed happily.

"You've obviously never seen *Die Hard*," he managed to choke out, sounding mostly like himself instead of a dying frog.

"*Die Hard* is fine enough, but it doesn't alter lives."

"Now, you just don't know that," he said, pushing off the couch. He needed some air that didn't smell like her or cookies or…life changes.

Nothing was going to change in his life, especially some sad sack old movie. Worth and meaning were fine enough on a movie set, war heroes could toast their heroic home-front brothers, and everyone could be so damn happy you wanted to smash in a TV screen.

But that was not real life, even when the words felt a little too real. A little too revealing. "I think I'm going to go...try to dig us out." Anything, *anything* to find some air.

"Those drifts are almost as tall as your shoulders. We're lucky we have power. I don't think you're going to get anywhere."

Gabe shrugged, trying to smile at her. "Can't sit around in here twiddling my thumbs."

He ignored the little flash of hurt that chased over her face before she smoothed it out. He focused on finding his coat, his boots.

"I didn't expect the movie to bother you," she said quietly.

Oh, he hated that quiet, hurt voice women could wield, far better than any man he'd ever known. Alex and Jack might get stoic, silent, but it was never that quiet quavering infused with hurt.

Becca had laid that on him a time or two, and it had been enough to eat him alive then. Coming from Monica, it felt like razors cutting his chest to ribbons. But what might happen if he gave in to that feeling? If he said he was sorry, if he told her all the things that bothered him?

He knew how those stories ended. He wouldn't go there again. Not with her. Not in this place where he'd found the closest thing to home he was ever going to get.

"It didn't bother me," he ground out as he shoved his foot into his boot.

"I told you not to lie to me," she said, and it was laced with all that hurt.

"I don't know what you're trying to do," he grumbled, shoving the other boot on.

"I'm trying to understand."

The look he gave her probably wasn't fair, but at least he bit back the words *Stop trying to be my shrink.* He knew she wasn't trying to. He understood that to an extent, after the conversations they'd had, but it was easier to lash out with that, make her back off with *that*, then try to understand this panic in his gut.

"I thought we'd gotten over this," she said quietly. "I…I know I said I used it as armor, but that's not what I'm doing. Not even close."

"Then what *are* you doing, asking if that movie got to me? Just being friendly?"

"I didn't ask. I observed it. Not because I'm your therapist or want to be, but because I'm your… We're…" She huffed out a breath without finishing. It made him sick to his stomach that he was desperate to know what she'd call them. What she wanted them to be.

Nothing. You can only ever be nothing.

"When you're friends with someone," she began again. "When you have a care for someone, you want to know what's wrong."

Gabe wanted to inure himself to that tremulous note in her voice, because there was no shield or armor, not when she was showing her emotions too plain. On the surface and vulnerable. He never, ever wanted to see her vulnerable.

"I don't know, you want to be there. Understand. Offer a shoulder. And, yes, maybe I'd fix it if I could, but because I care."

"Don't need a shoulder or understanding. Definitely don't want it." He got to his feet and shrugged his coat on. He'd go out that door and shovel his way back to Revival with his two bare hands if he had to. Anything would be better than this hell where emotion clogged his throat and feelings ripped at his insides and this awful, stupid part of him wanted to give in.

To her. To the hurt. To the change.

He reached for the door, and she all but leaped between it and him. She swung out her arms, slapping them back against the door as if she could actually block him.

"You think you're going to stop me? I could have you off that door in five seconds flat."

"When you see Jack or Alex hurting, do you ignore it?" she demanded, ignoring his threat. Ignoring every damn warning she should heed.

"I'm not hurting," he said, and those words seethed out of him, that boiling emotion likely undercutting any chance he had at having her believe him.

"Then maybe that's what I'm trying to understand," she said, her voice breaking.

God damn it all to hell, why did she care this much? He didn't want it. "Monica, I will give you five seconds to get out of my way before I physically remove you from blocking that door."

But she went on as if he hadn't spoken. "Maybe I'm trying to understand why it seems you are so often hurting when you claim you're not."

"Claim. Isn't that undermining my feelings? As if I don't know what I'm thinking or feeling?"

"You don't, or worse, you just don't want to feel those things, so you think you can fight them by being an asshole to everyone who cares about you. I don't know if you've noticed, but no one at Revival, including me, takes it very seriously. No one, *no one*, believes that's who you really are."

He stepped forward, the tide of fury sweeping through him so hard and fast he slapped his palm hard against the wood of the door, right above her outstretched arm. "Of course it's who I really fucking am."

She dropped her arms from the door and reached out to him. *She* reached out to him, pressing her palm to his heart, splaying her fingers out right there in the center of his chest. His breath was coming too hard, his heart beating too fast.

"I can't believe that. Do you remember what you said to me after we kissed that night? Out by the car?"

He remembered everything. Every second of that kiss, every roiling, traitorous hurt that had swelled inside of him, and every word she'd uttered in response to him. It haunted him.

"You said my actions had to back up my words. Well, yours don't. You are one of the kindest, most generous and giving people I've ever met in *deed*. Sometimes in words too, but then you cover it up with that surly attitude, and it isn't you. That isn't you."

But he wanted it to be. He *needed* that to be him. At least on the outside, at least in those actions. He needed to protect himself, and he'd learned how. He'd finally learned how. He couldn't let her undermine that, even with words like *care*.

But her hand was pressed there, against his shirt. He could feel the warm, firm imprint of it, and things inside of him seemed to shift, reach out for that touch. He had the horrifying, unstoppable desire to tell her.

Everything.

And then, as if on cue, the lights cut out.

It was still light enough outside that they weren't plunged into total darkness, but it broke whatever moment they'd been having.

Gabe stepped away from her, and all of that churning emotion Monica had seen in him, *felt* in him, was gone. She supposed tied up and buried deep, deep down again.

She'd seen glimpses of it here and there, but she'd never allowed herself to be quite so vulnerable in return. She'd never allowed her voice to break or her hand to touch him gently. Even though she hadn't gotten anywhere, she felt cracked open at the possibility she could maybe break him.

With care. With concern.

What would she do with what spilled out? Would she be able to stay this person who only wanted to know him, or would she fall back into old, bad therapist habits to protect herself and maybe even him?

"Should get a fire started before it gets dark out," he said, his voice all military, unemotional command.

She stayed where she was, leaning against the door, as he stalked toward the hearth. She simply stood and breathed and watched him start the fire they'd let die last night.

Last night, when she'd allowed herself to be thoroughly, repeatedly *taken* by this man, and she couldn't even muster up any feminist outrage over the word *taken* because what was taking if she was giving?

Which did not have to be relegated to the bed. Maybe this was temporary, but even if temporary they should have a better understanding of each other. They weren't having sex and then never seeing each other again. All of her future was tied up, at least peripherally, in Gabe Cortez.

She pushed herself off the door. "Truth or dare?"

He snorted. "What?"

"Truth or dare," she repeated, only feeling moderately stupid, but maybe if she was stupid, she'd catch him off guard for once.

"I'm not a teenage girl at a slumber party." The fire crackled to life, and his temper crackled with it.

She would not be deterred. "Fine. No game. A deal."

He unfurled from his crouched position over the fire, crossing his arms over his chest as he did so. "Fuck your de—"

"I will ask you one question," she said firmly, and maybe that was her mom voice that usually made Colin jump to attention, but Gabe didn't need to know that. "You have to answer said question to my satisfaction. No lies, no evasions, no half-truths."

"This sounds like a barrel of laughs and all, but—"

"In return, you can ask me two questions. Same rules apply."

That had him hesitating, which she'd count as a point.

"Why are you doing this?"

"I want to get to know you better."

Oh, what storms raged beneath those calm, dark waters in his eyes. Under the taut way he held his body. She wanted to reach out again, but instead, she faced him. A fighter's stance. Ready to fight for something more. What exactly, she didn't know, but she'd fight until she did.

"Everything that's happened in this cabin is temporary. That's what I want, and you said the same thing. That no one would respect you if this went any further than this week."

It felt like a slap, no matter that it shouldn't. It was true. She'd said those things. He didn't want more with her. She needed to accept all that. "I know what I said."

"Then what does it matter if you understand me?"

"We have to be friends after. If we leave not having understood each other any better, there's no hope we accept the…there's no hope *I* accept…" God, she hated struggling for words. "There's no hope we put this behind us. Because we'll be in the same sniping place we were before, but we'll know the sex is good. And every time we snipe…" She gestured at the couch.

"So this is all because you're afraid you won't be able to control yourself. That's sad, Monica." He grinned that empty, sharp grin.

She didn't react, didn't budge. She simply held his gaze. "I get one question. You get two. That is the deal I'm putting forth. Aren't you curious?"

"Why would I be curious?"

She nearly wilted at that, but he was studying her too hard, as if looking for that wilt or stab of hurt or…or maybe he was looking for something else. Something that would never make sense to her.

She only stared. Maybe her eyes were a little too wide and she wasn't as collected as she'd been, but she wouldn't give in to him. Not this fake, mean side of him that had to be protecting all that softness inside of him.

That sharp, empty smile slowly changed, turning down at the corners as his jaw tightened. "I have a condition," he finally ground out.

She tried not to let her elation show. "All right."

"Two rules. One, you have to ask first. Two, we play this little game once a day, and only once, until our deal is over."

"Christmas."

He shrugged.

That would give her six more days of questions, although she'd be in Denver for the last two. Four days of in-person questions. Which meant she had to be careful, and she had to choose wisely. "Okay." Okay.

"I don't suppose you have any alcohol I could black out with first?"

Her lips curved ever so slightly. "No, I don't keep alcohol in the cabin."

"Figures," he muttered. He glared all around the cabin as if it had done him some personal affront. With the quickly fading afternoon light sneaking in through the windows, bouncing off all that snow outside, he glowed close to gold.

Someone should sculpt him like that—scowling and bronzed, the picture-perfect image of an angry, vengeful god.

Except, for all Gabe's bluster, she didn't think he had vengeance in him. Anger, yes. Fury, absolutely. But the thirst for vengeance required a kind of belief that you could bend the world to your will.

It struck her as interesting and confusing that confident, and at times bossy, Gabe seemed quite comfortable with the fact the universe ran the show and the rest of them were just pawns.

"Ask your damn question," he ordered, bossy as hell.

She had so many questions. A million whys and hows and whens. But she had to be careful. Strategic. What were the things she needed to understand about him to go from being lovers to friends?

She supposed the simplest place to start was a question she'd already asked him before. "Why'd you join the military?"

He sucked in a breath, then let it out slowly. A coping mechanism he'd developed all on his own. "My stepfather didn't give me much of a choice."

Then he was silent. She waited for a while, thinking he'd find his voice again and explain that, but he didn't.

"So, my turn?" he asked instead.

She frowned at him. "No. You have to answer it to my satisfaction, and your stepfather not giving you a choice isn't an answer. It's a sentence that creates a million other questions."

"I'm sitting for this," he muttered, stalking over to the couch and collapsing rather dramatically on it. She moved slower, lowered herself onto the corner of the couch carefully. She wanted to touch him, wanted to curl up next to him, with his arm around her, and have this conversation as if...

But there was no *as if*. She kept her distance, and she watched his scarred hand rather than his face. "How did your stepfather make you join the military?"

"Powerful man. A powerful man who always hated me."

"*Hate* is a strong word. Sometimes when we're young—"

"I was young, and then I wasn't. He hated me. This

was no up-for-interpretation, stepdaddy grounded me a few too many times. Hate. Pure, unadulterated hate. I was a stain. He loved my mother—well, his version of love. I was his not-fair-skinned, not-easily-folded-into-the-family reminder she'd loved someone else. Although in fairness, I did start a fire at their wedding. Quite on purpose."

Monica gasped. Silly, all in all, considering she'd heard far worse. Still. She couldn't imagine… She couldn't…

"It was the first time they sent me to therapy. Hardly the last."

He said it so offhandedly. So…dispassionately. She could hardly reconcile this man on the couch with the man she'd gotten to know over the past six months. "You…"

He gave her one of those rueful, awful smiles as if the world was a cruel, cosmic joke all the time. "Have to save questions about that for tomorrow, I guess."

Except, now that she'd started it, part of her didn't want to know how this story ended. All she wanted to know was that he was whole and real and here. A good man. She didn't want to know about the tragedies that had shaped him—they hurt too much.

But she'd opened up Pandora's box, and here was all the hurt he'd tried to convince her to avoid.

When would she ever listen?

Chapter 18

IT WAS A STRANGE THING TO BE HAVING THIS conversation, Gabe thought. Not because of the place or time or even her, but simply because he'd never expressed any of this to a living soul.

Oh, he'd told his mother plenty of times that Evan hated him. Before they'd married even, he'd begged his mother to stay away from the man with cold eyes and cruel words.

She'd been lost somehow. Evan's money or charm or sick ability to find the weaknesses in people and destroy them with it.

Destroy everything.

She cleared her throat. "Why did you... You were a boy and you... At a wed..." She shook her head as if she couldn't wrap her head around it.

He almost wasn't sorry for letting that part slip out. He wanted some of her horror directed at him. He might have been the injured party overall, but he was certainly no innocent victim.

"Why did I set a fire at my mother's wedding?" he asked flippantly, but how could he be anything but flippant when he'd somehow confessed all these old horrible things to her? What was there to explain? He'd been angry, hurt, scared, and he'd lashed out in a way he still couldn't fully remember deciding to.

"I guess you'll have to save that question for another day, too," he said, smiling blankly at her.

It didn't provoke her anger as he'd hoped it would. She simply looked sad. The color had leached out of her face and her eyes looked impossibly blue. Impossibly... kind. But kindness didn't last. Kindness, care, love—it all faded. Always.

He'd answered her first question, now he'd ask his two, and then he'd find a way to get out of here. Besides, what could this question really reveal about him if he told it right? "Have any experience with emotional abuse?"

"As a therapist, some," she said softly.

"That's what he did. He never hit my mother that I knew of, but he broke her down just the same. Changed her, manipulated her, until she was someone else. Someone who didn't care about me. Because as long as she cared about me, she couldn't give everything to him. And even then...he did everything in his power to get rid of me."

Gabe tried not to catalogue the long list of things, and the way his mother had slowly and methodically withdrawn her support, her love, until he'd been left completely alone, used only as free babysitting and a target to blame anything that went wrong on.

But he didn't have to give those pieces to Monica either. This wasn't about all the things that led up to the worst, and it wasn't even about the worst. He'd never, ever give her that part.

"When I was seventeen, I got into some trouble, and he used that. Said I had two choices, I could join the army or he'd make sure I was punished by the full extent of the law."

Her pale eyebrows drew together. "But you joined the navy."

"I didn't have very many choices, but I wasn't about to let him pick which branch of the military I went in. As fuck-yous go, it wasn't great, but it was all I had." He flashed a grin.

She clearly found no humor in it. "And your mother… She just…"

"She just stood by him while he gave me that ultimatum. She never said anything. Not even goodbye. He gave me the choice. I took my things and left. The rest is history."

She swallowed, and he could tell it stuck in her throat. Her shiny eyes were a dead giveaway she'd been moved by his story.

Moved by pity. Which he wanted less than nothing to do with.

"It all worked out." He rubbed his scarred shoulder. "Mostly."

"Do you have any contact? Does she—"

He recoiled some, hated himself for the show of weakness. "I answered your one question, fully and wholly and with a few more details than I needed to. Your questions for today are done." Why he sounded more raw than forceful he didn't want to examine.

She bobbed her chin, then uncurled herself from her position in the corner of the couch and moved over to his corner. She slid her palms over his cheeks, gentle and… It felt like admiration. Like she was in *awe* of him.

A trick of the fading sunlight and the crackling firelight, surely.

Then she lowered her mouth to his and kissed him. It was gentle, sweet, and it said a million things words never could. He wanted to shove her away from him almost as much as he wanted that to last forever. Gentle kindness and care.

She slid into his lap, and he wanted to focus on that. Arousal only. But he was afraid if he let that take over, it would come to mean more than he could ever let it. So he pulled her back by the shoulders, ending the kiss.

"My turn."

Again, she only nodded, still holding his face, still looking at him like she wanted to soothe it all away. As if it were possible.

"Did you love your husband?" He shouldn't have asked it, but it had more power than his control, apparently, the need to hear the answer he already knew. If she said it, in his lap, looking him in the eye, then he'd know. He could eradicate all these horrible hopes out of his dreams.

"Yes," she said in a whisper, fierce and so full of truth it felt like a stab. "I'll always love him. He was a good man, and he's why I have Colin."

She would always love another man, a dead man, the father of her child, and all Gabe could ever hope to be was peripheral. He'd come behind the memory of a good, dead man, and the needs and wants of a very much alive child who deserved everything his mother wanted to give.

"What's your second question?" she asked softly, and he ignored the tear that had fallen onto her cheek. She was probably crying for the dead husband anyway. Why would she ever cry for him?

"Why me?" He hated himself for this question more than the first. The first was pathetic, but at least it was a reminder. This was that hope again, that little voice that whispered, *Why wouldn't she cry for you?* "Why only me since him?"

"I'm not sure I have an answer for that, Gabe." She let out a shuddery breath. "There was school, there was Colin, and a million armors I didn't even realize I wore, but I guess more than that… I never argued with anyone the way I argued with you. At first, that was annoying. No, it's still annoying, but it set you apart. You didn't keep your distance. You challenged me. People had stopped challenging me a long time ago."

"Challenging you on what?"

"I don't know. People treat you differently when you're a mental health professional. I mean, you should know that, you treated me like a scourge. But usually it's more avoidance or a careful way of talking. People seem…afraid sometimes, like I can read into things, put things together, confront them with truths they aren't ready to confront. It can be hard to have friends who don't look at you a little sideways."

He knew something about that. People were careful with wounded soldiers too. Even his mother called him on occasion now that he'd been hurt. She'd never come to see him, but she had reached out. All the people he'd met since he'd been in that accident had treated him differently than he'd been treated before. It wasn't always a bad different, but it was different.

"Gabe," she said, her voice a pained whisper.

He didn't know what she was asking him for, didn't want to know. The only thing he knew was that when she kissed him, he needed to end it. Stop this. It was going way beyond his control, and he needed to nip all of it in the bud, blizzard be damned.

He sank into it, into her, instead. This kiss, this sweetness, some unspeakable thing he'd never have the words for.

Comfort. Care.

No, it couldn't be that. So he stripped off her shirt in a quick, rough motion, but when she returned the favor, her hands were slow, gentle. She lifted his shirt off of him like he was delicate glass.

What a bizarre joke.

He maneuvered them so she was straddling him, so he could move her against him. So he could increase the pace, the heat, lose themselves in something hot and edgy instead of all this soft sweetness.

But she wouldn't let him move fast. She slowed everything down, no matter how hard he tried to fight it. She kissed him gently, lightly, and the minute he took it deeper, hotter, she drifted away, planting kisses down his chest.

When she reached the waistband of his jeans, she unbuttoned him, unzipped him, slow, tantalizing movements. She slid onto the floor and pushed his legs apart. She looked up at him once, only once.

Part of him wanted to look away from all that, but he wouldn't be a coward. Maybe he couldn't extricate himself from this like he should, but he wouldn't look away.

She tugged at his pants, and he lifted so she could pull them all the way down and off, taking his boxers with them. She ran her palms up his thighs, still watching him. He watched right back.

If she thought a blow job was going to magically fix all the cracks inside of him, grow his heart three sizes, make him run through the town yelling shit about Christmas, let her think it. Let her be disappointed.

Then, every intelligible thought in his head died because she touched her tongue to the base of him and licked all the way up. The sound that escaped him wasn't human as she took the length of him into her mouth on something like a sigh.

Maybe there was a heaven, and maybe it felt like hell and salvation combined. The slick slide of her tongue against him, the silky strands of her hair fluttering over his legs. It was all he wanted. The heat of her mouth, the smooth glide of her between his legs.

His blood pumped harder, his breath coming in spurts, and if he let her do this, finish this, she would have that power. She'd have done something all for him, and in this moment, the moment where they'd talked about things he hadn't wanted to talk about…

He couldn't let her have it. He pulled her off him and up against him roughly and it was worse, having her here, looking at him with those big, blue eyes still swirling with emotions he wanted nothing to do with.

"Take off your pants," he ordered.

Monica considered the order. Part of her wanted to fight it. He did not get to tell her what to do, and she'd never let him. She immediately bristled at the thought of letting anyone tell her what to do.

But he'd softened her completely and she couldn't manage the bristle, the worry over her own pride or whatever. All she wanted to do was give him what he wanted. Offer him some solace even if it was sex solace and he wanted to distance himself from it. From them.

In *this* moment, she wanted to give him whatever he

wanted. Well, and some care, which he clearly did not want. But he needed it. God, she knew he needed it. He wouldn't be so scared of it if he didn't desperately want it.

Taking her time, she pushed down the sweatpants she'd changed into after they'd last done this. She didn't feel self-conscious now, even in the daylight or what there was left of it. She wasn't worried about herself, how she might look pudgy or unsophisticated or whatever. She only wanted to give him something. Anything he wanted. No. Not just what he wanted—what he *needed*.

He reached for the box of condoms, but she beat him to it, grabbing a packet and tearing it open carefully. Then she kneeled in front of him again, where he still sat on the couch, taut and beautiful. She rolled the condom on, watching his face harden as she made slow, slow work of it.

His hand curled around her upper arm, and she thought he was going to jerk her up again, but he didn't. His grip was firm, but he didn't move her, and when she moved her knees from the floor to the couch on either side of his body, he simply held on.

With her free hand, she cupped his face again, watching his eyes as she lowered herself onto him. She sighed at the now-familiar sensation of Gabe filling her, and she had the uncomfortable realization she would want this and him long, long after this was over.

Maybe in the future, she'd be able to convince herself the only thing she'd miss was having an adult around and sex, and any guy could fulfill that role, but here and now, she knew it was him—him alone that could make her feel this way. Jagged edges and all.

His dark eyes were their usual storm, his mouth its

usual grim, blank expression. So she pressed a kiss to his lips, soft and gentle as she lowered herself on him completely. She stayed there, still, her mouth gentle against his, and thought about words. How could there ever be words to express what this gave her?

She kissed his cheek, the hard line of his jaw, and then his earlobe. "I love this," she whispered, knowing it would hurt him. But sometimes words had to hurt before they could heal.

He stiffened, his hand dropping from her arm, but then both his hands clamped over her hips. Rough and hard as he pushed himself up into her.

She didn't relent though, no matter what sizzling pleasure zapped through her at that movement. She slid her hand behind his neck, pressing soft kisses over his face even as he tried to make it fast. Rough. It was like a fight. A battle. He wanted fast and over, she wanted slow and relishing, but they both wanted the end result. Desperately.

"Fuck me," he growled.

She pulled back, looked him right in the eyes as she lowered herself slow, raised herself slower. She might have relented to his pace if he'd asked, if he'd said anything, but this order wasn't one she was going to follow. Not here. Not now. "No."

He held her gaze, pushing into her again, his gaze all fury... Except, no. Underneath that glittering anger was something else. Something she recognized because she saw it so often in her work.

Panic. Bone-deep fear. She might not understand why he felt that, but she could see it.

"Fuck. Me," he ordered.

"No," she returned just as forcefully, refusing to let him

change the pace. She moved against him slowly, gently, no matter how hard he held her or how much he ordered.

He let out a breath, rough and ragged. His grip didn't loosen, but some of that panic, that desperation, faded into weary acceptance.

She hated to see him weary, but she'd use that acceptance for everything it was worth. She kissed him, all lips and tongue and a sweetness she could tell he didn't know what to do with. He didn't need to know. He only needed to accept it from her.

She whispered his name into his ear, smoothed her fingers over his hair, over his neck and shoulders, and she moved at this deliciously painful, leisurely pace. Till she was so lost in finding the edge and flinging herself over it she forgot about giving or receiving or anything other than the way his body fit to hers, the way she felt whole and perfect here in his arms. A swelling joy that twined itself in with physical sensation of bursting, pulsing pleasure.

She held on to him through the wave, murmuring his name, kissing his skin, scarred and unscarred inches alike. And still she moved against him, waiting for him to find that same moment, that same joy.

"Gabe. Gabe, please."

He shuddered through his release, his arms smoothing from her hips up her back until he was holding her. He leaned his cheek against her chest, and she held him back, resting her cheek on the top of his head.

Something too big and wonderful moved through her—a realization, painful and perfect at the same time. She practically laughed because she'd somehow tumbled all the way in love with him, and neither of them were ready for that, even a little bit.

Chapter 19

GABE DIDN'T KNOW HOW TO DESCRIBE THE PAST hour or so. They'd extricated themselves from each other, gotten dressed in silence, and then started talking about the loss of electricity.

As if nothing before had actually happened or mattered. He tried to believe that, but Monica was quiet and withdrawn as they lit candles and collected blankets and figured out what to eat for dinner that wouldn't require electricity.

They spoke, he supposed, but not really. You could speak to someone without ever communicating a thing, and that was definitely what they were doing.

Which suited him just fine. Down to the bone, in fact. Rather cut his tongue out than do more damn talking.

He slapped together a sandwich, though he didn't feel hungry in the slightest. But all he'd eaten all day were cookies, and he was certain that's why he felt hollow and unsteady. A man needed a damn protein in his life.

"Did Revival lose power?" Monica asked, he supposed in an effort to make stilted conversation that wouldn't begin to change the fact things had shifted. Somehow. Someway. And they were stuck in this godforsaken Christmastime hellhole of a cabin.

"Don't know."

"You haven't talked to anyone?"

"Texted about being stuck. Just asked if everything was okay up there."

"And?"

He maybe knew what she was getting at. He definitely ignored what she was getting at. "They said it was okay."

"What did you tell them?" she asked, eyes glued to her sandwich making.

"About what?"

"About where you were…" She trailed off, blinking down at the bread. "About where you are. Surely they're worried."

"Does it matter?"

She frowned at him, making eye contact for the first time since everything had grown decidedly weird. It was almost comical to think he'd once thought her cool and blank. Oh, she could pull that off, but there was always this…glimpse of her true emotions if he only looked. It all swirled there in her eyes. Pain, hurt, confusion.

He refused to give in to that. He was his own man, and her emotions were her own business. Seeing hurt there didn't cut him to ribbons—he simply wouldn't let it. So he held her gaze, then gave her a very deliberate smile.

He'd have been lying if he'd said he didn't enjoy the way her face changed over to anger. He didn't love that it was him angering her, but he loved that she had sharp, tough, near-violent pieces hidden under all that calm strength.

Just like him.

He bit into his sandwich, but it tasted like ash.

"Actually, it does matter," she said, some strange tone to her voice. "If you've told them you're here, you know what they'll think."

He shrugged, chewing and swallowing, no matter how tasteless the food was. "Maybe I lied."

"Maybe you did," she returned, all calm and cool, but something simmered underneath. Part of him wanted to make it boil. Oddly, it wasn't the same part of him that wanted to get the hell out of here. They were like two confusing sides to the same ugly coin.

"But we should have our stories straight, shouldn't we?"

There was something too sweet in her voice, too innocent. It made it a lot easier to pretend than it would have otherwise. "Guess we should." He smiled at her again.

She fisted her hands on her hips, failing so hard at keeping all her usual calm that his smile turned a little more genuine.

"What did you tell them?"

Weird to be ashamed that he'd done both. Told a truth and a lie. Weird to be ashamed at all. What did any of this matter? Not a thing. There was no future here, and that meant any razzing they suffered at the hands of their friends would be short-lived.

"Told them I was here."

Her hands dropped to her sides, her mouth hanging open for a second.

"I said I'd picked up a package in town for you for one of Colin's gifts, came over to drop it off, waited for the snow to clear up, but it just kept getting worse and worse until I was stuck."

She worked her jaw back and forth, and she managed that mask of distance for about a second before the swirling emotions were back. "You said all that in a text?" she asked, her voice rough.

He wouldn't let that sway his tactic. "More or less." Decidedly less.

"Do you think they'll believe it?"

"Doesn't matter."

"What *does* matter, Gabe? Anything?"

He raised an eyebrow at her, standing there while her breath heaved in her chest, anger swirling around her. He didn't understand it fully, but some sick, twisted part of himself that would never deserve her wanted to push her further. See her explode spectacularly.

"Maybe it doesn't."

"Oh, what utter bullshit." She spun around, stalking into the living room. He thought for a fleeting second she was going to go down the hall and hide herself away in one of the two private rooms.

Instead, she whirled around again, pointing a demanding finger at him.

"I'm going to tell Becca, and Rose, for that matter. They're my friends. The only friends I have here. Actually, aside from my mother, they're my only friends period. I'm going to tell them. I *have* to tell them the truth, everything that happened, or I'll go a little nuts. So…"

"So?"

"So? So I'm going to tell them!"

"Okay."

"Don't you have something to say?"

He bit into his sandwich, spoke around it. "No."

"But—"

"You were the one who didn't want to tell anyone," he said, not wanting her anger anymore, because it was spurring his on. If he let his boil over…well, things could go wrong. All wrong.

Like earlier. Too much feeling. Too much want, and not the sexual kind.

"You agreed!"

He shrugged. "I didn't care."

She hefted out a breath, some mix of exasperation and some emotion he didn't understand. Would prefer not to.

"I care," she said, her voice grave, still standing all the way across the room.

"I know, hence the whole 'let's not tell anyone' thing *you* suggested."

"No," she said firmly, crossing her arms over her chest, holding his gaze. "I mean I care. About you. About this." She waved her hands up in the air. "I have an obnoxiously big and uncomfortable amount of *care*."

The panic was back. From this morning when she'd been sleepy and beautiful and he'd had this idiotic flash of desiring all the things he didn't want, perfectly imagined in front of him. As if he wanted them so desperately he could conjure them out of thin air.

"No," he said, putting the sandwich down carefully.

"No?"

He lifted his gaze to hers because he needed to make his point. Once and for all, so she couldn't keep needling him, getting under his skin, changing who he was. "No."

"Gabe, that wasn't a question. It was a statement of fact."

"I reject it."

"You can't…" She threw her arms up in the air. "I could punch you."

He spread his arms wide. "Go ahead."

"I wish I could be like you," she said on one of those whispers that ripped out his soul and stomped on it a few times. "So damn untouchable, aren't you?"

"That's me."

She laughed. Bitterly. "Do you think I'm that dumb, or are you just that good of a liar? Or do you just lie to yourself? You don't seem like the type to believe your own lies, but I've been wrong about you before. I could be again."

He didn't say anything, though he had to clamp his jaw shut to make sure he didn't. She wanted to think him untouchable, well, he'd prove it. All night long, just like this if he had to.

He'd survived far worse hells than Monica looking like she was about to cry, saying shit about him that was probably true.

She stepped toward him though, one foot, then the other, and he didn't feel as good about his chances. He might have survived a grenade, a crash, *war*, but Monica Finley with that soft look in her eye, desperate and a little lost, was somehow worse.

"How do you do it? Lock it all away? I wish I could do that."

"Ignore it and it'll go away," he managed to croak. "Isn't that what you're supposed to do with bullies?"

"Bullies, maybe. Emotional issues, not so much."

"We don't *have* to figure it out. Sometimes in life, you don't figure things out. You just go on and nothing is figured out. That's life."

She paled and flinched as if he'd reached out and backhanded her.

She shook her head. "You have to figure things out to move forward."

"No, you don't."

Monica could only stare at him. She wasn't even sure what the hell they were talking about anymore, but...

She had to figure it out. She had a ten-year-old who depended on her, patients who needed her. She had to figure everything out, make sense of it, analyze it, and then decide on the best course of action.

Except when it came to caring about Gabe, loving him. God, she was an idiot for loving him, but she did. There was no best course of action here. A relationship with him undermined her role as therapist at Revival. It just *did*.

Added to the fact he didn't want her. Not her or her care, and she wasn't stupid enough to throw herself at a brick wall.

He wasn't her father. There was no PTSD to cure, so she'd have the person she'd once known back. There were only all these impossible roadblocks.

She jumped when her phone rang. With shaking hands, she pulled it from her pocket. *Mom*.

She felt so perilously close to tears, but she had to answer. She had to hear how Colin was doing and talk to him herself and...

She swiped to answer the call and swallowed, realizing she had to keep the tears out of her voice. If she wasn't careful, her mother would sense it. She'd demand to know what was wrong. What could Monica possibly tell her? *I don't know*.

Not figuring something out sounded like her absolute worst nightmare and yet...here she was, not figuring it out. She had no answers, and the thing she wanted most in this world right now, to cry to her mother and ask for advice, just wasn't possible.

"Hi, Mom. How's it going?"

"Good. How are you?"

"Well, we've had a bit of a blizzard. Power's out. I'm good on provisions and lots of firewood to keep me warm, but my phone is getting low, and I don't know when... Just in case I don't answer tomorrow, don't get worried."

"A blizzard? And you're alone stuck in that cabin? With only firewood?"

She glanced at Gabe, standing there staring at her with that inscrutable gaze. No, she wasn't alone, but a part of her wished she was. Alone was better than not knowing what to do. "I'll be fine. I promise."

"Well, you save that battery for emergencies. We can talk more later."

"Let me talk to Colin first."

"Save your batt—"

"Mom. Please." She needed to hear Colin's voice. She needed something to remind her she was not the utter failure and fool she felt like right now. She needed someone who loved her. Someone she loved, and it wasn't complicated at all. He was hers and always would be.

"Hi, Mom," Colin's voice said into her ear.

She nearly choked on a sob, but she kept it inside. Swallowed it down and turned away from Gabe, so he couldn't watch her desperately try to keep it together. "Hey, baby. How's it going?"

"Awesome. Grandpa took me to the shooting range, and I got to shoot his big gun. He said next year he'll take me hunting."

"Oh. Joy." But it was normal—her father pushing the boundaries of what she wanted Colin to do. Normal and good. She took a deep breath as Colin kept talking.

"And Grandma let me help make the cookies and didn't get mad at me like you always do."

Well, that one hurt.

"She froze some for you."

"Good. I can't wait to be there and see you."

"Oh, and they bought me a bunch of books and I've read like three."

"You…read three books." She was forever trying to get Colin to read. She'd tried bribing and ignoring and offering a million incentives and…

With her parents, he was happily making cookies and learning to hold a weapon and reading.

So much for not feeling like a failure. "I miss you."

"Okay, Mom. Grandma says I gotta go."

"I love you."

"Bye."

"Bye." She looked at the phone, the call already ended, and indeed her battery was at 20 percent, so she should save it.

He'd been with her parents for a day. One and a half days and he was someone else. More than happy without her.

The tears started spilling over, and she tried to breathe through all that. She was being silly. Overreacting. She tried to think back to those parenting handbooks she'd read a million times over. She tried to think about what she'd tell a patient who was having similar feelings about their parenting.

But she couldn't think beyond the persistent whisper. *Failure. Failure. Failure.* She couldn't find her rational center over this twisting stab of pain and guilt. She *did* always yell at him when they baked together because he never listened. She tried too hard to get him to read. If she'd been chill about it…

A sob escaped her mouth, and she slapped a hand to it, trying to muffle the sound. Trying to hide what an utter mess she really was.

"I'm just going to…" She started moving toward the hallway. She'd have her cry in Colin's bedroom.

Another sob and it was hard to make her feet move. She should run and slam the door and hide and—

Gabe's hand touched her shoulder. She tried to jerk away from it, but he simply turned her to face him and then pulled her into his chest. A hug. Firm and comforting.

This time, she couldn't stop the sobs, no matter how hard she tried to breathe through them or swallow them down. She could only sob against the hard, warm comfort of his chest.

"Shh," he murmured, stroking her hair.

She sucked in a halting breath. "He doesn't need me," she sobbed into his chest.

"Come on. He's your kid. Of course he needs you."

"He's having more fun there. He's…reading. He's… I'm *failing*."

Gabe's hand kept stroking her hair, a slow, calming movement that somehow made the sobbing ease, even if her tears didn't.

"He's with his grandparents. Grandparents are always more fun. They're probably stuffing him with sweets and never making him sleep. He's having the time of his life. You can't compare."

She looked up at him. He seemed so…sincere. So genuinely trying to make her feel better. It wasn't that she was surprised he'd try to make her feel better, because he was kind. It was just that she didn't think it would come from words and hugs.

Still his arm held her to him, there in the entrance to the hallway, his other hand at her hair. "My grandma died when I was like eight or something, but she used to sneak me candy and let me watch things I wasn't supposed to. Grandparents are the fun ones, the ones who make your kid resent you. That's how the world works."

She laughed at that between the tears. "My grandma used to let me put sugar on my Rice Krispies, even though Mom specifically told her not to."

"See?" He let her go, but then he was wiping her cheeks delicately. His big, rough hands being unreasonably gentle. "No reason to cry."

She wanted to cry for a whole new reason, but that would be fatal or something. It would just kill her.

"What if I can't get out?" she asked. "What if we're stuck here for weeks? What if I miss Christmas with him? I've never missed a Christmas with him. Never not been with him on his birthday or mine or Valentine's Day or even Columbus Day. I have never, ever been away from him for even a day."

Gabe shrugged, and his expression was all kind regret. "You're doing it right now. You'll have to do more than that someday."

She frowned. "That's a mean thing to say."

"No, it's a practical thing to say. If you don't accept that time marches on, you can't march with it, and then you miss everything."

"That's very wise." She blew out a breath. "I haven't cried in front of anyone like this since…" She shook her head. "I can't even remember when. I was alone when I found out about Dex, and I always hid if I was going to have a jag."

"Blizzards are a bitch."

She managed a laugh at that too, and she took note of the way he was starting to edge away. His instinct might have been to comfort, but he wasn't comfortable with that instinct.

It saddened her to think it had probably been beaten out of him, if not literally, then figuratively.

She made sure to look him in the eye even though she was embarrassed by her outburst. She was more grateful than embarrassed, or at least, she'd try to be. "Thank you."

"It was nothing. Just a little sense to stop the hysteria."

She rolled her eyes. "I know you're trying to piss me off now. Please don't. You did a nice thing. Just say you're welcome and move on."

"You're welcome."

Then they stood there, looking at each other, like a few too many other moments since they'd been stuck. Those *sparks* everyone had been poking at them over. Because it didn't matter that her head hurt from crying or that she loved him and that was stupid. When she was with him, breathing the same air as him, she wanted him.

God, how she wanted him. "We still have two days," she whispered.

He watched her, quietly and stoically for the longest, most horrible minute. "Wouldn't want to waste it."

Chapter 20

GABE WOKE UP THE NEXT MORNING WRAPPED UP IN dancing candy cane sheets, a warm woman tangled up with him.

Sadly, they weren't naked. It was too damn cold for that. Anything that wasn't covered or wrapped up in the approximately ten blankets they'd put on the couch bed felt like ice. He was pretty sure his nose would never thaw. But underneath the layers of blankets and clothes, there was a warmth he had no interest in leaving.

He tried to shrug the blankets closer to his face without actually unwinding his arms from around Monica, but that didn't help, and since she was currently laying on top of his arm, he decided to use her instead of the blanket.

He nuzzled into her neck, cold nose against warm, smooth skin, until she shrieked awake. Then she slapped him. Hard.

"Sorry," he murmured against her neck, trying not to grin against it.

"No, you're not."

"No, I'm not."

She sighed but curled closer. "It's *freezing*."

"I hear that happens when your electricity goes out and it's below zero. The snow is insulating us somewhat though."

"Somewhat my butt." She shivered, wrapping her arms around him more tightly.

He yawned into her hair, his face slowly thawing out. It was nice. Nice not to have to jump up and worry about chores, nice to be lazy and doze. Nice to have someone to wake up to, mumble sleepily to, feel…

He blinked open his eyes, everything inside of him unaccountably stilling at the horrible realization.

This was more than nice—it was like heaven. It was a joy to wake up with someone in bed with him, lack of heat or no. It was a comfort and a bone-deep contentment he'd never, ever, *ever* had. And it was as temporary as the snow outside.

He *knew* he could go without sex for months, and he also knew he could find sex if he wanted it. There didn't have to be a lack of that after this was over. And if all else failed, he had his own damn hand. Dry spells happened. He knew how to handle a dry spell.

But he'd never… Well, he'd never had someone to wake up with, someone to cook meals with and just… *live* with. Which was what this blizzard had forced him and Monica to do. Now he'd experienced it, and he wanted it. To last. To be real.

It was like waking up in that hospital room all over again. His world changed, leveled, and the people he'd counted on, cared about, taken away.

Alone. He'd be that dark, ugly alone again. The only difference was the lack of physical injuries, and he had the sinking suspicion there'd be plenty of emotional ones to make up for it.

There wasn't anywhere to go with this realization. He was stuck in this bed, the damage already done, even if he pulled away and started acting like a dick. Whether it was today or two days from now, *the end* was a reality that was going to crash down on him. Hard. Painful.

So why not enjoy it for those few more days? What was done was done, and no number of minutes or days would change the awful end result. Why not put it off?

Especially when it was damn cold beyond these blankets. At least there'd be work to do eventually. Here, all he could do was wallow, so he'd enjoy what he had and when he had to go back to not having her...

Well, he was used to that. Having someone and then not. He'd learned early and often that was life.

He started disentangling himself from her, suddenly not so worried about the cold. Sometimes cold was better than warmth. "I'll go start the coffee."

"Wait." She held on tighter. "I have to ask you my question."

He stiffened in spite of himself. He would have rather she not been able to feel that physical reaction, but he couldn't exactly take it back. "You really want to do that again?" He hoped he sounded dismissive. He was afraid he sounded pained.

She burrowed closer, pressing a kiss to his neck. "Yes, I really do."

"All right." After all, yesterday's question had ended in sex. Even if that had made everything weird. Weird sex was still sex, and the sex was good, no matter the circumstances.

Damn good. The best. Seriously, what the hell was wrong with him?

"What experience with therapists made you hate them so much?"

He should have predicted that was where she'd go

with today's question. He'd laid the seeds, and it was his own fault for allowing them to sprout. If he'd been thinking, if he had any self-preservation skills left, he would have made up some story in advance.

He should lie, and even as he told himself to come up with one right that second, he knew...

She'd asked him not to lie to her and he'd agreed.

"The fire thing... Well, believe it or not, people don't take it lightly when you set fires indoors at weddings." He said it lightly, even as his gut clenched against old memories of anger, confusion, pain. Having to sit at that table with a bunch of strangers while Mom and Evan sat with his kids at the head table. He'd realized at some point he was sitting with the help: photographer, reverend, florist. A little boy, left alone at his mother's wedding.

Even now, he didn't feel much regret at fooling around with the lighter he'd found in the bathroom. Even now, he got a grim kind of satisfaction remembering the way the flame had licked up the paper decoration that had hung in the hallway that led back to the main reception area.

Warped, sure, but he could accept warped. He wasn't a liar, and he didn't hurt people. He'd take messed up in the head over anything Evan was.

"Imagine that," she murmured. Her leg was curled over his, her arm over his chest. She reached up and began drawing her fingers over his cheek, down his jawbone, then back up. Sweet. Comforting.

Just as he had last night, he felt a tightening in his chest. When she'd been crying over Colin, thinking she was a failure when she was the best mom he'd ever known. That clutching, painful knot that hadn't dissipated till he'd reached out and held her while she cried.

Now the clutching, painful knot was there in his chest because she was offering him the same. Comfort. Touch. Care.

"Evan wanted me punished or sent away, but eventually they agreed on counseling. Over the years, that would be a constant. I don't know how many offices I was dragged into, how many people tried to twist what I felt into something else or shove a pill down my throat so I felt nothing at all."

"That isn't what counseling should be," she whispered against his neck. "I'm not a psychiatrist, but counseling isn't about telling you what you feel."

"But that's what they did. Told me what to feel. Told Evan what he wanted to hear. I was warped and damaged and a threat."

She leveraged up on her elbow, looking down at him, her eyebrows drawn together. "That can't possibly be true."

"And yet…"

"No, I meant…you're none of those things. I'm not denying that those things happened to you. I'm expressing my utter confusion."

"He paid them off, Monica. Or threatened them. I don't know. But they were working *for* him."

"Surely… You take an oath. You… Surely someone told him go to hell."

He snorted a laugh at the idea of anyone saying that to Evan Milan. "No, not a… Well, I suppose there were a few they had me see that… I'd forgotten that." Forgotten in all his bitterness and rage that there *had* been a few friendly faces. It was just he'd never seen them again.

"What?"

"There *were* shrinks they took me to who we never went back to. I suppose they didn't fall in line with what Evan wanted them to say."

Monica was quiet, her fingers still trailing up and down his jaw.

"Would you?" he asked, even though it was a stupid question. Of course she never would, and if she would, she'd never admit it.

But she was quiet for a few moments as if she was really considering it. "For money? No, I couldn't manipulate a patient for money."

"No amount?"

She shook her head. "Maybe it's because I've never had to live in real poverty, but I can't imagine any sum that would assuage the guilt I would feel. That being said…I can't say I'd never do it."

He frowned at her. "You can't?"

She lay back down on the pillow as if considering her words. She looked downright angelic with her blond hair spread out all over the pillow, her blue eyes wide and serious.

"Maybe I've watched too many episodes of *Law & Order*, but I can think of a few situations where I'd capitulate, mainly involving any threats to my loved ones I couldn't circumnavigate."

"Most people would just say no, they wouldn't do it."

"I'm under no illusions that I'm a saint, Gabe. Or that I wouldn't do something that repulsed me under the right awful circumstances. Maybe that comes from working with military men. Maybe I'm just too practical to fancy myself the most noble. Sometimes people have to do ugly things they never thought they would. That I do know."

No one he'd ever spoken to had articulated it quite like that, even Alex and Jack. They didn't discuss the things they'd done, the questionable choices they'd sometimes made because of war. Because they'd had to.

But she'd put it all into words that shifted something inside of him. *Sometimes people have to do ugly things they never thought they would*.

He knew in that moment she'd understand. All of it. The darkest pieces of himself, and she'd assuage all that guilt, all that wrong and warped. She'd say he was fine, and she'd mean it—another terrible realization in a long line of them. Because no matter that it was irrevocably true, that he was one hundred percent certain, it didn't change basic facts.

She'd always love her husband. Colin would always come first. Hell, being a therapist would always come first. If he hadn't lived through hell, maybe he could believe he could contort himself into the spaces that were left.

But he'd tried that too often and too much as a kid to think it was possible. There was only so much room a person had in their life, and she didn't have much of any.

He wouldn't cut himself to pieces to fit into them.

It was an odd thing to have this conversation while actually touching each other, practically being on top of each other. While he spoke, thought, breathed, Monica could feel the tension in him. The way he held himself still or purpose-fully relaxed. She could *feel* all that emotion roll through him, and it made it all more honest somehow. Connecting.

She shouldn't want that, but after last night, she was under fewer and fewer illusions she had any control over this thing between them. She'd *cried* in front of him, sobbed like a baby. He simply undid her completely, and she knew he wasn't trying to.

But very much against her will, she'd shown him a million vulnerable sides of herself, sides she'd held under lock and key so long she'd forgotten they existed. As if it was second nature, he'd opened that lock and Monica had poured out. Not the mother or the therapist, just a person.

She hadn't been smart enough to ward it off, strong enough to walk away from all that. She'd fallen in love with him knowing nothing could come of it.

Can nothing *really come from it?*

She didn't know. She wasn't sure she was ready to answer that question. She certainly wasn't anywhere near ready to ask it. So she focused on the other questions.

"What's your second question for me?"

"Second?" He narrowed his eyes. "That was not my question, cheater."

She shrugged in that same negligent way he always did. "It was a question. I answered it."

He scowled at her, and she wanted to press a kiss to it. Press herself to him. She wanted to forget questions and realities and the future. For the first time maybe in her whole life, she wanted to dwell in a moment, relish it, and not worry about what was next.

But he asked his question.

"Cats or dogs?"

She huffed. "That is not your question."

"Oh, but it is. A very serious, important question that will tell me all I need to know about you."

She rolled her eyes. Well, if he didn't want to take it seriously, that was fine. *She* still would, and she'd answer his questions with complete and utter honesty. "Dogs. Cats creep me out."

He laughed way harder at that than he should have.

"What's so funny about that? Cats *are* creepy. You never hear them coming, and they have those eyes that glow and just…stare."

When he finally stopped laughing, he grinned, twirling a piece of hair around his finger. "That's just exactly what I told Bec when she informed me I was living under the same roof as a cat. Not that I've ever seen said cat, thank God."

"Oh God. Becca's cat?" She shuddered for dramatic effect. "It has these weird, yellow eyes that glow, and I swear, with enough plotting, it could eat your heart out before you even woke up."

"You've seen the fabled Hannibal?"

Monica nodded. "On the day of the wedding, we helped Becca get all the dresses out of her closet upstairs, and there he was. Glowing, creepy cat eyes ready to like…pounce and eat my soul."

"But is it creepier than the goat?"

Monica fisted a hand to her heart. "How dare you insult Ron Swanson?"

"I'm deeply, deeply sorry for such an affront."

Then they were both laughing, wrapped up in each other and a million blankets, warm in this little world they'd built while outside it was frigidly cold.

She wanted this. Camaraderie. A relationship. All those things she'd had with Dex. This was different. Gabe was different—*she* was different. But she wanted

that experience again. Someone in her life. A partner.
Since Dex's death, no one else had even come close to
making her want that.

Of course, the man who did… She wanted to laugh
for a completely different reason. He wouldn't agree to
it in a million years.

But why was that? He didn't want to settle down or
build what his friends had, but why? Was it as simple as
not wanting something, or did it go deeper, into all the
ways he'd been hurt growing up?

Well, maybe that'd be her question for tomorrow.

He dropped a casual kiss to her temple. "I need
coffee," he said on a yawn. He unraveled himself from
her and the blankets, and got out of bed, cursing as he
walked to the kitchen, presumably at the cold.

She watched him in her kitchen, gathering the things
he'd need, then fiddling with the coffeepot. As if he
belonged there, doing little things for her—for them.
She wanted him to belong there.

"We're going to have to make an effort to get out of
here today," he stated casually.

It hurt, of course, that after everything, he'd still be eager
to get out of here. But beneath the hurt was also a panic.

She didn't want to lose this. A man in her kitchen
making her coffee in the morning. A man who held her
when she cried over feeling like a failure to her son. A
man who relaxed when she traced his jaw.

Every second of being with him only reinforced
what she wanted. What she was starting to think she
needed—a partnership, *this* partnership. She liked it. It
made her feel good, and it didn't stop things from hurting. In fact, some things hurt worse.

But then he held her. Kissed her or made her coffee and… There had to be some way…some way. She just had to figure out how to get through to him.

"Why today?" she asked, attempting to sound as casual as he had.

"We'll run out of firewood if we're not careful. Who knows when the power will come back, and I don't particularly want to freeze to death. Seems like a nasty way to go."

"Well, there are a few piles of wood in the back. They're just under approximately eighty gajillion feet of snow."

"Eighty gajillion *is* the scientific term. I don't know how much good it'll do if it's wet, but we can give it a shot. All else fails, if we can manage a path to the Shaws' we can see if they have any extra wood or if they have power."

Monica scooted beneath the blanket, trying to hide the wide grin splitting her face. He wasn't trying to escape. He just wanted wood. It was a good sign. A positive sign that if she found the right combination of words, she could convince him that they could find a way to work things out.

Telling him she had fallen in love with him was certainly not the right tack to take, but if they had time, if he wasn't running away, she could find the right path, the right words.

She could find them a chance.

Chapter 21

GABE FROWNED AT THE WHITE, FLUFFY HAT MONICA handed him.

"I'm not wearing that. I have a hood. And I'm a man."

"A hood is not nearly as good at keeping your head warm as a hat. Now, if you want to put your hood over the hat because your precious manliness cannot handle a simple, white stocking cap."

"It has a...thingamajiggie on the top," he replied, pointing to the ball-shaped tassel.

"It's just one little pom," she said, jiggling it as if that would make it somehow less offensive.

"I was a Navy SEAL, Monica. Current or former SEALs do not wear pom-fucking-poms."

"Who are you afraid is going to see you? The great god of masculinity?"

"I'm not wearing a hat with a pom on it. That's final. The much bigger issue at hand is we don't have a shovel." He picked up the pots they'd gathered. It was the best option they'd been able to find for snow relocation.

"There's a utility shed out back that might have some, but with the back door iced shut, we'd have trouble getting to it."

"Have to get to the wood anyway. Might as well try." Gabe opened the door and braced himself against the icy wind and blinding whiteness of it all.

Once his eyes adjusted, he could notice the sky above was almost as blindingly blue as the world below was blindingly white. But that was good. Sun shining might cause retinal damage, but it would also help melt some of the snow.

"I don't suppose you have any sunglasses I wouldn't be ashamed to wear?"

"How do you feel about purple?"

"I can pull off a purple as long as they don't have sparkles."

She rolled her eyes and went back inside, rummaging around in the kitchen for a few seconds. Gabe nudged the snow in front of him. Quite the mixture of hardpack and fine, blow away.

Monica returned to the doorway and handed him a pair of black sunglasses with a smirk. "Do I really strike you as the purple sunglasses type?"

"A few days ago, I would have said no, but I've seen your Christmas sheets. Now, nothing about you would surprise me."

They both stepped forward, Monica trying to lever herself up into the snowbank. She sank to about waist deep. He tried to stifle a laugh, but she looked a little too ridiculous.

"I can handle this. You stay inside."

She shook her head and began pushing through the snow with her gloved hands. "I might as well help. I don't want to freeze for lack of firewood any more than you do."

"Too bad we didn't have electricity for your hair dryer idea."

"If we had electricity, we could stay happily inside for the foreseeable future. Now hand me a pot."

He handed her one of the pots without saying anything. There was nothing to say when that scenario would be a little too much of a fantasy he shouldn't have.

Staying in the fictional world of snowed-in cabins and just him and her. Which was a fantasy she wouldn't share because she missed her kid.

Somehow thinking about Colin in terms of this fantasy made it worse. He wouldn't mind if the kid were here. Sure, it would cut back on the sex considerably, but he liked having Colin underfoot. He liked being with Monica. Put the two together and...

He wished he were Alex or Jack, wished he had that kind of certainty in right things and building. To them, the situation would be a no-brainer: build a foundation, forge a relationship and a future. He didn't know how to be the kind of strong that just *built* whole worlds.

Alex had built Revival with Becca at his side. And she'd built plenty of Revival herself, with the therapeutic horsemanship. Jack had built a new life after his old one had imploded. He was building something so that Rose could trust it.

Gabe had to uncomfortably consider Rose for a second. The fact she'd had an even worse childhood than he had, and yet slowly, she was coming to accept Jack's strength, a future with him, and a kid.

Gabe couldn't allow himself to fall into the foolish trap of thinking he could do what other people did. After he'd set that fire at his mother's wedding, he'd spent years trying to atone for it, trying to turn himself into something Evan would accept or at least would pretend didn't exist.

He'd gotten excellent grades and never gotten in trouble at school, no matter how much he'd wanted to sometimes. He'd tutored Evan's two kids from his previous marriage, Jenna and Zack. He'd sat with them and the three kids his mother had had with Evan later, through nightmares and illness. He'd been the best older brother to them he'd known how. He'd done everything he thought of to earn himself a place in Evan's house.

The harder he'd tried, the more Mom had withdrawn. The harder he'd tried, the more Evan said he was the bad seed making everything problematic at home.

And then Jenna…

Gabe didn't want to think about it. Not even in a fantasy world, where Monica could understand and believe him. It didn't matter if she'd believe him when no one else had. She might believe him, but it would plant a seed of doubt, and those doubts always sprouted. Evan made sure of it.

Gabe shook his head, trying to physically eradicate the old thoughts, the old fears. Monica would need someone more whole, more sure of himself. The kind of man she could inherently trust to be around Colin. The kind of man who didn't have any sort of blights on his past. A man not connected to her job who might undermine how she looked to her patients.

He needed to get that through his own head. Imprint it on his soul, so he'd stop having these moments of hope. There was no hope for him.

"Gabe?"

He looked up and realized he'd been standing in the same position while she'd scooped and pushed her way through the drifts all the way to the corner of the cabin.

"Coming," he muttered, following the makeshift path her small body had cut through the snow.

"Where exactly did you disappear to?"

He could've pretended like he didn't understand what she meant, but he didn't feel like being kind right now. Kindness had gotten him into this mess. A soft heart and a stupid brain dropping his guard enough to entertain these feelings.

He snorted as he made his way to her. When the hell had he gotten stupid enough to allow himself *feelings?* Feelings he could never, ever allow himself to articulate.

It would be a beginning, and then it would be an end. Ends always came, no matter how hard you worked, and he couldn't let an ending risk his sticking with Revival.

Jenna and Evan had made sure he couldn't stay with his mother, but in the wake of all that, he hadn't wanted to remain. He hadn't wanted to watch them all turn on him. Better to leave. Better to not try and soldier through.

He couldn't leave Revival, which meant he could not allow himself to think there was any future with Monica. All futures ended. Whether in threats or in fire, all plans blew up in his face.

"You already had your question for the day," he muttered, harsh and mean, as he approached. He made himself watch the hurt chase over her face. Life was hurt, and life was pain. Better to give it to her now than pretend there could ever be anything different between them.

"With this weather, the snow should start melting. I should be able to get out of here soon, maybe even today."

She was silent at that, and they moved slowly through the huge drifts of snow to the back of the house. There was indeed a shed in the back, and they worked in utter silence to clear the snow around it so they could get to the door.

"Even if you could drive out of here today, it wouldn't

mean you have to," she said quietly. He stared at her in horror for a few humming seconds, sick to his stomach at the sheer amount of hope on her face.

She wanted him to stick around. As though she felt the same thing. Cared about him and fantasized about a future between them.

She hadn't had anyone in her life for ten years. Maybe…maybe he was actually special to her. Maybe he was supposed to be here, and maybe they were supposed to…

Hell, when would he ever learn? He'd had the same thoughts once upon a time. He'd made it through BUD/S training, become friends with Alex. He'd motivated people and saved lives, and he'd started to believe his shitty adolescence had been worth something. Like he'd gone through all that to be there, helping people.

He'd allowed that feeling to grow and grow until the Navy SEALs was his entire life. Until all that mattered was the next mission. They suffered losses, and still he'd believed that he was exactly what and where he was supposed to be.

Then Geiger had thrown himself on that grenade and saved the rest of them. Geiger had been dead and the rest of them couldn't be Navy SEALs anymore. And for what? What had been accomplished? What had he ever done to make Geiger's sacrifice worth it?

He hadn't belonged in Evan's house. He hadn't belonged in the SEALs. Gabe Cortez was a man who didn't belong anywhere.

He couldn't ever let Monica turn him into the kind of man who believed again, because men who believed only ended up blown up and alone.

"No matter what, I'm not staying past tonight." And with that, he managed to jerk the shed door open. Then he pointed. "Look. Shovels."

―∿∿∿―

Monica hadn't said anything to his proclamation of leaving. She'd worked with him to clear some paths around the house, to dig out the firewood and take it inside to dry out. They'd dug out paths to their trucks, and they didn't speak.

He never even tried to, and she was just...numb. Confused. Silent because she had no words to fight the kind of broken finality his words conveyed.

She'd find some of her own words. She just needed time. Too bad time was running out.

No. That was silly. Even if he went back to Revival tonight, that didn't mean she'd lose her chance forever. There would be time. In fact, time might be best. Something had clicked in Gabe. A kind of fear. A fear she didn't understand, but it had to stem from the tragedies he'd faced.

She'd known men with worse backgrounds, that was for sure, but it was different when it was someone you loved.

She sighed heavily, working on fixing a very piecemeal dinner of peanut butter and jelly sandwiches and canned fruit.

Gabe crouched by the fire, moving logs this way and that with a poker. Something had changed in him this afternoon. There'd been flashes of it here and there since this whole thing started, but it was sharper, harsher tonight. It wasn't just considering silence, or even that weird silence from yesterday. This had a darkness to it, a heaviness.

She hated this feeling of premature despair. That it was all over before she'd even had the courage to try to start it.

She frowned harder at his back. She had never let someone tell her she *couldn't*, and why would this be any different? No, she couldn't make miracles happen and erase his past or magically heal all his scars, but she could get through to him if she tried. *Love* was powerful that way, and if he didn't love her back…that didn't mean her love couldn't be powerful.

That's what he hadn't had growing up, so it made sense he might not believe it existed, might not want to trust it. She'd just have to prove it did and that he could.

Talking healed. The entire basis of her professional career. Talking could heal.

Her stomach turned. She was much better at listening, at guiding. She'd grown up in a household that held itself together no matter the cost.

Things had eased once her father had started seeking help for his PTSD, but by then she'd been twenty. It was too late to undo all the stoic, military acceptance her mother and father had impressed upon her.

"It's never too late," she muttered to herself. She'd raised Colin differently, and her family *was* different now. And most of all, *she* was different. She'd dreaded this week alone, but it had turned into an awakening.

She didn't want to do this on her own anymore. She could, and if she had to, she would, but she didn't *want* to. She wanted a partner.

She wanted Gabe.

Now, she just had to find the courage to tell him,

and the right approach to convince him. She squared her shoulders. Her childhood might have made expressing emotions hard, but it had also taught her the value of hard work, and the importance of not giving up when the going got tough.

But as she marched a plate over to Gabe's crouched form, a million words jostling for space in her brain, a knock sounded at the door.

Blinking, Monica turned to stare at it.

"Expecting visitors?" Gabe asked dryly.

She didn't bother to respond. She put the plates down on the fireplace hearth next to Gabe, then opened the door.

"Oh, Caleb, hi." Caleb Shaw ran the Shaw ranch and had rented her this cabin. Though he was Rose's brother-in-law, Monica didn't know him very well besides a few conversations over rental agreements.

"Hey. Just wanted to give you a heads-up that the road out is fairly passable. Probably another day or two before we get power, but…" His gaze drifted to Gabe, so Monica's did too.

He'd gotten to his feet and was scowling.

Caleb cleared his throat. "Anyway, didn't mean to interrupt your evening. Just wanted you to know we're not so blocked in anymore. Path out will still be rough and slick though, so be careful."

"Thanks, Caleb."

He tipped his hat and then headed back to some kind of vehicle clearly made for traveling over snow. What little light remained of the day glowed in the west, and Monica sighed. It was beautiful, this snow-covered land of vast space and even vaster sky. She couldn't say she enjoyed this long, bitter winter, but she'd fallen in love with Montana.

She smiled a little ruefully. Just as she'd fallen in love with the harsh, bitter man behind her. Because under all that bluster, something big and true and honest existed. Strong and good.

"Friend of yours?"

She frowned at Gabe's voice, finally closing the door against the pretty Christmas exterior. "Caleb Shaw."

Gabe just made a grunting sound.

"You know, my landlord, so to speak."

"So to speak," he repeated with an odd edge of something she *really* didn't understand. Because surely that was not some kind of twisted jealousy lurking there.

She could only blink for a moment. Jealous? Of a married man who was her *landlord*? Which surely he knew. "He's married to Rose's sister," she said, baffled beyond belief.

"Your point?"

"What's *your* point?" she returned. She wanted to laugh, but his eyes were too dark, his scowl too deep.

"I don't have one." He shrugged, then picked up his coat. Because he was going to leave, retreat. Then he was going to build up all those boundaries he always kept around himself.

She couldn't let it happen. She stood in front of the door, even as her heart began to pound in panic. "You can't leave."

He shook his head, a little sad but a lot determined. "The roads are passable. There's no reason to stay." He zipped up his coat as if it were some final goodbye gesture.

"Except that I want you to stay, and I think you want to stay."

Chapter 22

GABE WASN'T SURE WHICH WAS WORSE. THAT HE *DID* want to stay, though he knew he couldn't, or that she could see it on him. That desperate film Evan had always called *trying too hard*. As if he could erase what he really was.

What are you, really?

But a Navy SEAL knew how to handle the onslaught of fear and pain and memories. He knew how to still himself, compartmentalize all those jangling feelings into boxes. Boxes he could bury and set aside so the mission could be accomplished without outside forces risking the outcome.

There was no place for the past, certainly no place for this overwhelming warmth of feeling wanting to spill out of him. There was only his mission: extricate himself from this dangerous predicament. She was the enemy, and he had to escape her.

"If I wanted to stay, I would," he said flatly.

He couldn't have been more caught off guard by the bright pop of laughter that echoed out of her mouth. His jaw even dropped a little bit as he stared at her. Laughing. *Laughing.*

"Would you?"

"Yes, I would," he replied through gritted teeth. He wasn't sure what he'd expected her reaction to be. Amusement was not it.

But that was just another lie to himself. He'd expected her to pale. To be hurt. He'd expected her to back off.

Maybe some small, stupid part of him had hoped she might plead with him. Beg him to stay, beg him to care.

That hope was a terrible, terrible trap. He didn't want her to plead or beg, because that would be its own trap.

He was screwed, and it had to stop. He wasn't a kid anymore. He'd learned his lessons. He'd fought in a war. He was a part of Revival, and he wouldn't fall for the trap of loving someone again.

"I don't know what you want from me." Because this was about her, not him. She had gotten something wrong, didn't understand things.

She laughed again, but it ended sounding sad. She looked at him, shiny, blue eyes and the kind of pleading he'd craved for too long. It froze him to his core. That she might finally be someone who could—

No. No, he couldn't let himself believe that and survive. He'd survived plenty, but not that.

"I told you. I want you to stay." She stepped forward, reaching out and unzipping his coat. "I want you to stay here. With me."

"If this is about sex, just because I leave doesn't mean our deal has to end right this second. Christmas. Christmas was the deal."

"Don't do that," she whispered.

But, of course, he had to do it. "If it's about the questions, go ahead. Ask me a million. But no matter what you say or do or ask, I'm not spending another night here."

She pushed the sides of his coat apart and then pressed a palm to his chest. There was no way she didn't feel the way his heart galloped out of control.

"What are you so afraid of?"

He tried to remind himself she wanted to rearrange

him until he was some fixed, healed thing. He'd never be that. He hadn't been that when he'd joined the navy. It was too late. He'd gone too far. She wanted the challenge. It wasn't about him. It was about him being messed up.

He knew it wasn't true, because he saw the way she loved her son, loved her friends. Still, he tried to convince himself. Lie to himself. Anything to protect himself. "I'm not afraid."

"It's one of my questions, so you can't lie to me." She used her other hand to cup his jaw, and he held himself as stiff and cold as he could against all that warmth.

"I don't want to hurt your feelings or anything, but I think you've…you've got it all twisted."

"But you don't?"

"I know what and who I am." He reached up to pull her hand off his face. It was so much harder than it should have been, but he managed. He managed to pull it away from his cheek, to drop her delicate wrist.

"But what do you *want*, Gabe? What does it matter who and what you are if you don't want anything? Aren't working for anything?" She pressed her dropped palm next to the one against his chest, as if she were trying to give him CPR.

As though he were dead and needed to be revived.

What did he want? He didn't want to tell her he didn't know. That he'd learned to stop wanting things. Stop trying for things. He hadn't even wanted the SEALs, not for him. All he'd hoped was prove to Evan that he was better than him. Not some morally bankrupt liar who manipulated the weak and vulnerable, but a man who saved them, protected them. A hero.

He'd gotten a certain amount of satisfaction out of

that. It had suited him, military life. He'd started to believe he could make life on his own terms.

Then, boom.

Three strikes and a man was out, and he didn't plan on getting out. No, he'd done his time, survived his explosions. Monica wouldn't be another one. He couldn't stomach the thought. If not for her, for the kid and...

"Are you going to get out of my way, or do I have to make you?" he demanded.

"Do you want to know what I want, Gabe?"

"No."

She just smiled, smiled big and broad as if he'd said, *Yes, please. God, tell me every last wish or want, and I'll make them all come true.*

"I want it all," she said, her hands still there against his chest, *pushing* as if she could push him into wanting this. "All of you. *Us.* I want you to come to Denver with me to pick up Colin. I want you to eat dinner with my family, and then I want us to come home and be with our family here. I want you. You in my life. In Colin's life. I want to be *with* you."

Boom. Boom. Boom.

I either call the police or you join the army voluntarily.

Geiger is dead.

I'm sorry, I can't clear you for active duty.

Boom. Boom. Boom.

She wanted to be with him? Under no circumstances could he ever let that happen. "No, you don't."

She laughed again, but this one was harsher. "I love when men tell me what I want or don't. Women are such lucky creatures that way, always being told what we feel isn't quite right because the men don't see it that way."

"Well, this is fun and all, but I'm going." He moved to step around her, but she only moved with him.

"No, you aren't. You're listening."

"Pass." He didn't want to forcibly move her, mostly because he was afraid if he so much as nudged her, he'd want to hold on, fall at her feet, beg her to take this panicked, squeezing horror away.

"You'll listen to me. You'll listen to me ask the tough questions, and you'll listen to me push you when you're being a concrete wall of... I was going to say stupidity, but you aren't stupid. You're afraid. I can't begrudge you that. Fear—"

"I have faced far worse than you, Monica Finley."

"Undoubtedly. Undoubtedly." She swallowed, as if just by knowing he'd faced horrors, she felt some echoes of them. "You've seen things that would make me weep, that would cut the legs out from under me, and you have survived all those things because you had to. Because you learned to disengage, to compartmentalize and put it away. But life, real, nonmilitary life, doesn't work that way. You have to engage. You have to... No, that isn't even right. You don't have to. Everything is a choice."

"My choice is getting out of here. I won't say it again." If in any world he could have predicted her next words, he wouldn't have given the warning. He would have pushed her out of the way and walked straight out, ears plugged and words ignored. But he had no idea and absolutely no warning.

"I love you."

He opened his mouth to tell her she didn't. She couldn't. No sound came out. Her mouth kept moving as if she was speaking, but for a few moments, he only heard the roar of his own heart, some pounding, deafening thing that matched the horrific, splitting pain in his chest.

Boom.

Monica let out a shaky breath. She wanted to laugh. Hysterically. There'd been no forethought. Those three words needed more buildup, more…tact. She'd meant to lay a foundation. She'd meant to get a ball rolling.

Instead, she'd blurted out an avalanche, and he stood there looking horrified. Assaulted, maybe. Buried under a sudden metric ton of snow and rock.

But it was true. She loved him, and boy, did Gabe need to hear that. Monica might not be particularly fond of this horrible, naked, vulnerable feeling, but she also understood it was a step. Because whether he reciprocated or accepted or anything remotely positive, those were her feelings.

Love. So much love for him, and so much hope for them. Her mother had taught her something about the resilience of love, the hope of it. It would be some kind of insult not to believe in it here and now. No matter how vulnerable she felt, the way it twisted inside of her so she felt sick to her stomach, she knew Gabe *needed* this and deserved it.

Love. *Her* love. Even at her pride's expense. "I know that isn't what you want to hear."

Still, he didn't say anything. She wasn't even sure he heard her. She'd dealt with enough men in trauma situations to know sometimes they went somewhere else when facing something hard. She'd seen waking nightmares, fugue states, total shutdowns.

She wasn't sure what Gabe's was—maybe all three. It wasn't exactly clear to her why something *good* would make him shut down, but she supposed it all connected to his fear.

But there was no going back. No pretending. There was only a future she could see, a man she loved, and even though he was so...hurt, broken, she was so very sure he felt the same. He just needed more time to work through it.

Talking. Time. Love. Those were the only true things that could heal, so she had to believe and trust in them.

"Gabe?"

"I don't..." He shook his head, and some of that shock cleared. Unfortunately, it cleared into that blank, dead thing he did so well.

Her stomach sank even as she reminded herself to hold on to hope. Patience. She reached out, and he all but scrambled backward. In any other circumstance, she might have found that funny, that she could cause an ex–Navy SEAL to *scramble*.

But it only sliced at her in this moment, all the ways people had failed him. All the ways love had failed him. She wouldn't, and her love wouldn't. If she could reach him.

"I take it that was a bit of a surprise. I mean, *I* was surprised at how... I didn't expect it to happen, certainly. But it did. Do you want me to tell you why?"

His eyes widened in horror. "No. God, no."

"Then maybe that's what you need to hear."

"I don't know what you're doing," he said, his voice rough. "I don't know what you're thinking."

"I just told you."

He inhaled, held it for a second, and then it was as

if a switch had been flipped. He was done stuttering. Done faltering. He opened his mouth to speak, but she couldn't let him.

"I know you've got a ways to go. Some demons to face, maybe. Scars to heal, certainly, but I think you love me too, or at least…you could. So I don't want you to say something you'll regret," she said all in a quick rush.

"No, I won't regret anything I say," he returned flatly, and his gaze was on hers, dark and empty and the thing she didn't want to see at all.

Certain.

"Ask me what kind of trouble I got in that my step-father had the pull to threaten me with jail or demand I join the army."

"W-What?"

"Your question," he said, calm and blank. "Ask me: What prompted jail or the military?"

There was no way she wanted to know this. Whatever it was, he was using it as a weapon, and she had to remind herself that's all it would be. No matter what he said. No matter how awful. It wouldn't be a lie, because Gabe wouldn't lie. But that didn't make whatever came next the truth.

"All right," she said, trying to find her own calm. "What happened that gave Evan the opportunity to manipulate you that way?"

"He found me with his daughter."

"Gabe, I hardly think—"

"I was seventeen. She was thirteen."

Monica swallowed. *Not a truth*, she reminded herself, even as her stomach felt hollowed out with a pounding panic that made her think she might throw up.

"She was naked."

She tried to suck in a breath, because with breathing, she could focus. *Not a truth. Not a truth.* He'd phrased that all very carefully, hadn't he? *With* his daughter. Ages. That didn't mean...

No, it didn't mean. She raised her chin, leveled him with her best neutral-therapist expression. "Were you?"

"What?"

"Were you naked?"

His jaw hardened, his eyes narrowing. But after so many ticking seconds, he shook his head.

Relief coursed through her. "Were you touching her? Did you ever touch her while she was naked?"

Again, he paused, looking more and more furious. "No," he ground out. "I had just walked in the room, but—"

"So you walked in the room. She was naked. Were you physically attracted to her? Did you want to have sex with her? Did you—"

He turned away. "Stop."

"You brought this up, so I'd say they're fair questions. Was there ever touching? Heavy pet—"

"She was my sister!" he exploded. "She was *four* when my mother married Evan. Four and sweet and... I used to sing her lullabies when she had bad dreams. I was her brother in every way that should ever count. But Evan used her. He twisted her to think there was something more or different, so she... She was too young to know what she was doing, to know Evan was using her." He breathed heavily now, chest heaving, fists clenching, and it physically hurt to watch him work through all that. Lock it down, put it away, erase all those explosive feelings inside of him until she couldn't see them.

But they were still there. They'd always be there.

"Is this the part where I'm supposed to stop loving you?" she asked quietly.

"You wouldn't, would you?" he murmured, not looking at her but some spot on the wall behind her. She should have been ecstatic at his words, but something in his expression only made her feel uneasy. Then he was advancing on her, and she felt herself scrambling back because there was a menace in his gaze she didn't understand. Didn't think she ever would.

"You'd love me no matter what. Understand. Absolve. You would stand by me, no matter the cost."

"I would," she whispered.

"With a few exceptions."

"N—"

"Colin. Your job. You see, I know what it's like to play second fiddle to other things. Always. She loved him better. Everyone loved him better, bigger, and he sucked it all up until there was nothing left for me."

"Evan isn't here."

"No, but he's here." Gabe patted his chest, and she wanted to argue with him. "He warped me, shaped me. I am who I am because of him."

"You are who you are in spite of that monster."

"You'd like to think that. Hell, I'd like to think that." He looked down at her, and she realized now why she couldn't figure out this expression. It was too many things: fury and pain, blankness and calm certainty. His eyes glittered, but his mouth was relaxed in surety. "You're right, you know. I do."

"You...you do what?"

"I love you."

"Gabe." His name whooshed out of her, and she moved for him, but he held out a hand, and that bubble of hope burst. Quick and painful.

"But I don't want this. You or love or a life with your kid. I don't *want* it. I don't want to love you, and I really don't want you to love me. I want nothing to do with your future. I won't be that little boy again, and love would make me."

"No, it—"

"Yes, it would." He was so calm. So sure. Any mixed emotions had disappeared, and there was only this aura of…leadership, almost. Like a man who'd given an order to blow up a village and simply knew it was the right thing to do. "You asked me what I want. I don't want this."

She reached out for something solid and found the door behind her. Somehow, she was still standing even though he'd ripped the floor out from under her. She tried to breathe past the shock of pain, the horrible realization that he'd found a way to undermine everything she'd thought, been sure of.

She could fight his refusals. She could even fight his insistence she didn't love him or he didn't love her. *She* knew the truth. He'd never convince her otherwise.

But him admitting he loved her and saying he didn't want it? She had no words for that. No way to fight the crushing blow it was. She couldn't make him want anything. He had to make that choice on his own, with absolutely no help from her.

"Goodbye, Monica," he muttered.

Then, he finally got what he'd wanted this whole time. She moved out of the way of the door, and he walked out of it.

Chapter 23

GABE HADN'T ALLOWED HIMSELF TO THINK OF JENNA in years. That night had haunted him for so long. As big of a betrayal as any, but then war had suddenly made that old life seem trivial, and his mother and Evan had made it very clear no one in the family wanted anything to do with him.

Who cared if the sister he'd once protected had been used against him and his family wanted to cut him off forever? There were worse horrors in the world.

He shouldn't have told Monica. Shouldn't have brought it all back up. But he'd thought... In the heat of the moment, he'd thought he'd say it in a way that would disgust her, but he should have known better. Should have known she'd see right through him.

Still, no regrets, because it had brought him to the realization of what he had to do. He couldn't manipulate or blank-face stubborn Monica into understanding. He had to use the truth.

He pulled the truck to a stop in front of the bunkhouse, almost marveling that he'd gotten here. He didn't remember the drive. He'd been in a numb fog that felt suspiciously like shock.

What a joke. Shock was for grenade blasts and dying men.

Not some weird fantasy world that had come to life for a brief, brief period of time and had come to its rightful, necessary end.

He stared at the bunkhouse through his windshield. The night was dark, but Becca's Christmas lights glowed against the huge drifts of snow. He could make out paths to and from the house and the stables and barn, clearly plowed by one of the ranch vehicles. But no one had attempted to dig out the bunkhouse. It stood nearly covered halfway up, some places higher where the wind had blown the snow against the building.

He would have to dig himself in. That was fine. Good even. No use fooling about with a snowplow attachment to the UTV. He'd dig himself in the old-fashioned way.

He turned off the truck and followed the first path from the shoveled-out drive to the barn. He hunted for a shovel and then got to work.

He counted each shovel strike against the snow, each toss of the snow off the shovel. *One, two, three. One hundred and one, two, three.* Count, count, count, so his mind couldn't dwell, think, bargain, argue.

One hundred and fifty.

"Gabe."

Gabe jumped a foot, immediately disgusted with himself for the complete lack of awareness. But it had taken all of his focus and attention to keep his mind on the numbers, not the thoughts or feelings.

"What?" he muttered, not even bothering to look back at Alex. He focused on the fact he was almost to the door.

"What are you doing?"

"What does it look like I'm doing?"

"Okay that wasn't the right question. *Why* are you digging into the bunkhouse when you know you can stay in the house? Better than trying to warm the bunkhouse up after it's been shut up. Come on."

"No." Gabe didn't have to look at Alex to know his expression would be all confusion. Both at the fact his order was being refused and at the whole situation.

"Don't be stupid. If you're all worked up about PDA, Becca and I will stand on opposite sides of the room."

Some dim corner of Gabe's brain acknowledged that was supposed to be a joke, but he couldn't find it in him to smile or joke back.

"Go away."

There was a heavy silence, and if Gabe could have thought straight, he'd have played this differently. Acting like a surly, injured animal was only going to make Alex start poking. But the best he could do was count. Count and move forward.

"So I guess the question is: Are you pissed with yourself because you slept with her, or because you *didn't*?"

Gabe stopped midtoss, the snow dribbling off the shovel and back to the little square he'd just cleared. Slowly, he turned to face Alex. Red and green lights danced across the brim of his hat and Gabe couldn't see his expression.

"What are you talking about?"

"You and Monica. Being trapped in a cabin with her for a few days… Full disclosure, we have a bet."

"A bet."

"Me, Bec, Jack, and Rose."

"On whether or not Monica and I slept together."

"Yes."

"You, Alex McGuire, bet on someone else's sex life?" The most un-Alex action was almost enough to penetrate the numbing fog pushing him down.

"Well, truth be told, I wasn't going to, but the losers

have to clean up Christmas dinner. I was told by not participating, I would be considered a loser. I really don't want to do dishes."

Gabe just grunted, focusing back on his work. He was almost there, and then he could do two very important things. First, get rid of Alex. Second, drink himself into oblivion.

"It's freezing out here, Gabe. Come on. Let's go."

"Almost done."

"You can't stay out here."

"Sure I can."

"Gabe. I'm going to be pissed if Becca gets bundled up and comes out here just because you're being stubborn. Drop the shovel. We'll dig out the bunkhouse and get it warmed up tomorrow. Now is not the time."

"Sorry, Dad, last time I checked, I get to make my own choices."

"Come inside," Alex said in that commander's voice that had all of Gabe's temper snapping against that cold fog of numbness.

He slammed the shovel hard into the snow, turning to face Alex fully. "I'm not going in that house. You'll have to knock me out and drag me. Either figure out a way to do that, or fuck off."

Alex crossed his arms over his chest, and though Gabe couldn't see his face due to the darkness, he could perfectly picture Alex raising his eyebrows.

"I see. So you did sleep with her."

"W-what?"

"You'd be pissed if you didn't, but not shut-down pissed."

"I have no clue what you're talking about," Gabe

muttered, yanking the shovel out of the snow and going back to work.

"The only thing that ever pisses you off is something you can't control or shrug off as being one of life's great cruelties. The only thing that ever truly pisses you off is feeling something you don't want to feel."

"I didn't realize you were itching for a fight, Alex. I guess I could knock you on your ass again, if you wanted me to."

"You could. But maybe you could try to listen instead. You make very sure everyone knows you've got a chip on your shoulder, but not why. And why would anyone push? You're fun-loving Gabe. Quick with a grin and a joke and a sidestep should it get a little too real."

"Been there for plenty of your real moments."

"You have. So why don't I be there for yours?"

One, two, three. Gabe counted, breathing with it. Shove, scoop, lift, throw. *Four, five, six.*

"You have forty-eight hours."

Seven, eight... He turned to look at Alex. "What?"

"Forty-eight hours to get yourself out of this little snit on your own, and then Jack and I interfere."

"What the hell does that mean?"

Alex smiled, turning into the Christmas lights glowing from the house. The smile was one Gabe had nearly forgotten. The kind Alex used to flash at a guy who tried to challenge him.

"Doubt you want to find out, brother."

―⁓⁓―

Monica had promised herself, over and over, on the plane ride to Denver that she wasn't going to cry when she saw Colin. After all, she'd spent days crying at this point. Crying and trying to figure out a solution to this horrible, horrible heartbreak.

There didn't seem to be one. Maybe she'd find a Christmas miracle, but before she could, she needed to pick up her son. She needed to have Christmas with her family and enjoy that. Really, really enjoy it.

Heartbreak happened. Loss definitely happened. In those breaks and losses, leaning on and loving her family had always given her the strength to keep on moving.

So, yes, when she saw her parents drive up to the airport's pickup curb, Colin's dark head visible in the back window, she started to cry. Not a particularly pretty cry either, but she hefted her carry-on bag into the trunk of her parents' car and then slid into the back seat next to Colin.

She pulled him to her, rough and tight. "I missed you so much." Teardrops dripped into his hair, and she felt a kind of relaxation take over her body. Whatever had happened or would happen back at the ranch, she had this amazing boy.

He'd grow up and go on his own someday, but he'd always be hers.

"Ugh, Mom. Really." But Colin didn't squirm or push her away. His displeasure was all verbal, while he snuggled a little closer inside her tight embrace.

She held on to him the whole way back to her parents' house. Mom had a roast in the slow cooker and the house smelled like Monica's childhood Christmases—meat and baking with the faintest hint of evergreen.

It made her joyful and sad all at the same time. She'd celebrated her son's first Christmas in this house, but her childhood Christmases had been spent anywhere and everywhere. Still, the smell tied all those years together. The smell and her parents and...

She didn't want to cry again. So, at dinner, she incited her father into an argument over presidents. She guessed gifts with Colin under the tree. She put Colin to bed in his old room, and when she went downstairs afterward, her mother handed her a drink.

"Alcoholic," Mom assured her.

Monica lifted the boozy hot chocolate to her mouth and took a sip. "You're the best mom."

Mom laughed, then patted the couch cushion next to her. "Have a sit, my girl."

"Why does this feel like every teenage inquisition I was ever treated to?"

"It's different."

"How?"

Mom pointed at the mug. "The alcohol."

Monica laughed, the weird, nostalgic relaxation washing over her all over again. "I miss you."

"We miss you too. I'd point out you can move back, but I suppose you already know that."

"I love you both, and I miss you both, but I love it there. More than even I had hoped I would."

"So why are you sad?"

Monica looked at the prettily decorated tree. She could tell where Mom had let Colin help decorate because a bunch of Broncos-related ornaments hung in a clump at the center. She'd once done the same with her favorite ornaments, but Mom had always spread them out after Monica had gone to bed.

"Monica."

She blew out a breath. "Well, I made the mistake of falling in love."

Mom tsked. "Not with another military man."

"Afraid so."

"Irresistible, aren't they? Let me guess, the dark-haired one who made eyes at you the whole time we were there."

"Made eyes at me," Monica scoffed.

"Couldn't take them off you. The minute your father and I were alone, I told him that man was in love with our daughter."

"What did Daddy say to that?"

"If I remember correctly, he grunted and changed the subject." Mom sipped from her mug thoughtfully. "Love shouldn't make you sad, sweetheart."

"No, it shouldn't. And it doesn't. Loving him doesn't make me sad at all, but..." Monica studied her mother. This woman had made a marriage with a difficult man in a difficult situation. She'd stayed with him through war and PTSD, and Monica had never once doubted her mother's love or devotion to her father, even when she'd doubted her own.

But Mom was also a force. She let her opinion be known, and Monica had made it a habit to never ask for advice or help. Mom usually gave it whether Monica wanted it or not, but with some hindsight and some rough patches in her own life, Monica realized she'd been remiss, because her mother was one of the strongest, most self-reliant women Monica had ever known.

"When Dad... After he came back and he wasn't... When he..."

Mom raised an eyebrow. "You've become a therapist

for men with PTSD and you're afraid to say the words to me?"

"I think I'm afraid to utter the words under his roof."

Mom smiled a little at that. "When your father came back from Desert Storm suffering from severe PTSD... Go on."

"How did you keep believing? How did you stick by him even when it was so bleak?" And it had been bleak. Monica remembered the fear. The bursts of temper. At her. At Mom. At himself. It had been sad and scary, and Mom had never once acted it. Not in front of Monica.

Mom looked at her mug. "I made vows," she said carefully. "I wasn't going to break them."

"Is that all that got you through?"

"Some days." She lifted her gaze, her lips twisting wryly. "I'm not going to lie to you."

"You never have."

Mom chuckled a little at that, then sighed. "I know my practicality can be harsh sometimes, but I always thought that was best, and it got me through a lot of days, too. The reality was your father wasn't the man I loved, but I believed the man I loved was still there. Or if not, that someone was there I could love. Love..." Mom smiled. "That was what got me through. Oh, I worried. I was deeply afraid whatever love he had was dead, but mine wasn't. I don't believe in a lot of intangible things, Monica, as you well know, but I believe in love."

Mom reached out, cupped Monica's cheek. "I believe in it because I've been surrounded by it. Your grandparents, your father—before war and then after his own—you, my baby girl. Oh, the love I've felt for you. Honestly, that was what got me through. Love. My mother, you. It all gave me the strength to keep loving him, even when he wasn't him at all." Mom dropped her hand. "So, your man has PTSD?"

Monica shook her head. "No. Actually, he doesn't. But he had a horrible childhood with very little love, and I don't think... He doesn't seem to believe in it."

"So he doesn't love you back."

"That's the worst part. He said he did. He said he loved me, but he doesn't want to. He says he doesn't want it. Love. Us. A relationship. I spent two days trying to...understand that. But I can't. And I can't fight it. If he doesn't want love, to love me or me to love him, how can I fight that?"

"I wish I had a very practical answer for that. A map or steps you could follow."

"But you don't. Because it's impossible. I *can't* fight it."

"If you love him, you can fight anything. Trite advice, but the truth." Mom shrugged. "Even when you don't know how, even when you think it's useless, even when it would be easier to turn around and walk away. That's what I did with your father. I guess I was too stubborn to give up even when it felt hopeless. For you. For me. For the man I loved. I just kept fighting, and you know, the damnedest thing happened."

"What?" Monica croaked through her tight, scratchy throat.

Mom smiled, but a tear dropped over her cheek. "One day, we were sitting down, eating breakfast. It was a day like any other. He looked up at me across the table, and he said, 'Lorraine, I'm going to see that therapist.' No warning. No inciting incident. Just suddenly, after years, long, painful years of ups and downs, he finally agreed.

Love isn't a thunderstorm. It's the way a river cuts through rock over time." She reached out and squeezed Monica's arm. "I'm sorry you didn't have that chance with Dex, but if you have a chance now…"

"How long do I fight though? Just…forever?"

"As long as you love, you fight. Unless it's hurting you or Colin in a damaging way. Love hurts, but it should never damage."

"My, you got wise," Monica managed, though her throat felt too tight and everything hurt and ached.

"Lord, what I've had to go through to find that wisdom. I don't wish it on anyone." But Mom said it with a grin.

Monica didn't know that she felt sure or settled or even brave enough to follow all that advice, but here, curled up on the couch with her mother, talking as both mother and daughter and two adults, with Christmas lights shining, she felt something a lot closer to hope than she had the past few days.

Chapter 24

HANGOVERS WERE ONLY PAINFUL IF YOU LET THEM be. They could only affect your life if you were planning on having one. The snow greatly impeded any chores getting done, and Alex had been doing just fine without Gabe the days he'd been…stuck elsewhere.

Elsewhere had him leaving his bed and searching for more alcohol. It would make the pain go away. The pounding head, the swirling stomach.

He blinked blearily at the empty bottles that littered his small, squat dresser. They were all empty. It seemed impossible, but the evidence was right there in front of him.

He'd have to go get more. The thought of leaving was as unpleasant as any, but not nearly as bad as sobering up. He'd run through the shower, wake himself up a bit, and then head into town for more booze.

He'd get enough for weeks. Months. Years. If that much in two days hadn't fixed anything, he needed to up his game.

Unfortunately, the shower's cold water brought too much clarity. He could think straight. Worse, he could feel…everything. The physical pain. The emotional pain.

He wrenched off the shower and dried himself off. His head was pounding, and he felt unsteady on his feet. He gripped the sink, trying to find some center of not-going-to-puke.

Once his body settled a little, he slowly lifted his

head. Then he could only stare at himself in the mirror, wondering who the man looking back at him was. That man looked haggard. Haunted. *That* man looked like... well, everything Evan had ever hoped he'd be. A lonely, drunken loser.

Gabe spun away from the mirror and jerked on his clothes.

Fuck Evan. Fuck old memories. Fuck...

He didn't even want to think her name. It conjured up too many memories of her smile, her touch, her laugh. Saying she loved him as if that was something either of them would ever survive.

He took a deep breath. He wasn't going to lose himself in alcohol today. If only to prove he didn't need to. But he wasn't going to sit here and *think* either. If he allowed himself to think too much, he'd be liable to convince himself of something that could never be true.

When he stepped out of the bathroom, he stopped abruptly. Jack was sprawled out on his old bed, and Alex was sitting in an uncomfortable chair Gabe never used.

"What are you two doing?"

"Thought we'd help you drink yourself to death," Jack said, nodding toward the dresser, where his empty bottles were lined up, but a brand-new and very full bottle sat at the end.

Tempting. Especially with Jack and Alex here, likely with advice or some shit. Best to handle this the way he always handled things. Flippantly and distancing. Throw in a few good smiles, if he could manage them, and he'd win whatever battle this was going to be.

Even though he'd decided to lay off the booze, he wasn't about to tell them that. It would play into their hands. "What else is there to do in this godforsaken wasteland?"

"You could leave," Alex said calmly, his dark gaze only adding to the way those words landed like blows. "You don't have to live in this wasteland if that's how you feel."

Flippant. Be flippant. Smile. But he couldn't get his mouth to curve. He could only stare at Alex as if the man had thrown a machete into his chest.

"You'll note he said you *could*, not that we want you to," Jack added.

Gabe slowly turned to meet Jack's gaze. "Is there a difference?"

"Yes," Alex replied calmly.

"We want you to be happy," Jack said, sitting up in the bed, eyes never leaving Gabe. "If that meant leaving, we might be sad, but we'd support it."

"You need me here. You can't run this place without me." He sounded too rusty, too desperate.

They don't want you either. It whispered along his skin like needles, and only when he began to see spots in his vision did he realize he'd stopped breathing. He sucked in a breath that sounded horrible and telling in the silence of the bunkhouse.

"We do need you," Alex said quietly. "We need you, but we love you. So happiness matters."

Gabe didn't know what to do with that. How could he absorb… It didn't make any sense. If they needed him, they wouldn't have been suggesting he leave. If they loved him, they wouldn't have suggested he go.

Bottom line. Bottom line.

Except if he reversed situations, quite against his will, he knew he'd say the same to either of them. They'd pushed Alex to get help when he'd needed it and been refusing it. They'd given Jack a family and people to trust and lean on when he'd needed it. Now they were giving him his freedom if he needed it.

He didn't. He wished to God that was what he needed, but no. What he needed was a mystery. "I wouldn't be any happier anywhere else." Which didn't sound casual or flippant or like a throwaway comment. He wanted it to sound like that. *Needed* it to sound like that, but it sounded pained and desperate and weak instead. "So, just…go."

Alex and Jack exchanged a glance, but then they both just settled back into what they were doing. Jack lay back down and sprawled out. Alex picked up his phone and began to scroll.

"What are you doing?" Gabe demanded, ignoring the slow beat of panic in his body.

"I think I'm going to take a nap," Jack said on a yawn. "Rose was up half the night puking. Didn't get much shut-eye."

"And I'm going to catch up on my reading."

"I don't want you two here," Gabe said. "I… Go away."

"It's Christmas Eve," Jack said as if that explained their continued presence.

"Even more reason to go. You have families now. You have…other lives. Go be with your wife. Go take care of your baby mama. Go."

"You're our family, too, Gabe."

"No, I'm… No."

Jack sat up again and Alex put his phone down, and they were both looking at him as though he'd hurt them in some way. "Your friend. Your partner. I'm…that."

"Our family," they said in unison.

"Brothers," Alex said.

Gabe wouldn't do this. Not now. Not when he wasn't... He couldn't do this. "If you won't go, I will."

"No. No, that is not an option."

"You're not my leader anymore, Alex. We've been over that," Gabe said through gritted teeth. He looked around the spacious bunkhouse for his boots. They had to be somewhere around here.

"Just where are you going to go on Christmas Eve?" Jack asked, too much gentleness in his tone.

"Go home to your families," Gabe said, realizing too late it was a shout, and not a particularly effective one when he sounded panicked and out of control.

"As if you're not a part of those families?" Alex scoffed. "We are one big family. A weird-ass conglomeration of family, I'll give you, but a family nonetheless."

"No. You have wives and kids. It's different. It's more."

"It isn't more. It's just different."

Gabe looked away from Jack's eerie calm. "Nice thought and all, but it isn't true."

"Of course it is. Firstly, you're a part of the reason we even have those things. Who threatened to fight me when I was screwing things up with Becca?" Alex demanded, with none of Jack's calm. "Who promised to be here for Jack when Rose was trying to skip town? You don't get to decide you're not a part of this just because someone else joined. It's not all or nothing. You or them."

"No." Gabe whirled, pointing toward the outside world. "It's them."

"No, it's us."

"I don't want you. Any of you."

"What utter bullshit," Jack said and actually laughed. "If that were true, you wouldn't have busted your ass with us to get Revival up and running. You wouldn't have stuck with us in that rehabilitation center when we all know you were cleared before we were."

"Th-that isn't true." Exactly. He'd been given an option, because while his injuries had been extensive, they hadn't required the same kind of rehabilitation, but it had been close enough that he'd been given an option.

"Christ, Gabe, where is all this idiotic denial coming from? Do you think Becca would ever forgive me if I said, 'Oh, Gabe wanted to be left alone on Christmas Eve so we left him there'? She loves you, too, and more, she doesn't need all of me to function. She doesn't have some one hundred percent hold on my love or devotion, nor would she need it."

"God knows Rose doesn't even need a quarter of me to function. It's not some all-consuming thing that takes you away from everything else. Love is just…there. No piece of pie you have to dole out carefully."

Gabe wanted to argue with that. He'd only ever known people whose love was all or nothing.

Except here. Alex and Becca gave parts of themselves to this ranch, to this foundation, to friends and community. Rose had a whole slew of sisters she gave to with or without Jack.

And more, so much more, over a decade of friendship that had survived being SEALs and losing Geiger and their futures. They'd always given to each other.

But…but…

"Is this about your family?" Alex asked quietly. "Why you're not seeing them on holidays?"

"They don't love me." He honestly couldn't believe the words had come out, but there they were, flopping on the floor like a grotesque dying fish.

He figured Jack and Alex would try to argue with him. Try to tell him he had to be wrong, because families always loved each other, unless someone very much didn't deserve to be loved.

Me. Me. Me.

Bang. Bang. Bang.

"That doesn't mean we don't," Jack said firmly.

Horrible words. Horrible lies. But Gabe felt like he was being cracked open. Worse, somehow, than when Monica had said it. He could convince himself she didn't know him. Could never understand him. She might, but he could work hard to believe she didn't.

He couldn't work up the same denial with Alex and Jack. They knew him better than anyone. Even if they didn't know his family stuff, they knew *him*. The boy he'd been, the man he'd grown into.

"You love her," Alex said simply.

Bang.

"How do you know that?" he demanded, though his demand sounded more like a whisper.

"I know you. I love you. I've also felt the same kind of panic. Maybe not for exactly the same reason, but only love works a person up quite like this. Where you're ready to burn it all down because your fear is bigger than your faith."

"I don't want to believe it. I don't want to trust it."

"Why not?"

He turned away from them. The two friends who knew him, who could see through him, who'd built their own lives and weren't walking away from him, weren't letting him walk away from them. "Easier that way."

"When do Navy SEALs need the easy way out?" Alex demanded.

"I'm not a Navy SEAL anymore."

"Maybe not in practice, but in action, you'll always be one. You know better than to let fear—any fear—rule you," Jack said. "It's hard. God knows civilian hard is this whole other thing from SEAL hard, but it's still hard. Harder, I think, because it's all about our insecurities, weaknesses."

"Love means being vulnerable when we were taught to never show that, but allowing yourself love—giving and receiving it—it's stronger, braver, harder than anything we ever had to do in the military."

Funny, the man who'd never meant to join the military found those words the most enlightening. He'd wanted to prove something by becoming a SEAL—to Evan, to his mother. That he was worthy of their love. Worthy period.

He hadn't. Not to them and not to himself. Instead, he'd found love in the failures. Losing a man, losing the SEALs. Admitting things to Monica. In all of those horrible, dark places, all the good in this life had sprouted.

So, maybe… God, could he really trust the sprouts not to die? He turned back to face Alex. Jack. His brothers. His family.

"You're turning us into Oprah, so you're going to need to believe us and go make up with the woman, so we can stop," Jack offered dryly.

"It's Christmas Eve," Gabe said weakly.

"I have it on great authority they're going to be here

tomorrow for Christmas dinner. I'd suggest fixing things before my wife gets even a whiff of discord. It would be really unmanning to have her swoop in and fix it for you."

"She would, too," Gabe muttered. Becca would swoop in and somehow, with her goat-rooster magic, sew everything back together. But that wouldn't be right. He was done making his choices for other people and, more, letting other people make his choices for him.

He was a lot of things, and probably not good enough for half the things he wanted, but he wasn't a coward.

Maybe his mother had simply made a choice, the wrong one. And maybe he could make the right one.

"Do either of you know where I can get a puppy?"

Monica hefted Colin's bag, now made twice as heavy by the presents bestowed upon him, into the back of Dad's car. Colin and Mom were still inside, deciding on what airplane snacks to pack for Colin, but Dad had helped Monica pack up the car.

She had figured she'd be excited to go back. Excited to have Colin to herself again, to have their little Christmas traditions just him and her.

Gabe had ruined that.

She hefted out a heavy sigh that puffed wisps of air into the cold afternoon.

"You don't seem that excited to go back. You could stay. I'd pay for the ticket change."

She smiled. Her father's frugality made that offer extra special. "I want Colin to spend Christmas at home. And as much as there's some unpleasantness to face, I learned from my parents it's best not to put it off."

"Want me to off him?"

Monica laughed, but it caused a little stab of pain. "You made that offer a lot when I was with Dex."

"He made you cry a lot."

"I was a teenager."

Dad shrugged. "Doesn't matter much when you're the one watching your daughter cry."

She, of course, hadn't been able to understand that back then. She hadn't been able to separate normal parent over-protectiveness from his PTSD episodes. She hadn't been able to accept he might have just been worried about her.

Then she'd become a parent, and a lot of it had made sense in retrospect. Still, she'd never talked about this with her father. Maybe it would be good to. "Did you still hate Dex at the end?"

"I never hated Dex."

"You were downright mean to him."

Dad grunted, crossing his arms over his chest and leaning against his car. He squinted across the street. "Yes, but I didn't hate him. I hated the idea of him. Some little punk air force brat touching my beautiful daughter. I didn't want you to get married so young, get tied to someone so young when you had so much life left to live." Dad moved restlessly, which wasn't like him at all. "Doesn't help any, but I regretted it after."

"He thought it was funny. Way funnier than I thought it was."

"Sorry," Dad mumbled. But he eyed her. "So, now I got to deal with some smart-ass SEAL touching my beautiful daughter?"

Monica heaved out a sigh, mirroring her father's pose. "What made you finally get help?"

"Don't tell me the shit has PTSD."

"No. Not that it would change things, but no. He had a rough childhood though. He doesn't trust love."

"Then I guess that's your answer."

"What?"

"Why did I finally get help? Because I'd never had a reason to doubt your mother's or your love. I doubted my manliness, my bravery, my sanity, but I never doubted I had people who loved me. I got help not because of any one thing, but because you and your mother never gave up on me, and eventually that built and built and built until I trusted it more than I trusted my pain."

"Daddy…that's…I think the most words you've ever said to me at once." And they made her teary.

"Don't get used to it," he said sternly. But no matter how stern his words were, he'd softened. A great deal. With love and time.

"A man with scars needs a woman like you," he murmured.

She swallowed at her tight throat. "And what does a woman like me need?"

"A man who'll want to treat her like a queen," Dad replied as if it was obvious.

She wrinkled her nose, hugging herself against the cold air. "I don't want to be treated like a queen."

"Of course not, but a good man will *want* to treat you that way."

She wished it didn't make any sense, but in a strange way, it did. She wanted a man who wanted to try, that was for sure.

"Now, before that monster of yours comes tearing out here, I've got one more thing to say."

"What's that?" she replied with a smile, expecting some sarcastic joke.

Instead, he turned to face her, making eye contact. "Thank you."

She stared at him for what felt like the longest time. "F-for what?"

"The years."

"I-I don't understand." And her father's uncharacteristic emotional forthrightness scared her down to her bones.

"The years you hounded me to get help. The years you begged me not to give up. I resented hearing all those things from my daughter, and I wasn't always kind about it. But I needed it. And I thank you."

She didn't have words. Even if she did, she wouldn't have been able to speak them. He reached out and brushed the tears from her cheeks.

"None of that." Then he pulled her into a hug.

Her stoic, military father had thanked her, was hugging her.

"Merry Christmas, sweetheart. You're a good mom, and the best daughter, and I imagine the second strongest woman I know. Your mother only wins because she's older, but if you beat some sense into that idiot SEAL, you'll be damn close."

She laughed and cried into his shoulder. "Got any tips on how to do it?"

"When a sledgehammer fails, just be the rock."

She thought about that the whole flight home, and she came to the conclusion that both her parents were right. Love was the river and love was the rock, and somehow, she had to be both.

Chapter 25

IN THE END, GABE HADN'T BEEN ABLE TO FIND A puppy. Or a dog of any kind. He'd even asked around for a few cats. He could wait, he supposed. But he wanted some kind of gesture. A "we're in this together" kind of gesture. Partnerships. Foundations.

Built on a llama, apparently.

Because, somehow, that's what was sitting in the back seat. A llama. An actual llama. It had been Rose's idea, and Becca had jumped on board so fast his head had spun. She'd said it was unique, and she'd done that horrible squealing thing she did when she got really excited.

Jack and Alex had expressed some concerns, but Becca, she of the goat and the rooster and apparently plans for a pig, had shot down every single one of their reasonable concerns.

Then he'd found himself in Becca's truck, being driven to a llama ranch. A ranch full of llamas, including two llamas that hadn't taken to the herd or something? The guy running the place, Dan Sharpe, who'd seemed strangely familiar even though Gabe had never met him, said he was happy to have one inside llama, but his wife had put her foot down at two.

And suddenly, Gabe had a llama. Apparently, its name was Macaroni. Dan assured Gabe a change in name wouldn't confuse it.

A llama.

"What am I doing?" he muttered as Becca helped him transfer the llama to the back seat of his truck.

"You're professing your love with a weird animal, and I couldn't be prouder. Or happier. Or—"

"She might not be as ecstatic about the llama as you are." Or the love. Forty-eight hours wasn't so bad in the grand scheme of coming to grips with years of childhood fucked-upedness, but he'd been mean. A little cruel.

He figured she could and would forgive stupidity. He wasn't sure he wanted her to forgive cruel.

Becca added another blanket around the llama, cooing to it softly before she closed the back door and turned to him. "If she doesn't want to keep it, I do."

"So, the real reason you agreed to this comes out."

She reached up and cupped his face, patting his cheeks. A little hard to be considered a pat, really. It was very close to a slap. "Off you go. Grovel, plead, beg, but don't you dare make my Christmas dinner tomorrow awkward."

Gabe gave her a mock salute, but he stiffened when she sniffled.

"I'm *so* glad you found—"

"Don't you dare start."

"—someone," she continued, ignoring him completely. "I'm so glad you're giving this a shot, and I'm so, so, so glad fate brought me the best pseudo-brother a girl could ask for."

"Make sure you inform Jack I'm the best."

"Only until Rose has the baby. Then he gets to be the best for making me a pseudo-aunt, but I'll switch back when you and Monica get married."

"Have it all planned out, do you?" Married. Christ.

He had a ways to go on that front. Maybe it didn't fill him with dread or anything—after all, he wouldn't try to get over years of fear and shit for just anyone.

Married.

Becca grabbed him in a tight hug. "No jokes, okay? Just be honest with her."

His initial reaction was to lean away, to carefully disentangle himself from all Becca's care, but he didn't let himself. He hugged her back because it helped with the nerves, leaning on someone. Believing in them and what they said and felt. "I'll do okay, and if she kicks my ass, you'll patch me up, right?"

"We all will." She brushed a sisterly kiss across his cheek, then released him. "I want an update, even if it's only text."

He nodded, then got in the driver's seat of his truck. On a deep breath, he shoved it into drive.

"Stay put, Macaroni," he muttered. Because yes, he was in love and talked to llamas. That was his life now. Normal, normal life.

Panic was also a part of this new normal, because it beat through him like a wild thing. But it was a weird panic because he felt no compulsion to turn around. He wouldn't go back. Couldn't.

He followed the Shaw's drive over to Monica's cabin, then frowned at the prettily lit house. It looked like a fairy-tale Christmas cottage, but Monica's truck wasn't out front, and she clearly hadn't been home yet, because there was some snow that had blown up over her stoop at least partially blocking the door. Based on the flight information Monica had given Becca, she should have been home by now.

"Well, Macaroni, we might be screwed."

The llama shifted in the back seat, but that was about all.

Headlights splashed across the dark, and then her truck was pulling up next to his. She was here, and he had to actually do this.

He stepped out of his truck the same time she did.

She stared at him as if she couldn't believe he was there, but it gave him some hope he didn't see any traces of horror at him being here.

"You're here," she said.

"Yeah. Yeah, I am."

Colin scrambled out of the passenger side door. "Gabe!" With the exuberance of a child probably hopped up on sugar, Colin lunged at him.

Gabe scooped him up easily enough, even with the ache in his shoulder. Something like relief washed through him. Hell, he'd missed the kid. "What'd you do, eat your weight in cookies at your grandparents?"

"Kinda."

He dropped Colin back to his feet, then grinned down at him, ruffling his already-messy hair. "Missed having you around, runt."

Colin all but beamed, and Gabe kept his gaze on him, because he was afraid to look at Monica's expression. He crouched down, so he could be eye level with Colin. "Hey, can I, uh, talk to your mom out here alone for a few minutes?"

He saw the way the kid's faced changed. Hurt, probably, but something else too. Something closer to fear than Gabe could stand. He reached out, gripping Colin's shoulder and squeezing. "And if all goes well and she doesn't punch me for being a jerk, I'll come in and have some cookies or something after we're done talking."

Colin glanced back at Monica, then leaned close to Gabe's ear. "Tell her she looks pretty. Gets her every time."

Gabe barked out a surprised laugh as Colin took the keys from Monica, then bounded for the front door.

Gabe stood back up, and neither he nor Monica spoke until Colin had gone inside and slammed the door behind him.

"I brought you a Christmas present." Still she said nothing, just stood a safe distance away looking…something. He wasn't sure what it was. Maybe it was just exhaustion. "You look pretty," he added.

Her mouth curved the slightest hint. "He told you to say that."

"Yes, ma'am, though it's never not true."

"Uh-huh."

"So, your present."

"Gabe—"

"It's symbolic, so you have to let me give it to you."

"Symbolic of what?"

He pulled open the door to the back seat of the truck and pointed inside. Monica peered over at the llama.

"What the hell is that?"

Not *quite* the response he'd been hoping for. "It's a llama. A housebroken pet llama, I'm assured."

"You brought me a symbolic llama for Christmas."

"Well, technically it's my gift to Colin. My gift to you was sex. You said I could keep my gift card. Also, I couldn't find a puppy. But if you don't want it, Becca's going to take it, and obviously I didn't want Colin to see it before I ran it by you and—"

"Gabe. Breathe."

"Right." He took a breath, let it out. *Breathe. Think. Stop babbling about a fucking llama.*

"Llama aside —"

"Its name is Macaroni."

"Oh, no, don't tell me its name." She hesitated, then stepped forward, then reached out and stroked her hand down the llama's neck. "How is it so weirdly cute?"

She was close to him now, him standing next to the open door, her reaching inside the truck. He wanted to reach out and touch her, hold her, say all the words that seemed to clog his throat as she cooed over the animal.

"Monica?"

She turned her head, meeting his gaze.

"I love you."

—◈—

Monica wanted to fall into his arms at that, but she knew… Oh, there was some work to be done first. No matter that he looked so earnest and sincere and any fear that lingered in his expression wasn't that horrible thing that had driven him out of here a few days ago.

"I love you, too, but we already went through that."

"I was wrong to leave like that. Wrong to let fear… It's a strange thing to have lived thirtysome years, been a Navy SEAL for a decade or so, lived through a grenade explosion, and still realize that fear was the thing that motivated most of your life choices. Not desire, not drive, not anything but fear."

"Fear can be a powerful motivator. Or de-motivator. I was too afraid to go after you. I told myself I was giving you time, but I just didn't want to hurt like that again."

He reached out, his fingers brushing across her hair so gently she didn't even feel it. "I wasn't ready for you to come after me."

"What changed your mind in such a short period of time?"

"Love," he replied simply. "That you loved me, and you're too smart and good to make it up or lie. That Alex and Jack... You know, that first time Alex came to talk to you a few months ago, when we kind of... I hate to use the word *manipulated*. Jack and I *encouraged* him to go to you. We pushed him. Egged him on. Tried to get him to fight us."

"Men," she muttered irritably.

He smiled, and this time when he reached out, his gloved fingertips brushed her cheek. "That was love. That we stood up to him. That he went to you. It's easy to accept love when it helps someone else. It's scarier, harder when it's just...you. But they've also been in my life for so long, and nothing has changed that. The worst day of our lives, and we're all still here. So, this morning, they...they just showed up. And they stayed, no matter what I said. They always have. I guess I don't have any reason to believe they won't always."

It moved her in a lot of ways. Because she knew what an important step it was for Alex and Jack too, these three men who'd gone through hell together, to be here on the other side reaching out for love and lives and, just as important as that, pushing each other to do the same.

"I will, too," she whispered. "Show up. Stay."

His mouth curved, and it had none of his normal sharpness. Only sweetness. "I know. It'd never have gone this far if I didn't, on some level, know that."

If only it were as simple as all that, but she had more in her life than just Gabe. "But I need to know you'd do the same. I can love you, Gabe. I can't really fathom being able to stop, but I can't have you in my son's life if you aren't willing to show up and stay. I need that promise from you."

"I love him, too, you know."

As if her heart wasn't already raw and aching, beautifully big and bursting, and then he added that to this emotional day.

"He told me he likes you best because you treat him like a man," she managed to say between her tears. "And I like you best because he thinks you do, and I know you don't always."

"Hell," he muttered, pulling her to his chest and holding her there.

She gave herself the space to cry there against his chest for a few minutes, to feel and absorb in a way she usually forced herself to move away from.

"It was a lie. Not wanting you, not wanting a future with you both. I wanted it so desperately I couldn't see straight, but when the thing you want is the thing you most fear..." He squeezed her tighter, and she was happy to be squished against his hard, warm chest. "It's easier to convince yourself you don't want it or can't have it than face the fact that having it just requires some work...and some faith. I can't promise that faith will never falter, but—"

"I'll be here to remind you it shouldn't."

He pulled her back, so he could look down at her, the array of colorful Christmas lights dancing across his face.

"And what will I be here to remind you of?"

She smiled. "That I'm not just a therapist or a mom."

"I can think of a few ways I'd enjoy doing that."

She gave him a little shove, but he kept his arms tight around her. The llama made a noise from the back seat. It was the weirdest little thing, but she was already halfway in love.

"So, what on earth is the *llama* symbolic of?"

"My promise to you, and Colin, to take care of responsibilities together." He glanced at the llama. "No matter how weird they are."

"That is a *very* symbolic llama."

"I'll admit, I looked for a dog first."

"It's a default, symbolic llama then."

"I suppose. Doesn't matter though. You know why?"

She shook her head.

"I love you. I want to build a life with you. All the things I said I didn't want are what I want more than anything. I've been too afraid of that for so long, and then you came along, and it was suddenly real. The truest, most beautiful thing I'd ever wanted. I'm not very good at the words—"

"Those'll do," she whispered, moving onto her toes to press her mouth to his. "Come inside." She sighed and looked over his shoulder at the back seat. "Both of you, come inside. Colin is going to flip."

"I was told a name change wouldn't confuse him, if he wants to change it," Gabe said, picking the llama up out of the back seat and then setting him down on the snowy ground.

He made a little noise, too cute for words, and then pranced a bit through the snow.

"Oh, no, he's Macaroni. There's no doubt about that."

And there wasn't any doubt about *this*. She walked to the door, pushing it open.

The llama did another little, weird prance and noise, and then happily ran for the door. Gabe followed, perfectly silhouetted by Christmas lights. Tall and strong and hers, really hers. She glanced at Colin, who'd fallen to the floor, mouth dropped open in awe as the llama edged toward him.

Gabe stepped up to the threshold and grinned down at her. "Merry Christmas," he murmured.

"You know you can't be a grinch anymore, right?"

"Of course I can."

She shook her head, grinning up at him. "No, Christmas Eve is officially our official moment. You made Christmas promises, Gabe." She tapped her fingers to his chest right above his heart. "I'm afraid your heart *has* grown three sizes."

He grunted. "Maybe two."

Since Colin was busy exclaiming over the llama, she reached up, pulling Gabe's mouth to hers. But she didn't kiss him. Instead, she looked right at him and grinned. "I'll make it three."

A promise she didn't intend to break.

Chapter 26

Gabe awoke wrapped up in a tangle of sheets. Santa grinned lasciviously from the pillowcase his face was shoved into. He rolled over to glare at the cause of these hideous, nightmare-inducing sheets.

She was still fast asleep, blond hair tangled around her face. She'd been exhausted already, then they'd been up late putting presents under the tree and deciding where on earth a llama was going to sleep in an already tiny cabin. They'd talked, too. She'd told him about her visit. He'd told her more about his conversation with Alex and Jack.

It was hard to believe, here in the morning light, it had all just worked out. There she was, in the bed next to him. That they loved each other and were going to make things work. Permanently.

He felt more than heard a presence and maneuvered up to his elbows. Colin was standing at the tree, the llama standing next to him, both staring at him with matching inscrutable gazes.

"Ah. Merry Christmas," he whispered.

Colin's eyes moved from Monica's sleeping form, then back to Gabe himself.

He and Monica had started broaching the topic of how they were going to explain things to Colin in the morning, but he didn't remember what they'd decided. It was possible they'd both fallen asleep before deciding anything.

They had *not* had sex, though Gabe probably

shouldn't explain that to a ten-year-old. Did ten-year-olds know adults had sex? He grimaced a little. He hadn't expected this responsibility to fall to him, but it wasn't one he was going to abandon.

Carefully, he slid out of the bed.

"Let's take Macaroni out, yeah?"

Colin nodded, then moved for the pile of boots and coats by the door. Silently, they both pulled on their winter gear as Macaroni watched them.

Gabe pushed the door open, and Macaroni loped out, immediately taking a few steps into the frigid Christmas morning before doing his business.

Since Colin was watching the llama in the slowly encroaching daylight, Gabe didn't expect him to speak. But he did.

"Are you going to live with us now?"

Gabe scratched a hand through his hair. The kid sure wasn't going to ask him any easy questions. "Cabin's a bit small for all that, but I'll be here a lot, and you and your mom will be with me on the ranch a lot, until we figure out something more permanent." Gabe blew out a breath and watched it puff into the cold air. He thought there'd be time to parse this all out, but kids weren't exactly big on deep discussions and taking things slow, were they? "I love your mom."

Colin pulled a face, but then he shrugged. "Yeah."

"And, well…" Gabe tried to think about what he might have wanted back then, if his mother had chosen someone else. A good man. The kind of man Gabe wanted to be. He owed that to Colin.

So even though it made his hip twinge, he knelt on one knee in the snow so he could be eye level with Colin.

"And I love you too. You're a part of whatever changes we make. So you've got to promise me that you'll be honest with us when something's bothering you or not working. Because this is about all three of us, not just me and your mom."

Colin stared at him, a considering kind of expression Gabe couldn't quite read. His heart pounded a little too hard in his chest as he waited for Colin to respond in some way.

"Are you guys going to get married?"

Christ. He had to huff out a laugh as he moved back to his feet. Married. It had already crossed his mind, so that wasn't the shock. It seemed more inevitability than possibility, but it was a complicated question for a kid to ask, for Gabe to answer. Still, he wanted to be straight with Colin. Always. "I have to ask her first. Then she'd have to say yes."

"New Year's Eve."

Gabe blinked down at him, but the boy was still watching the llama. "What about New Year's Eve?"

"You should ask her on New Year's Eve. Because that's the start of a new year. Plus, there's this movie she always watches on New Year's Eve with a guy and girl and gross kissing and crying, so she'd probably like it."

"Yeah?"

"Yeah."

"That's soon." Like a *week* soon.

"Mom always says I should do my homework sooner rather than later. Don't know why this would be any different."

"Right. Homework and marriage. Very similar." Gabe blinked, looking out at where the sun flirted with the horizon. A new day. Christmas Day. A new year. A promise. Inevitability over possibility.

Hell.

"You'd be okay with it?"

Colin finally slid a gaze his way, so much like his mother—practical and certain and just a...force. A force all his own.

"You and Mom getting married? Yeah, I'd be okay." But his mouth twitched a little bit, and as he turned his head away from Gabe, Gabe caught a glimpse of a grin.

"Guess I'd be okay with it too." He rested his arm around Colin's shoulders, gratified when Colin leaned into it. "Maybe...tomorrow or the next day you can come to town with me and help me pick out a ring. If you think you can keep it a secret."

He puffed out his chest. "Of course I can keep a secret." He leaned a little harder, looking down so Gabe couldn't see his face at all. "Would I call you *Dad* when you guys get married?"

Oof. Amazing how he wanted to sink to his knees and say yes almost as much as he'd been desperate to run away from this a few days ago. But, God, he wanted to be something of a dad to this kid. And he knew, deep in his bones, he'd do a damn fine job at that, whether he deserved the opportunity or not.

Deserved didn't matter when he had people in his life who loved him, whom he loved.

Still, he wanted to be careful. Evan had never been careful, and Gabe wouldn't follow any of those ugly footsteps. "That's up to you, Colin. I'd be your stepdad, and you'd always be mine to me, but...well, it's up to you. Maybe something to talk to your mom about. She also has to say yes first."

"I never knew him, but I know you."

Gabe was speechless at that.

"She'll say yes. She told me she liked you. That she'd always be friends with you."

"She did, huh?"

"So, she'll say yes and then I'll call you Dad."

Oh, to have the faith and trust of a ten-year-old. "I'm going to have to trust you on that, buddy."

And he would.

Becca's squeal nearly broke Monica's eardrum. She engulfed Monica in a hug. "You kept the llama!"

Monica laughed, hugging Becca back. "I did. Since I hear you were partially behind getting him, he's now a part of your Christmas celebration."

Becca leaned down and gave Macaroni a pat. "Welcome to the menagerie, Mac." Then she stood back up, eyes suspiciously shiny. "I assume if you took the llama, you took the man too?"

She glanced back at the truck, where Gabe and Colin were hefting the presents out from the back. "You assume right."

Becca gave her another squeeze, then hurried forward to help the men. They brought everything inside and settled into the afternoon being, well, a family. It was a beautiful Christmas cacophony as the boys swiped appetizers and Monica helped Becca and Sandra with dinner prep.

"Where are Jack and Rose?" Becca fretted.

"Maybe Rose wasn't feeling well. Want me to call?"

Becca shook her head. "Not—" Before she could get the words out of her mouth, the door opened and footsteps echoed through the house.

"There they are." Becca wiped her hands on a towel and headed straight for the door.

Monica followed. She wasn't sure she'd ever get over the wave of warmth that swamped her every time she saw Gabe's and Colin's heads bent together, as they were now, sprawled out on the rug next to the fireplace. They were whispering about something, and Monica made a mental note to ask Gabe about it later.

She'd managed to have a short conversation with Colin this morning while Gabe had been getting ready, and Colin had been acting shifty and sly. Happy, though. Giddy even, to have Gabe in the cabin. Monica knew it wouldn't always be this easy or simple, but for Christmas, she'd enjoy it.

Becca was scolding Jack and Rose for being late as Jack shrugged out of his coat.

"Sorry, got a bit held up," Jack said, grinning. He helped Rose untangle from all her winter gear, and Rose grinned up at him.

"My, you two are suspiciously, overtly happy," Monica observed.

"Oh, are we?" Rose said, faux innocently as she slowly pulled the glove off her left hand.

"Ring!" Becca and Monica shrieked in unison.

Rose held out her hand proudly. "And a doozy at that."

They oohed and aahed over the ring, offering congratulations and some friendly ribbing from Alex and Gabe.

Becca's mom reappeared with a bottle of champagne and glasses. She poured, finding some sparkling cider for Rose, Jack, and Colin. When they all had glasses, Alex took the lead.

He held up his glass. "To Rose and Jack."

Everyone echoed the sentiment, clinking glasses, taking happy sips.

"Wait, I have a toast, too," Rose said, holding up her glass again. "To a Christmas miracle." Rose's gaze moved to Gabe.

Gabe raised his eyebrows. "What miracle? You finally saying yes to Jack? That's just you coming to your senses."

"That isn't the miracle," Rose returned, pointing at Monica, then Gabe. "You two are the miracle."

He exchanged a confused glance with Monica. "Huh?" they asked in unison.

"A few months ago, when you were grumpily working on our house, Rose mentioned you needed to find someone," Jack explained. "She thought you were lonely."

Gabe scowled, but Monica leaned her head against his shoulder. Whether he liked that it had been noticed or not, he *had* been lonely. Now he wouldn't be, because he was hers. She glanced at Colin, who was leaning against Gabe's other side. *Theirs*.

"Jack said it would take a miracle to find someone for you," Rose continued.

Jack lifted his glass. "So we should toast to Christmas miracles."

Monica wanted to be offended, but it was hard to find any kind of outrage in the midst of all this love and joy and Christmas cheer. She lifted her glass, clinked it with Gabe's, and grinned. "To Christmas miracles," she murmured.

"That you are," he returned, wrapping his free arm around her shoulders and pressing a kiss to her temple.

"Aww," Becca said with a sniff. "Now *this* is the perfect Christmas. And the only thing that can make it more perfect? Let's eat."

The room dissolved into laughter and chatter, everyone filing into the kitchen to load up their plates before coming back to the living room, where the tables were set up.

Gabe held her back from following the crowd, so she tilted her head up. "What were you and Colin whispering about?" she demanded.

"Ah, we're planning a bit of a shopping trip."

"And that's a secret?"

"It is." He grinned down at her, overly pleased with himself for a man with secrets. "You're not invited."

"Hey," she protested.

"Man time," Gabe said with a smile before something in his expression went very, very sly. "You wouldn't happen to know your ring size, would you?"

"My ri—" Her head jerked up so hard it nearly hurt. "What?"

"Colin's quite sure New Year's Eve is the moment, and he wants it to be a surprise. I'm a little more…careful. I want to make sure you don't need more time, so he won't be awfully disappointed. But if *I* put it off, I think he'll be fine. So…"

"So," she repeated stupidly. She could only gape at him for a few more moments. Rings and asking and… "Gabe." The funny thing was, she thought she *should* be wary. She *should* think it was too fast and too soon.

But she didn't *feel* any of those things. "Do you need more time?" she asked, her voice little more than a whisper.

His smile widened, and there wasn't an ounce of hesitation in him. "No. Might have been Colin's idea, but I wouldn't have been too far behind."

She swallowed at the lump in her throat. "Then I don't need more time. I might need to measure my finger, but I don't need more time."

"Good," he murmured, then pressed his mouth to hers.

"Gross," Colin groaned as he reentered the room, plate heaped with food.

"I think you're going to have to get used to it, baby," Monica said. "And me saying this: I love you both. More than anything."

Colin rolled his eyes, immediately plowing into dinner. "I love you both, too," he muttered, looking anywhere but at them.

"And I love you both, too," Gabe added, even as people filed in with plates.

As Christmas miracles went, it was the best one she'd ever get.

Epilogue

Five Years Later

"I WISH HE'D GET HERE ALREADY," MONICA GRUM-
bled, pacing from the living room to the entryway and
then back again.

Gabe glanced at the clock. "You gave him till one.
It's only twelve forty-five."

"Do you think they're having sex?" Monica
demanded. Whether or not Colin assured her he and
Katie Lane were just friends, Monica had her doubts.
And fifteen-year-olds, whether *just friends* or not, were
definitely thinking about sex.

Gabe didn't quite stifle his laugh of surprise. "Er, um,
well."

"Oh my God. You think they're having sex! He's
fifteen! If my baby is getting naked with that—"

"Very nice girl whom you like, I should point out,"
Gabe interrupted her outrage. "And they're with her
family. It's *Christmas*. The Lanes and the Shaws don't
strike me as the type to let Colin and Katie sneak off and
have sex under their noses."

Monica crossed her arms over her chest, scowling at
him even though he looked beyond handsome there in
the glow of the Christmas lights. His wedding band even
glinted. Her handsome, good, sturdy husband.

It soothed, the way it always did when she worried,

that she had this man in her life. They'd built the house and moved in four years ago, and Monica only ever missed the cramped cabin around Christmas, when she was feeling particularly nostalgic.

It was hard to believe it had been five years since that first Christmas together. Hard to believe even now she was standing here in the house they'd built on Revival property, with her husband. There had been so many challenges and so many adjustments. To morph from a family of two to a family of three, for Colin to get used to having two parents instead of one. But things were good lately. Really good.

She rested her hand on her stomach. More adjustments and more challenges were coming, but Monica knew they'd face them, conquer them. Together.

"And you're not going to grill him when he gets here, because you can't put off telling him any longer," Gabe warned.

Her scowl turned into a nose wrinkle. "I just…" She knew it was time. Time to tell Colin and the others. Her stomach was starting to round, and she couldn't hide it much longer.

They'd suffered a loss early on in their marriage. It had hit them all hard, even Colin, and they'd only just this year decided to try again. It had taken a while, but here they were.

They'd been cautious about telling anyone, especially Colin. But Gabe was right. She needed to get over her worry, her fear, and tell him.

She sank onto the couch next to Gabe. She looked up at him, needing some reassurance, and wasn't she lucky she had a husband who always obliged? "Do you ever get so happy you worry something terrible is going to happen and take it all away?"

He tucked a piece of hair behind her ear. "Yeah."

She harrumphed. "Well, as long as I'm not alone," she said gloomily. She'd expected some kind of pep talk, not easy agreement.

But he slid his arm around her shoulders and drew her close. "I learned a long time ago the bad times will come, no matter what you do. The best we can do is enjoy the good while we have it and build whatever we can that'll withstand the bad."

She kept trying to frown, but it kept tugging up at the corners. "My, you've gotten wise in your old age."

"You're not far behind in the age department, and don't you forget it." He dropped a kiss to her mouth. "Whatever happens, today, tomorrow, in ten years, we'll get through it."

She nodded—ah, there was her pep talk. "I know. Sometimes I need to hear you say it, but I know." She leaned forward, brushed her mouth against his. "I love you."

"I know," he replied very solemnly.

She hit him, but he only grinned wider.

"I love you, too. And in five years, I've never gotten tired of saying it. I have never felt as though I didn't mean it. I love you more, somehow, with each passing year. Day, maybe. You've opened up a whole new world to me. One of trust and love and faith and family. Even when we're yelling at each other or at Colin, I never doubted it. Not for a moment."

She could only gape at him, tears falling onto her cheeks. He always told he loved her, but they weren't ones for poetic, emotional words like that.

The door banged open, and then Colin's heavy, quick footsteps sounded even as the door slammed again.

Gabe touched his nose to Monica's and looked her straight in the eye. "Tell him. It's Christmas. No excuses."

She nodded, turning to smile as Colin skidded into the living room.

"Not late. Early even," Colin announced proudly. He looked at Monica, then Gabe. "Shit, did someone die?"

"No one died," she replied, wiping the happy tears off her cheeks. "And don't say 'shit' in front of me. Sit down. We have some news for you. Good news."

"You're getting me a car!"

Monica glared, but Colin grinned at Gabe as he sat himself on the fireplace hearth. He'd turned into all limbs almost overnight. A teenager, talking cars and college or the marines or whatever that would get him the hell out of Montana ASAP all the time. So close to adulthood he could taste it.

It broke both Gabe's and Monica's hearts a little bit, but they knew Colin needed that space. To dream. To spread his wings. Much as it pained her.

Besides, they still had three years to convince him he was very, very wrong.

"So, what's the news?" Colin asked, vibrating with energy. He usually was, but always a little bit more so after he'd spent time with Katie Lane. Monica didn't like to think about that.

Monica grabbed Gabe's hand, and he squeezed, which was what she needed. A gentle urging. Some courage. "Well, in a few months…May actually, you're going to be a big brother," Monica said carefully.

Colin's eyes widened. He grinned, before sobering. "It'll…be okay this time?"

"We can't promise that, of course, but so far, the doctor says he or she is very, very healthy. In fact, we get to find out if it's a brother or a sister next month."

Colin's grin was immediately back. "Cool. Cool."

Monica laughed a little. The tears were back, but she didn't shed them even as she turned to Gabe and rolled her eyes. "So very *cool*."

"Yeah," Gabe said, brushing a kiss against the back of her hand. "The coolest."

Gabe parked in front of Revival next to Jack and Rose's truck. The kids were out building snowmen under Alex's watch. He held his youngest at his hip, so bundled up you couldn't even be sure there was a baby under there. His oldest played happily with Rose and Jack's two.

Gabe's heart squeezed. It was amazing the way they'd built this family when it had all started with a tragedy.

When Colin stepped out of the back of the truck, Mac jumping out behind him, the kids forgot their snowmen and came running, both for Colin and the llama.

"Guess what, guys," he heard Colin announce. "I'm *finally* going to be a big brother!"

The kids squealed happily, because Colin was their favorite since he always greeted them with tosses into the air. Mac danced through the snow, happily basking in the attention of the little ones.

Monica grabbed the bags of presents and treats from the back. "I've got them. You go tell Jack and Alex," she said, nodding toward the porch where Jack had joined Alex.

"I think Colin announced it to the world."

She grinned, gave him a kiss on the cheek. "Go tell them."

He followed her to the house, opening the door for her so she could go inside.

"So. Someone's going to be a daddy." Alex handed him a bottle of beer with his free hand.

Gabe took it, looking out at the yard where Colin was playing with the little kids. "I've been a dad for five years." It hadn't always been easy. As the reality of a new family dynamic had set in all those years ago, he and Colin had suffered their issues. But Gabe supposed that was fatherhood, no matter how you sliced it. And as long as love was at the core, you could get through any problems.

"True enough," Jack agreed. "Still, the baby years are something else. Hope you're prepared."

"I'll survive."

"Of course you will. With friends like us, you'll have so much advice, you might just drown in it."

"Yeah, can't wait." It was sarcastic, but at the same time, he couldn't. He'd somehow gotten here, and he couldn't wait for advice and babies and all this damn hope inside of him to be drowned a little out by stress and reality.

"So, how do you think we got so lucky?" Gabe gestured to all the kids playing in the snow. "Kids and weird-ass animals and the three strongest women I've ever encountered? A foundation that's helped countless men and women?"

"I'd say it was just that—luck," Jack offered. "And you know, maybe a little bit earned, with all we went through before we got here. And those countless men and women earned their help, too."

"Three busted-up former Navy SEALs couldn't have hoped for better," Alex said, jiggling the baby on his hip.

No, they couldn't have, and these three busted-up former Navy SEALs had found everything they couldn't have even dreamed of in the midst of the big sky of a Montana ranch and the biggest hearts of three amazing women.

"Merry Christmas, gentlemen," Jack offered.

Merry Christmas indeed.

About the Author

Nicole Helm is the bestselling author of down-to-earth Western romance and fast-paced romantic suspense. She lives with her husband and two sons in Missouri and spends her free time dreaming about someday owning a barn. You can find more information about her books on her website: nicolehelm.com.

Also by Nicole Helm